ANTS ACROSS THE PAGE

ANTS ACROSS THE PAGE

CONNIE AVERITT
WILLIAMS

ST. JOSEPH, MISSOURI USA

ANTS ACROSS THE PAGE
Copyright © 2022 Connie Averitt Williams

Paperback ISBN: 978-1-936501-66-3

For more information on Connie Averitt Williams, visit her website StrugglersandOthers.com

Editor: Debra L. Butterfield
Cover Design: Carrie Dennis Design

Printed in the United States of America

Dedicated to the memory of Ross and Pansy Burlingame.

Also dedicated to the students with learning struggles who power their way through school and come out on top. My hat is off to you, and to the teachers, aides, parents, and friends who love and support you on your journey.

ONE

Apple Valley, Indiana, September 1960

*This is when I learned that some people can whip
you into shape without doing anything.*

I remember that one particular moment in 1960, an everyday moment
when the school bus dumped me out and groaned on down the road,
setting me free from all things related to school. With a happy sigh I
strolled up our long gravel driveway past the pear trees, their branches
dropping ripe fruit in the grass with a plop here and a plop there. I picked
one up and took a bite, letting the sweet juice run down my chin. Cot-
tony clouds glided over the fields, pushed by darker clouds, not the kind
that crash their way across the sky, but the other kind—silent, gentle,
sliding into place above me. My nose was telling me that soon I would
feel the first pricks of cool water on my skin. Change was in the air.

When I came around to the side of the house, I saw a strange car
parked in the driveway. A woman stood on the back porch, her hand
on the doorknob. She didn't see me.

Oh, no. Not again. Dad bought us another woman.

That's when I tossed my fifth-grade history book into the grass and
raced to the barn where I knew I'd find Dad. "Hey!" I squeezed between the tractors. "Dad, where are you?"

"What, Luke?" His voice came from under the green John Deere
parked near the Dutch doors. He was on his hands and knees, proba-

bly hunting for a dropped bolt or something.

"Dad, didn't you hear that car pull up? Somebody's on our back porch. She's looking in the screen door and wiggling the doorknob." I took a deep breath. "She has a big stomach."

Dad's long legs moved, and his head clunked against something hard. "Ow." Dad was silent under the tractor, probably recovering from his head bonk. I swear, my dad usually looked like his face just wrestled with a chicken.

He sat up on his knees, holding his right eye. "Did you say someone's on the porch—a woman?"

I groaned. "Dad, did you buy us another woman?"

He crawled around to my side of the tractor and pulled himself up to his full height beside the huge wheel. As he rubbed the side of his head, his fingers scrambled the thick black hair around his ear. "We're not going to buy us a woman, son. I'm just going to interview a woman, and possibly hire her. We don't buy people, Luke. We hire them. There's a big difference. Don't go around telling people we buy women."

"But, Dad," I complained. "None of 'em like us. The last one practically drilled a hole in my ear with her finger in a washcloth. I'm too old for somebody to be doing that to me."

"You must've needed it or she wouldn't have done it."

That's when I noticed the new grease-lined scratch on his eyebrow. "I think she wanted to fix you, too."

"Well she's moved on to greener pastures." Dad sighed. "And we need somebody to help take care of us."

"I can take care of myself."

"And Stevie?"

I pointed at my chest. "I can take care of Stevie."

"Like you did this morning when he ran down the driveway in his socks?"

"You saw that?"

Dad rolled his eyes.

"Clean socks, Dad. He had on clean socks—and they matched!"

He rubbed his forehead.

"And I did get his shoes to him before he got on the school bus."

"Saw that, too."

"Whoops." I'd thrown them.

"There's a fifty-fifty chance he has them on the right feet today." Dad shook his head as he set down his favorite wrench, the one that was almost permanently connected to his hand.

I liked the way our life was now, free and loose like my favorite pajamas that our last helper lady threw in the trash. She'd tried to whip us into shape, forcing baths on us all the time and lecturing Dad about my lousy schoolwork. I was so glad when she left.

"We'd better get to the house." Dad wove through the tractors toward the front of the barn. "Luke, this lady needs us just as much as we need her. She's a widow, and she needs a job so she can take care of her baby, or was it a kid?"

My jaw clenched. "You don't even know if it's a baby or a kid?"

He stopped just inside the barn door, and we both looked across the yard.

The lady had returned to the other side of her car. The door was open, and she was studying something in her hand. Because she was short, all we saw was her head poking up like a brown-haired pea on top of the car, a '57 Chevy. Turning, she walked toward the back door again, her baggy blue jacket rustling in the soft September breeze.

"Who is she, Dad?" I asked.

"Aunt Louisa's sister's friend's other friend's cousin's cousin's cousin."

"You'll have to draw that in a picture later so I can understand it."

He grinned. "To be honest, I don't know exactly how it goes. I just made up the stuff in the middle. I do know it started with Aunt Louisa and ended with somebody's cousin."

"Man, you used to be real picky about who came to take care of us. This one—you don't even know who knows her?"

"I know my Aunt Louisa. And if she knows all those other people—well, it'll be fine with me. Aunt Louisa wouldn't do us wrong. She loves us."

The lady stood at the door, knocked, then squinted at the paper in her hand. As she turned to look around, we backed into the shadows of the barn. With a squeak, she pulled the screen door open, shouted, "Hello?" and walked into our house.

"I guess we'd better get over there." Dad picked up a rag and started to wipe the grease off his hands.

"Did you do the dishes today?" I asked.

"I've been working out here. I don't even know what the kitchen looks like right now." He stepped out of the barn.

As we approached the house, a voice floated out to us through the screen. "Is anyone here?" A strong, steady voice. "Am I at the home of William Bradley? Hello?"

Dad yanked the door and walked inside, and I followed.

She stood at the sink, her back to us. Dishes lined the counter like a platoon of flying saucers that had skidded across a tomato patch and stopped against a fence.

She turned to meet us face to face. "Hm. Looks like you had spaghetti last night."

Dad stopped and I bumped into him. "Yes, we did," he said.

Even though she was small for a grown-up, there was something powerful in her sparkling dark eyes that made me almost salute her. If this was to be our next helper lady, we were in big trouble.

She glanced back at the dish pile. "And, let's see, for breakfast you had…cement?"

"Oatmeal." Dad answered quietly. I think he was in shock. I know I was.

After a pause, Dad hung his greasy rag on the doorknob, stepped toward her, and held out his hand. "I'm William Bradley, Aunt Louisa's nephew."

"Aunt who?"

"Aunt Louisa, whose sister is a friend of someone who is a friend of someone you know, cousins and other people."

"Martha Taylor?"

"Never heard of her." Dad's arm was still outstretched.

"Martha said you are Esther Hines' sister's neighbor's nephew, I think, maybe." After shaking Dad's hand, she took off her coat and set it on our stool by the sink. I noticed there was a dark streak of grease on her thumb from Dad's handshake.

He didn't speak. He was staring at the lady's stomach. It pooched out like she was hiding a volleyball under her dress.

Dad cleared his throat and pulled out a chair. "Please have a seat."

She walked over and sat down. And wouldn't you know, the chair creaked and wiggled, so she jumped up.

"It'll hold you," Dad reassured her.

She eased herself back onto the chair and looked around the room, sort of like she expected rats to jump out of our dish pile.

"We don't have rats," I told her in my most reassuring tone.

Her eyebrows lifted. "Good to know."

Outside, Stevie's school bus rolled to a screeching stop at the end of our long driveway.

"That'll be my other son," Dad said. "He goes to a special school. I'll tell you that right off the bat, he's a Down's syndrome child." Dad's fingers twitched nervously against his pants pocket.

"Oh." She put her hand on her cheek and slowly nodded. "Okay."

Dad had already explained to me that Down's was another name for what kind of a boy my seven-year-old brother was—with his flat hands, his runny nose and constant sneezes, clumsiness, limited abilities, and a truckload of sweetness deep down inside.

"Did Martha Taylor tell you about him?" Dad asked the lady.

"No. Martha didn't really know much about you. She just said you were trustworthy." She paused. "She knew I'd be safe here."

So, Dad's good reputation had inched its way into other towns and places. People from afar came because Dad was—

Stevie burst into the room. "Cool car!" he shouted.

That's how Stevie was. He walked around all day with a foghorn voice and a smile plastered on his face that hit you like a big sneeze of butterflies. Anyway, Stevie got excited over a new crayon or an old crayon, or even a strange car in the driveway. And besides that, he never thought before he spoke. Instead, his thoughts just came shooting straight out of his booming mouth. "Cool car!" he repeated, walking to the sink. "Drink-drink."

I jumped to the cupboard to get a clean glass. Of course, there wasn't one, so I grabbed a dirty one, rinsed it, filled it with cold water, and handed it to Stevie.

"Cool water!" he said between glugs, sloshing drops all over his chin. He smiled at the lady, squeezing his almond shaped eyes into little slits. "Cool tummy," he sputtered, fumbling his glass against a pan as he set it on the counter.

"Watch out!" Dad warned—too late.

Stevie had started a dish avalanche.

Dad sprang forward and dove toward the counter. That probably would've worked, except the lady also dove with lightning speed, colliding with him, their arms getting tangled up while more dishes slid to the linoleum floor, crashing and rolling until the last pan lid bounced against a table leg with a loud ringing clang.

When it was done, Dad was sprawled across the floor in front of the lady, his arms stretched out like Superman with a rescued cowboy bowl sideways in his hands, dripping oatmeal globs. He had spaghetti on his arms and a broken plate under his elbow, which was slathered in red. Oh, no. Blood?

"Dad, your arm."

Dad, whose cheeks were a shade of bright red, carefully scooted back on his knees and looked up at the lady who was standing with her back against the sink. Her white blouse was peppered with tomato sauce spots.

Maybe I should tell you right now that my dad doesn't have much luck with the ladies.

"What are you doing?" she asked.

"Trying to get up." Still on his knees, he scooted farther away from her. "Are you okay?"

"Just dandy." She turned to the counter, pushing back the remaining pans with her bulging stomach and outstretched arms.

Stevie stood still, his mouth open.

I groaned. "Dad, your elbow, it's bleeding. I'll get something." I rushed to the nook by the kitchen door, grabbed a white sock off the washer, knelt beside him, and wrapped it around his arm.

"It doesn't even hurt." He rubbed the sock bandage with his other hand. "I'll bet it's mostly spaghetti sauce." He looked down at his thumb. "Oh, wait. I am bleeding here, just a nick. Get another sock, son."

"A sock?" The lady set Stevie's cup in the sink. "You use socks for bandages?"

I got another one, and Dad wrapped his hand. Turning to Stevie, who was starting to cry, he said, "It's okay, buddy. Why don't you go play cool trucks in the living room?"

"Okay, cool trucks." Wiping a tear, my brother clomped down the hall.

"I'll get the mop and broom and stuff," I said.

Nobody talked while the three of us cleaned up the mess. All I heard was the patter of raindrops on the roof.

When the lady returned our mop to the nook by the back door, she stood for a moment and stared at the washer. "Oh, boy," she muttered.

We always kept our clean socks in a pile on the washer. We called it Sock Mountain.

The lady sat down at the table again. Dad dropped into a chair too. I wanted to know what was going to happen, so I joined them.

"I suppose if I do come to work here, I'll need to start with the dishes." She looked around the room. "Or put up new wallpaper?"

I'd never noticed the peeling wallpaper. It had just sorta always been there. My eyes wandered to the faded curtains and the petrified pink penicillin splotches along the windowsill where Stevie had knocked over the bottle last spring.

"I suppose the rest of the house is like this?" She waved her hand, palm up.

"We don't have the gift of housekeeping," Dad said.

The way I figured, she wasn't surveying the room to see what her jobs were. She was looking for the fastest way out.

She swung her eyes back to Dad. "Worse than I imagined."

For a second, I wanted to punch her.

Dad sighed. "I wouldn't blame you if you walk right out that door and never come back."

She continued to view the room, her eyes glancing along the crooked picture of a duck on the wall. "I think you might need me."

What? No. We didn't need anybody. We were fine this way. We liked it this way.

Dad didn't say anything. He was looking around the room like she was doing, and I could tell he was noticing things for the first time—things that had always been there.

"Mr. Bradley, I have a feeling that I'm not what you imagined either."

Well, she had a point there. Nobody could imagine her—not with the big belly, quick-as-a-panther-reflexes, and bold mouth.

I could tell that Dad, who had a stiff spaghetti noodle dangling from his hair like a piece of straw, was trying not to stare at her stomach.

The lady sighed. Her eyes moved down to his thick, dirt-caked work boots, then rambled upward to his long, grease-stained pantlegs, and on to his favorite plaid shirt with the ripped sleeve. If his clothes could talk, they would be announcing, I do tractor maintenance all day. Every day.

The expression on her face looked like she was viewing a train wreck. Her gaze rested on his hair again, a mass of black tufts and pasta particles.

I ran my hand through my own hair. All clear.

The lady glanced down at her middle, then back to Dad. "Did you know I was expecting?"

"No. I don't even know your name."

"Margaret Bowman. Most people call me Maggie."

"William Bradley." Dad pointed at me. "This is my son, Luke."

"Hi." She smiled at me, and I smiled back. Her eyes were chocolate brown.

"I don't know who your folks know that I know," she said to Dad.

"Me either," he replied.

What a worthless conversation.

"I'll just give you the facts about me. I'm from Richmond. My husband, Ted, was a fireman." She drew a deep breath. "He died in June while on duty. Did you already know that?"

My heart sank down into my shoes.

"No, I didn't," Dad said. "I'm so sorry about your husband."

She continued. "Our baby is due December 27. My parents live in Brazil right now."

Dad's eyebrows moved up.

"They're missionaries. They came home for a while to help me at first, but they had to return."

Missionaries. She was probably really religious. I didn't know how Dad and I would handle religious stuff going on in our house.

She was still talking. "If you have a room for me, I'll stay in it."

"Uh…" Dad started.

"I'll get out a bulldozer and work on your kitchen. I might even try to sandblast some of the rest of this place. You can pay me whatever you told your Aunt LulaBelle's cousin's nephew's sister's friend's cousin's uncle's kangaroo's sister's niece—whatever amount you said. I enjoy cooking. I can handle laundry. I like kids." She turned to me. "You look like a good one."

"Thanks." Something warm flickered inside of me.

She shot a glance toward the living room. "And I'll take that little loud guy in there, too—Mr. Cool, who is wearing two left shoes."

Dad turned to me.

"What?" I raised my hands. "I'm sure I gave him a left and a right this morning."

The lady put her fingers on her temples. "I've had a splitting headache since six this morning. Do you have any aspirin?"

I hopped to the cupboard, opened it, and handed her the aspirin bottle while Dad rushed to the pantry, found a clean peach jar, and filled it with water.

"Thanks." She took the pills, then turned to Dad. "If I get a day off, I'd like it to be Wednesdays so I can go into town. I heard there's a group of ladies who make quilts."

"Fine with me." Dad nodded. "And you can rest on Sundays. I'll cook my famous hotdog lunch."

"Okay, then."

"Do you have your things in the car?" Dad asked.

"I have a couple of suitcases in the trunk. Eventually, I'll need to go to Richmond for the rest. When my rent ran out, I gathered everything and put it in my Aunt Joyce's garage."

Dad rubbed his chin. "Aunt Joyce?"

"You don't know her."

Suddenly, I was anxious to get away from this weird conversation. "I'll get your stuff from the car," I offered.

She handed me her keys. "Thank you. There are two suitcases in the trunk."

"Maybe you should rest a bit until your headache clears up." Dad stood. "Luke and I'll work on these dishes."

"Oh, that'd be nice. Would you mind showing me to my room?"

Her room? I stopped at the door. Where? What room?

Dad turned toward the hall, probably trying to think of way to invent a room in the next five seconds.

I escaped.

Raindrops were pelting me, so I grabbed a suitcase out of the trunk and dragged it to the covered porch before it got soaked. I ran back for the smaller suitcase, then brought them both inside.

Dad and the lady were in his room, staring at the bed, which was all tussled up worse than usual.

I spoke. "Whoops. It looks like we forgot about the peanut butter and jelly fight Stevie and Bo-Wad had in here yesterday."

"Bo-Wad?" the lady asked.

"Stevie's friend," I answered.

"Great." Dad, who'd seemed mostly calm so far, now had a bit of a choke in his voice. "And I put the last clean sheets on the couch for myself last night." He sighed. "Let's get these off the bed and throw 'em in the washer, son."

Even though I was still wrestling with the idea of a stranger sleeping at our house, I realized Dad needed my help. "She can use my bed," I offered.

"Yours has clean sheets?" he asked.

"Well, they don't have food stuck on 'em."

"Um…" The lady was about my height, and since I'm tall for a fifth grader, her eyes hit me straight-on. "Okay."

Dad began stripping off his sheets while I led her up the steep steps to the wide room I shared with Stevie. I showed her my bed, thinking how weird it was to have a woman invading our house like this, then went downstairs and helped Dad stuff the sheets into the washer. We shut the door to dad's room. Nobody would sleep there tonight.

While she was upstairs, we ate tuna-fish sandwiches and alphabet soup from a can. Then we tackled the mess in the kitchen.

At about 9:00 we set the last sparkling dish on the cupboard shelf. And since the rain had stopped and we didn't have a dryer, we hung the clean sheets out on the line. Dad always said he liked the all-night dewy smell.

We stood at the end of the hall and looked up the steps.

"Pretty long nap," I said.

"I guess we'll just leave her up there."

We pulled out the roll-away bed and shoved it into the nook below the stairs.

"I'll sleep here," Dad said. We threw an old quilt on top of the mattress, and we both flopped down on it.

"This'll work for you," I said. "But don't sit up too fast. You'll bonk your head on the underside of the steps."

"Yeah, I can see that happening."

"Dad. Are you tired?"

"What do you think? I've been up since 4:30, besides milking three cows, working on that John Deere all day. Oh, boy. Ray Phillips never came to get it. Oh, boy. I forgot to call him to say it was finished."

"Dad?"

"What?"

"Do you think you could read history with me tonight?" As tired as he looked, I figured he didn't need to add schoolwork to his evening plan, but it didn't hurt to ask.

"Of course." He sat up slowly to avoid bonking his head. "I'll go call

Ray while you get your book."

My brand new book, which was still parked beside the barn door, was soaked. I brought it in anyway. We sat at the very clean kitchen table while Dad read to me like he usually does because I'm no good at reading. Afterwards, we shook the book and hung it over a hanger on the kitchen doorknob, hoping the pages would dry out before school tomorrow.

Then we went to Stevie, who lay asleep on the living room floor surrounded by crackers and toy trucks. Sure enough, there were two left shoes on his feet. I pulled one off.

"Dad, I know he had a left and a right shoe this morning. Look, this isn't even our shoe. I've never seen it before in my life."

He took it from my hand. "Me either." He put the other one beside it, then hoisted my seven-year-old brother over his shoulder and walked quietly up the stairs, returning in a couple of minutes. "The lady is snoring like Uncle Ned's old lawnmower."

I walked into Dad's bedroom and stared at the two suitcases sitting on the bare mattress. When the lady put her stuff in his dresser, where would Dad's clothes go?

I went back out to the hall and stood beside him, wedged into his new tiny sleeping space under the steps, squinting as he tried to read his Today's Farm Equipment Newsletter by the hall light.

"What am I supposed to do?" I asked. "She's in my bed."

He set the newsletter on his chest and glanced at the living room. "The couch worked for me last night."

"Okay." At least I'd be close to my dad, this being a strange situation and all.

"I'm leaving the light on by the steps in case she needs to come downstairs," he said.

"Okay."

"Luke, why are you just standing there?"

"Dunno."

"Do you know what I think?" he asked.

"What?"

"She's only been here a few hours, and we've washed sheets and hung them out to dry. We've absolutely made our kitchen cleaner than it was the day after the fire-flood." He chuckled. "Now I'm sleeping in something that isn't even a closet, and you're a couch worm."

"So, what does that mean, Dad?"

"It means that in just one evening, she's whipped us into shape."

She whipped us into shape by doing nothing. Now that was scary.

TWO

This is when we started to use the word sarge.

I didn't sleep well on the couch. I heard a loud whack—like someone's head hitting the wall under the steps, probably at 4:30 when Dad got up to milk the cows. I knew he would be out in the barn for a couple of hours, then come back to make sure we ate some decent food before Stevie's school bus stopped by the mailbox at 7:30.

The next time I woke up, there were noises coming from the kitchen. I thought of Stevie out there alone, and I jumped up to make sure he wasn't trying to cook on the stove. Even though he'd started our terrible fire-flood two whole years ago, the memory was fresh enough to make me jolt out of bed when I heard sounds in the kitchen. Sometimes Stevie had trouble understanding what he could and couldn't do.

Stevie wasn't in the kitchen. She was, the lady whose name I couldn't remember, standing at the sink.

I tried to sneak out, but she saw me in the doorway.

"Hey," she said. "Who did all this cleaning in here?"

"Me and my dad."

"Amazing." She grinned at me. "I saw you on the couch. Where did your father sleep?"

"Under the stairs."

"What?"

"Under the stairs." I spoke louder this time. Maybe she was hard of hearing.

I walked to the intercom like I did every morning and set my finger on the switch. "I gotta check in with my dad."

I pushed the switch down to TALK. "I'm awake, Dad." I flipped it up to LISTEN.

"Good!" His voice came from the near side of the barn. "What about Stevie?"

Back to TALK. "Not up yet. I'll go wake him." Back to LISTEN.

"Thanks, son. What about that scary woman? Is she up yet?"

The lady raised her eyebrows as she moved my hand away from the switch. She pushed it to TALK and leaned toward the speaker box. "That scary woman is up," she announced.

So, her ears worked just fine.

Straightening up, she flipped the switch to OFF and turned to me. "We'll just let him think about that for a while. Now show me where that man slept last night."

Oh, boy. My dad was in the doghouse already.

We walked down the hall and I showed her the cot under the steps.

"He slept there? Aren't there enough bedrooms in this house?"

"No, well, not now."

"So, why did he want a live-in housekeeper?"

"I don't think he wanted one. He just got one. Most of our other lady helpers went home at night. You're the only one who came from so far away you gotta stay here."

"Apparently Aunt Martha didn't have all her facts straight." She sighed. "This reminds me of that game telephone. Ever play it?"

I shook my head.

"It's a game where one person whispers something into the ear of the person beside her. Then that person whispers it to the next, and so on. By the time it gets to the last person in line, the message has changed considerably."

What did that have to do with this?

"What I mean is—Martha Taylor told someone that I was looking for a place to stay and help someone at the same time as a housekeeper. And by the time the message got passed along to your dad, well, some things were changed—or forgotten."

"Like the baby on the way."

"Precisely." She stared at Dad's rollaway bed. "And some things were lost in the message that came to me too."

"Probably when the message went through the kangaroo," I said.

She laughed then. "Yes, the kangaroo. My, you're a good listener. I'm surprised your dad didn't boot me out after I started going on about bulldozers and kangaroos."

It seemed kinda nice to hear someone laugh in our house, even if it was this short, brown-eyed stranger, laughing at herself.

"What's in there?" she asked, pointing to the door behind Dad's rocking chair in the living room.

"The library."

"Really. You have a library? Then why can't somebody sleep in there?" She grabbed the doorknob and tugged. It wouldn't budge. Grasping it with both hands, she yanked it open and looked into the room. "Oh."

I actually hadn't been in there for a long time. It seemed smaller than before. Dad's gazillions of childhood books were still on the shelves, books about everything under the sun. But to get to the books, you would have to climb over a pile of ripped overalls and a trunk full of my mother's old clothes and picture albums that I asked Dad to show me once. He'd said, "Not now. It's too hard." That was before I knew the entire story of her death, the reason for my dad's frustration and anger—and the deep cloud of sadness that hung over him sometimes. I never asked again.

Beside the trunk sat the motorcycle, in parts, that Dad and I tried to fix once. We were interrupted in the middle of the project by the last annoying woman helper person who insisted that motorcycles should not be parked in the living room.

"We need to get this motorcycle out of here," the lady said.

There she was, trying to whip us into shape.

She placed her hands on her hips. "Maybe I could just wheel it out."

"Don't try it," I said. "I wanted to make this room into a clubhouse once, but I couldn't get the motorcycle to budge. It weighs tons."

She scoped the room with her eyes. "Wow, look at all those books. You must be quite the reader."

"No." Not even close. "They're my dad's."

"Hmmmm." She looked at me, eye-to-eye. "When does your school bus get here? And the little guy—when does his come?"

"His is 7:30. Mine is 7:45."

"I'll get him ready this morning. My treat."

"Okay, thanks." It might be nice to have someone else get Stevie ready for a change.

"Where do you boys keep your clean clothes?"

"Kind of all over. I think Stevie's latest pile is on the dresser upstairs. We usually just go fishin' for clothes in the mornings. That's what Dad calls it."

"I see." She rubbed her temple, looked around the room, nodded, then muttered to herself. "I can do this." Turning abruptly, she walked past me to the steps. "I'll go fishin', then. Go pour yourself some cereal."

I went straight to the kitchen and did exactly as she said. Maybe having her around wouldn't be so bad after all, even if she was a bossy one.

This year I'd made it through the first month of fifth grade before it happened—the terrible moment of discovery that flashed across my teacher's face, the quick wrinkle over her eyebrows that signaled disappointment.

My jaw tightened like a vise. I wished I could dive out the window and evaporate into the warm fall air.

"Luke?"

"Yes, Miss Finch." Pretty, young, nice Miss Finch. I'd been trying hard to impress her this year—to show her what a great student I could be.

"Try it again." She pushed her blonde hair away from her cheek.

My heart came tumbling down as I leaned over the dreaded book, hoping to shade my page from the lights, hoping to settle the movement of the letters as they scrambled like ants along the margins. "I lost my place."

She tapped her long fingernail on her book. "Left column, second paragraph."

"On May 20, 1506, Columbus died…"

"Left column. Luke, please pay attention."

Oh. "Uh, other Eurog…Europeans began exportation…"

"Explorations," Eddie, my friend and seat partner, whispered.

"Explorations…explorations after his fri…first voyage." Deep breath. "They, too, poned of find…" That didn't make sense.

Miss Finch's voice broke into mine. "Hoped to find…"

"Hoped to find a pass…passage of, I mean…sorry, Miss Finch." I glanced up at her face—she was biting her lip, and I lost my place again. "Miss Finch, I feel sick. May I go to the office?"

Sighing, she filled out a yellow office slip and handed it to me. "Go ahead." She looked past me to the tall girl who gobbled books like they were Aunt Nelda's chocolate chip cookies. "Elizabeth, would you like to finish reading the paragraph?"

As I trudged past the cloakroom and out the door, Elizabeth's voice flowed behind me like the Wabash River, speaking words as if they'd come straight out of her head instead of from a book. How did she do that so easily?

I dragged myself down the hall to the school office.

"Well, Luke, I wondered how long it would take before you showed up this year." Mrs. Barnes stuck an office thermometer into my mouth.

Of course, I couldn't answer her.

She pulled my old familiar card out of her drawer and marked on it, then looked at her watch. "Math test today?" she asked.

"No."

"Don't talk." She grinned. "Keep those lips shut."

I smiled back, but my heart wasn't in it.

"Spelling test?"

I shook my head.

"Reading test?"

Shook it again.

"You don't look sick."

I was very sick—sick of school. And it was only September.

She answered the phone while I clamped my mouth tight around the thermometer in the hopes that maybe, just this once, I had a fever so I could go home.

She examined the thermometer, then sent me back to class.

Discouraged, I slunk into my seat. One by one, other kids read aloud while I stared at my book like it was a brick, my heart sinking down into my shoes.

Stupid, stupid, stupid.

Miss Finch had figured it out—I couldn't read worth beans.

I'd just barely survived the school day. As the bus bumped down the road, Eddie sat beside me in his usual place, reading his Hardy Boys book of the week, *The Hidden Harbor Mystery*. My job was to flick him on the ears before his stop, which was always fun because they stuck out. Next, I would peel the book from his face and shove him off the bus before it was too late. We always had fun doing that. He tried to wrestle me, holding onto the book in his big mitts, scrunching up his nose so his freckles ran together.

We had a ways to go before we reached his corner, so I relaxed and looked out the window, thinking maybe the long rows of dead corn stalks would soothe the familiar bad feeling that was growling in my gut. Why couldn't I read like Eddie? What was wrong with me?

I needed to think about something else, Halloween, my favorite candy holiday only a month away.

I fingered the slip of paper in my pocket, the fine. The rain-soaked history book was going to cost my dad money. And after he paid for it, I needed to find some kind of job so I could pay him back.

Miss Finch had sternly informed me that we were supposed to read our history books in class, not at home. She told me that if I didn't waste my time just staring at my books, but actually reading them, I would be in less trouble. I'm not sure why she'd bothered saying so. I could tell she already thought I was hopeless, anyway. I wondered if last year's teacher, Mrs. Randall, had told her how dumb I was, or that she'd threatened to hold me back in fourth grade while Eddie and my other friends moved on without me. The very thought made my heart sink.

Eddie's reddish-brown eyebrows lifted, then lowered again. He was in another world, a world of mystery and adventure. I watched him read. There was almost a rhythm to it, a sweeping of his eyes across and across, and down until they'd gobbled the words completely. He turned the page.

I wondered what his eyes saw that mine didn't.

It wasn't the seeing. It was the smartness. He was smart, and I was not.

The good part of my day had been that I'd managed to dig the wet history book out of the trash can in our classroom and put it under my lunch box to take home. We would still need to buy a new book, but this way Dad could read history to me every night ahead of schedule. For once, I could understand history information before the rest of the class.

Eddie's stop was coming up. I started flicking him on the ear, making it wiggle. "Twang, twang."

"Ow. Stop that, you goofball."

"We're almost at your house."

He bent the corner of his page and shut the book. I could tell his brain was still somewhere between the Hardy Boys and me so I didn't disturb him anymore.

He turned and gave me his old familiar grin. "Thanks."

My stop was next. After getting off the bus, I walked up the lane and tossed my books on the porch, then faced the barn. Part of me was ready to do the normal thing—to go talk to Dad for a few minutes before Stevie's bus arrived. But another part of me wondered what the woman had been doing in the house. Was she rifling through my stuff, throwing away my junk drawer treasures like the last lady helper had done? Maybe I wasn't ready to face what was going on in there. I would go see Dad first.

He was sitting at his desk at the far end of the barn, almost hidden from view by the John Deere tractor. I stopped to breathe in a rich noseful of hay, cow manure, and motor oil.

Dad set down his pen. "Hi, Luke. How was your day?"

"Okay, I guess." Dad's duty was to ask about my day. My duty was to say, *Okay, I guess,* even if it wasn't true. "Dad, why didn't Mr. Phillips come get his tractor? I'm ready for our ice cream celebration when he pays you."

"He's on his way and bringing me another customer. We'll have a different tractor sitting in the John Deere place, a good old 1930 Massey-Harris."

"More ice cream."

As he turned to me, I noticed a wad of square white hanky taped just above his right eye.

"What is that?" I asked.

"I whacked my noggin this morning when I sat up and hit the underside of the stairs. Gave me a good knot. After you left for school, I ventured into the kitchen for some coffee, and Maggie insisted on fixing up my head with this hanky invention."

"Man, it's big. And it has a pink *M* on it."

"Hey, this is nothing! She took a full inventory of my face and arms, including yesterday's bang-ups." He held out his long arms, smeared with tractor grease. "She was holding ice on my head and poking at my bruises. Told me I should've had stitches on that old cut over my ear. I was afraid she was going to knock me out and perform surgery right there on the kitchen table."

I wanted to laugh, but instead I took a deep breath and did what I had to do. "Dad, we have to pay for the history book."

"Not a surprise."

I pulled the fine slip out of my pocket and handed it to him. "I need to do some work for somebody so I can pay for this."

"Uncle Ned could use help stacking firewood. He says his back is getting too old and creaky."

"Maybe on Saturday."

"I'll set it up for you."

"Okay." I liked helping Uncle Ned. While we worked, he liked to try out his jokes on me, and when the job was done we went inside and ate cookies.

Dad turned back to his desk.

"Uh, Dad?"

"Yes."

"I dug the old wet book out of the trash and brought it home. I want to be ahead in history instead of behind all the time. Can you read a little extra to me tonight?"

He glanced at me for a second. He'd tried all sorts of things to get me to read. Finally, one day last year he'd taken a deep breath and said, "Do you know what? I'll just read to you any time you need it."

And that's the way it'd been ever since.

"Sure, son."

I decided to change the subject. "What's been happening inside our house today?"

"I'm afraid to go in there. Haven't left the barn since the woman strapped this magnificent medical invention to my head. She brought a sandwich out at lunchtime. I think she feels sorry for me."

The sound of gravel crunching under heavy wheels came to my ears. Probably Mr. Phillips was here.

"Either that, or she wanted to make sure I was still wearing my bandage." Dad continued as he stood. "I protested after I looked in a mirror and saw how big it was." He peeled the hanky off, showing a knot, bluish bruise, and a red scrape. "How does it look underneath?"

"Ugly."

He tried to press the tape back into place, but it didn't stick, so he sighed and set it on the desk. "I have a feeling I'm going to be in trouble with the sergeant when she sees me without my first-aid patch." He grinned at me.

I smiled, too. "Sarge."

"Don't let her hear you say that. We might both end up with KP duty...again." He walked to the wide barn doorway to greet the two men who were outside.

I wandered past a monstrous old tractor, like a rusty green dinosaur, pulled by a big Ford pickup. Scurrying to the porch, I snatched up my books and lunch box, and stopped at the door. After carefully folding my still-damp history book over the hanger I'd left on the doorknob this morning, I walked into the kitchen.

The room looked pretty much the same as it had before school, but something was very different. An aroma filled the air, pulling me toward the stove where a pot bubbled. Our pot, the one Dad used for spaghetti, shone like a new car, and a cloud of steamy, beefy air floated just above it. To the side, on the clean counter, sat a pan of homemade biscuits. My nose had died and gone to heaven. I turned around. Where was she?

I set down my lunchbox and went to the stairs. The rollaway bed was gone, and in its place was the old trunk from the library, piled high with folded overalls.

She'd been busy.

As I walked through the living room, I saw the motorcycle in the corner. It was balanced on its kickstand, gleaming in the window light. The loose metal parts stood like soldiers in a row on a sheet of newspaper along the baseboard.

The lady appeared in the doorway of the library. "Good. You're here. I need a hand." She had a dirt smudge on her cheek, and her short hair was sticking out all fluffy around her face. She smoothed it down with her hand. "I must be a mess."

"How did you get the motorcycle out of there?" Who was she—Hercules?

"Well." She brushed off her hands. "I lifted off the heavy stuff, and I fiddled with the little doo-flickies on the wheelie-deelie part, then it just slid out here like a big roller skate. Come in here and help me."

She was putting sheets on the rollaway bed in the library. It was pressed against the books, with the little lamp from Dad's old room resting on a small table. As I helped her tuck in the corners, I noticed the fresh smell in the room. She'd opened the window, which seemed to sparkle. The old curtains, scrubbed into tatters, flapped gently against the screen.

I followed her to the kitchen as the roar of a truck, now without the dinosaur tractor, rumbled away down the lane. We went to the window and watched as it turned onto the road. Behind it, the man named Mr. Phillips putted along on his John Deere, a look of satisfaction on his face. "I was under the impression your dad was a dairy farmer," the sergeant commented.

"Well, actually he is," I said with a flash of pride. "But people keep bringing broken tractors, and he keeps fixing them."

THREE

*After she threatened to hang Christmas ornaments on the
motorcycle, she told us we were getting another female.*

Maggie didn't go away. I woke up every morning to the smells of
coffee and bacon, and the sounds of dishes clanking.

I still started my day by calling Dad on the intercom and
announcing I was awake. It didn't seem to matter as much as it used to
because now a grown-up was in the house with us, frying eggs in a pan
and pouring fresh juice into sparkling clean glasses. She made sure we
washed before we put on the matched socks and neatly folded clothes
she'd laid on the steps, including new jeans that went all the way down
to my shoe tops instead of hanging at mid-ankle. But I called Dad every morning anyway because that's what I'd done since forever.

Unfortunately, the hot breakfast and neat clothes didn't change my
life at school, nor did the fact that Dad read the history assignments
to me ahead of time, just like he'd promised. It was already November,
and I sat at my school desk staring out at the leafless trees.

"Luke, don't daydream. Take your test." Miss Finch had snuck up
beside me.

I looked up at her. "May I do the test in the hall? It helps if can read
out loud."

"Of course not." She glared at me like I'd just asked if I could rob a bank.

I read the first question again—something about the explorers from
Spain. I wished I could just tell the teacher what I knew, instead of try-

ing to go through the agonizing process of reading the questions and multiple-choice answers which were, of course, designed to trick people. I struggled down the page, trying to make the letters stop bouncing.

"Five minutes left," Miss Finch announced.

I glanced at the remaining questions and simply wrote a letter in each blank. *A, B, B, D, C.* Maybe I would get some of them right.

Miss Finch collected the papers, frowned at mine, and went on to Eddie's test, which was finished and turned over. He had drawn Ponce de Leon in the wilderness and labeled some of the objects around him. I wish I could've done that instead of what I'd just done.

Later, I sat beside Eddie and stared out the bus window. Sadly, Halloween was gone, along with my stash of candy. There was nothing to look forward to until Thanksgiving. I would try to think of something to be thankful for.

Flunking, big time.

Eddie slammed his book shut. "Done," he said as he dropped his latest Hardy Boys mystery on his lap. "Do you want to borrow this one, Luke? It's exciting." Even though Eddie knew I had trouble reading, he pretended I was good at it like he was. He shoved it into my hand. "Try it."

I didn't feel like arguing, so I put it on top of my schoolbooks. "Sure." Maybe someday a miracle would happen, the one where I opened a book and the words silently spoke to my brain with the greatest of ease.

"Guess how many Hardy Boy books I've read so far," he challenged.

"How many?"

"No, you guess."

I didn't feel like guessing. "Six thousand."

"That's hogwash, Luke. There aren't even six thousand Hardy Boy books."

I sighed. "Five thousand."

"Eleven."

I flicked his ear with my finger. "We're almost to your stop."

"You don't have to do that when I'm not reading. I can recognize my own house." He frowned.

I shrugged. "Sorry. I couldn't resist. Besides, it's tradition."

The bus stopped, and Eddie got off.

Eleven Hardy Boys books. I'd never even read one.

I got off the bus and trudged up the lane where I saw Maggie in the yard with a plastic bat and ball. She was playing with Stevie, who was home early today because Dad had taken him to the dentist after lunch. Stevie'd been begging me to play catch with him lately, but I'd been too busy trying to figure out how to pass fifth grade, and Maggie had stepped in. Seeing them out there together, I suddenly felt guilty. "My turn," I said.

"Thanks." Maggie dropped the bat and handed me the ball. "I'll start supper. If it gets much colder out here, come inside and get warmer coats."

I tossed the ball to Stevie. It bounced off his shin and rolled. When he threw it back to me, it hit the porch. After I retrieved it, I moved us closer together and tossed it as softly as possible. It hit his stomach and rolled down into his hands. He laughed for no reason, then flung the ball my way. After my frustrating day at school, it felt good to do something I could manage.

Dad called Stevie into the barn, so I dropped the ball and bat into the corner of the porch and entered the kitchen, stopping to enjoy the aroma of chicken and dumplings, and something chocolate, too, possibly cake.

I set my books on the table next to a green booklet titled, *A Man after God's Own Heart*, probably Maggie's Bible study book. I tried to imagine a bunch of ladies who made quilts sitting around a table every Wednesday talking about a man after God's own heart. I suppose they all wanted to catch one.

Maggie stood beside Stevie's marble contraption, a sort of knee-high gravity-powered roller coaster for marbles. "I found this in the hall closet," she said. "What is it?"

"Stevie's magnificent marble contraption," I answered. "You put a marble on top and it rolls down to the bottom."

"Show me how it works."

She waited while I found a marble in the junk drawer. I set it on the grooved top board, which slanted downward into a hose. We watched the marble roll down into the hose, curl around to the other side, plop onto another grooved board that dropped it into another piece of hose and so on, back and forth, until the marble slid out across the kitchen floor to the wall where it stopped with a satisfying thunk.

"Wow," she said. "Where'd you get this thing?"

"I made it."

"You made it?" Her eyebrows lifted.

"Yeah, for Stevie. Dad helped me."

"I'll bet Stevie loves it."

"He does. Well, he did. Our last lady helper made us put it in the closet. She said it cluttered up the house."

"It's amazing!" Maggie looked at me with admiration.

My insides started glowing. "Thanks." The good food smells added to my pleasure.

"Let's keep it out tonight so Stevie can play with it."

"Okay."

Dad walked in from the porch, with Stevie close behind. "Chicken and dumplin's again?" Dad asked. "How am I supposed to keep my slim, trim figure with all this good cooking these past two months? I'm outgrowing all my pants. Pretty soon I'll start to look like…um…"

"Me." Maggie rubbed her round stomach. "You were going to say me, weren't you?" She put her fists on her hips.

"I…uh. No, of course not." As he stepped away his eyes fell on the marble contraption. "What are we doing with this?"

"Maggie found it today," I answered.

"Cool marbles," Stevie added.

Dad scooped the marble up off the floor and handed it to my brother, who set it on top of the contraption. We all watched it roll through its course and plop out the end.

Dad looked at me. "Let's put this thing in the living room tonight for Stevie."

"Oh, good," Maggie said. "Add it to your collection in there with the motorcycle."

"Oh, that." He picked up the invention and headed down the hall,

Stevie tagging along behind.

"Dinner'll be ready in about an hour!" she shouted after them. "And some guy named Ralph Ross phoned and says he wants to buy that motorcycle when it gets fixed. I wrote his number by the phone."

"Thanks," Dad called.

Last week I had asked Dad why he didn't take the motorcycle to the barn. He said he'd left it in the house as a test to see what Maggie would do. She'd done nothing. So, this morning I asked Dad if Maggie had passed the test, and he said yes.

We'd already cleared a place in the barn. Tonight after supper, we planned to rig a ramp for the porch steps and get the motorcycle out of the house.

"Maggie?" I said.

"Yes?"

"Why do you let us keep the motorcycle in the living room?"

"It's your house, not mine. If you like a motorcycle in there, well, okay." She grinned. "Next month we can hang a string of lights on it and put an angel on top."

I smiled as I pushed Maggie's books to the side and got out my pencil. I opened my history book and copied the first question: 1. Why did English settlers come to Jamestown?

There was a picture of Jamestown in my book, little square houses in a triangular-shaped fort. I leaned my head over the book and began to whisper so Maggie couldn't hear me. "The Enblish...Englishmen... crowded adored there shi..."

"Aboard," Maggie said. "They crowded aboard three ships." She was now hovering over me like she'd done last night while Dad was gone to a dairy council meeting. She'd made me read to her for a change, and because I'd been through the pages at school, I kinda faked my way through it. At least, I thought I did. She didn't get mad at me or tell me I was stupi—

"You wrote, 'Why bib the Endish settles come the Jamestown.'" Her voice brought me back to the present. "And you forgot the punctuation."

I covered my paper with my hand.

Scratching her chin, she stared off into space for a minute. "Okay, I got it."

"What?"

"Go get the whiffle ball and bat off the porch."

"What?" What for? Does she whack stupid kids with plastic bats?

"Bring it in here."

I obeyed her, like usual.

She shoved my book aside. "Show me your left hand," she said.

I looked down at my hands. It always took me a minute to do left-right.

She grabbed my left hand and set it on the table. In fact, she stretched out my left arm, set my hand on its side, and formed it so I made the letter *C* with my curved thumb and fingers.

"What letter is that?" she asked, touching my fingers.

"*C*."

"Straighten your index finger and thumb so you make an *L*."

I did.

"Now don't move." She went to the junk drawer and rustled around, then returned with a blue pen and drew the letter L on the side of my hand. "*L* for left. Say it."

"What?"

"Say, '*L* for left.'"

"*L* for left."

"Look at it and say it."

"*L* for left."

"Put your hands in your lap."

I did. You don't disobey the sarge.

"Okay. Show me your left hand."

Easy. I did. I could still feel the scratch from her pen.

"Show me your right hand."

I did.

"Back to the left. Hold it out on the table again like before, with the *L* showing."

I stretched my forearm and held my fingers in the *L* position.

She laid the plastic bat alongside the inside of my arm, and she tucked the ball at my elbow beside it. "This is the letter *b* for baseball."

"Okay." I had no idea what she was trying to do.

"Say it."

"*B* for baseball. What are you talking about?"

"The bat is the stick on the *b*. The ball is the circle. *B* and *L* are on the same side of the stick."

I looked down. I saw the *L* on my hand, the stretch of my arm, the ball to the right of the bat. "*B* for baseball."

She set my paper next to the bat and ball. "Look at this word you wrote." She pointed at it. "Are these *b*'s or *d*'s?"

I looked at the *L* on my hand, and the stick and circle on the lines as they wavered on the page. Actually, the circle held still, the line wobbled. "*B*."

"Right," she said. "So, what is that word?"

"Bib."

"Why do you move your head over the book like that?"

I hadn't noticed that I did, and what was wrong with it, anyway?

"It looks to me as if you're putting the book in a shadow."

"I am."

"So, why do you do that?"

I might as well bare all. "It makes the letters hold still sometimes."

She was silent for a moment. "Okay."

Okay?

She pointed to the question in the book. "Find the word *did*."

I searched, then pointed to it.

"Hold the bat and ball beside your arm. Then compare it to *did*."

I set the ball back in place. I held my head over the book and looked down. The letters held still enough, but I couldn't really tell if I was looking at *did* or *bib*. When I looked back and forth from the bat to the page, I couldn't seem to compare the letters like she wanted me to. I felt my heart sinking as I slumped in my chair.

Sighing, she rested her hand on my shoulder. "Okay, let me ask about your history test. Was it one of those multiple-choice kind like the last one?"

"Yes."

"*A, b, c, d*?"

"Yes."

She sighed. "In a column or a paragraph?"

Frustration rose in me. "I don't want to talk about it."

Looking disappointed, she stepped back.

"What's this?" Dad asked from the hall doorway. "Why is the bat on the table?"

"To help me read." I looked up at Maggie. "I don't think it's helping." I hoped my voice didn't sound too angry.

She whisked the baseball equipment off the table and set it by the back door. "It was just an experiment."

A failed experiment.

Dad stood between us for a minute, thoughtfully rubbing his chin before he sat down. "Luke, would you like me to read?"

I looked at the sarge for permission.

"Go ahead," she said.

Dad gave her a questioning glance as he reached for my book. "Okay, Luke. Where are we?"

"Just a minute." I held my hand out with the *L* on it and looked at the word on my paper. I erased the *b*'s and made them *d*'s. Looking at the word again, I really couldn't tell the difference—even with the *L* on my hand.

Dad opened his mouth to start reading.

"I'll interrupt for just a second, if you don't mind," Maggie said. "Then you can get on with the reading."

Dad shut his mouth.

Now what?

She cleared her throat as she faced us, no longer self-conscious about her belly, which had gone from bowling ball to basketball to beach ball. Of course, I wouldn't say that to her.

She took a deep breath. "Two things. First, on Sunday I'd like to visit the church in town where my quilt lady Bible study is held, Riverside Church. Do you know anything about it?"

"Yes," Dad answered. "We used to go there."

"Used to go?"

"Yes. But after Ramona, my wife, died everybody always stared at us with that 'I feel sorry for you' look in their eyes. Then, Stevie got bigger and his voice got stronger."

Maggie was focused on Dad, her eyes questioning.

I knew what he was going to say next because I'd heard him tell other people. "Stevie loves to sing, and he sings really, really loud, and in a monotone fog-horn voice. And he sneezes all over everything. It got so that when I walked in with my boys and sat down, well, people quietly moved away from us. You know, little tiny half-cheek scoots across the pew, and pretty soon we'd notice we were all alone—like an island."

"We called it Sneeze Island," I volunteered.

"I've come to the land of Sock Mountain and Sneeze Island," Maggie mumbled.

"Huh?" I said.

She winked at me. Maybe she was trying to let me know that she was okay with being in Sock Mountain and Sneeze Island.

Dad turned to Maggie. "What's the second thing?"

"Oh." She wiped her hands on a dish towel. "I've been asked to care for another child."

"What?" Dad put his hand on his head. "So soon?"

I groaned. Had I blown it? "You're leaving us already?" I was beginning to like her, even though she was bossy.

"Uh, no." She grinned. "Well, it's nice to know I'd be missed. The child would come here."

"Here?" Dad asked.

"Here, with your permission. After school mostly, two or three times a week. Her father drives a delivery truck and gets home around eight at night. Her mother works evening shifts at Mercy Hospital, so on those days the girl will come home on the bus with Luke, and she'll stay here until her dad picks her up."

A girl? What girl?

Dad stretched back from the table. "When did all this happen?"

41

"Mrs. Peterson—that's the mother—asked me at Bible study. I told her I might be able to help her, but I would talk to you first, which I'm doing now."

Peterson? Elizabeth Peterson?

Dad leaned forward. "What would this entail? Just having another kid running around the house? I wonder what kind of kid she is."

"She seems nice. Maybe sort of quiet, from what I've observed."

Elizabeth Peterson? Oh, no! Owl-rimmed glasses, book in the face, taller than me, Elizabeth Peterson?

Maggie continued. "And I'll earn a little extra money, which I'll keep in a separate pot."

"Okay," Dad said.

"What pot?" I asked.

"A different one than where I keep the money your father pays me."

Once last year Elizabeth Peterson had sat beside me while I worked on my spelling page. She kept pointing at my words and saying, That's wrong. You forgot the *e*, and there are two *f*s in that word, and so on. She even wanted me to switch my pencil from my left hand to my right. It was so annoying, trying to be polite while she trying to fix me. Finally, I'd slammed my book shut. She turned away and left me alone.

Later, I saw her laughing with her friends and looking at me. It was one of those rare times when I wanted to sock a girl.

Maggie interrupted my thoughts. "I'll use the extra money to spruce up this place. I'll start with new curtains over there." She pointed at the window. "And I'll replace the dishes from the spaghetti explosion."

Dad sat up straight. "But this isn't your house. You shouldn't spend your money on my things. What if you decide to leave us, and all your stuff is in my house?"

I held my breath.

"Leave you? Are you trying to get rid of me already?"

"No. I don't plan to get rid of you. It's just that, well, you've already outlasted all your predecessors. I live day to day when you women-people are in my house."

"Really?" She clenched her fingers and set them on her hips.

He took a deep breath and went on. "If you're like the others, I'll just turn around one day and *poof*—you'll be gone on to something better."

She rested her hand on her stomach. "Right now, I'm not poofing anywhere."

I exhaled.

So did Dad, I think.

She walked over to the stove. "So, if I'm to be here for a while, I'd like to make it more pretty." She turned to Dad. "All right?"

Dad glanced at me. "What do you think?"

"I'm okay with the pretty stuff." But I wasn't sure I could handle having two females in the house telling me what to do.

"Okay." Dad fingered my history book. "Where are we?"

Maggie spoke again. "One more thing, William."

"Yes?"

"When you read to him, turn the book so he can follow along."

Something thunked in the living room. "Stevie?" Maggie rushed down the hall.

"Man, she's bossy," I whispered to Dad.

Dad's hand rested on the green workbook Maggie had left on the table. "What's this?" he said. "It's titled *A Man after God's Own Heart*."

"I think it's her quilt ladies Bible study book."

"A man after God's own heart?" His eyes crinkled into a grin.

"Yep." I laughed. "So, do you think those ladies should be studying about a wo-man after God's own heart?"

He nodded, then checked down the hall to see if Maggie was coming before he did a quick flip through the pages.

"Sometimes she writes in it," I said.

He stopped at one section and let his eyes linger. "Hmm."

"Dad, she'll be back in a minute. Don't let her catch you being nosy."

"Tell me if she's coming." He finished reading something and reluctantly shut the book. "Interesting." He pushed it to the side, then turned to me. "Scoot closer, son."

I did.

"Luke, why is there an *L* on your hand?"

I sighed. "You don't want to know."

He turned my open history book so I could see it. "We'd better do what the sarge says."

As he began to read, Maggie stepped into the kitchen. I wondered if she'd heard Dad say sarge. She quietly returned to her work. Apparently, Stevie was okay—noisy, but okay in his own clumsy little world.

As Dad unfolded the story of the first English settlers in our country, Maggie worked by the stove, clattering dishes on the counter.

When we finished, Dad clapped my book shut and handed it to me. Even though it was now completely dry, I still hung it on the hanger, sort of like a doorknob decoration.

Maggie set the napkins on the table. "Maybe we can keep that history book somewhere else," she said. "It's been dry for a long time, but it stinks."

"Okay, I'll take care of it after supper." I would find a better place.

"I'd like you two to set the table while I go get Stevie cleaned up." As she headed down the hall, her voice floated back to us. "The sarge has spoken."

FOUR

I can see the headlines now: Pregnant Woman Beats up Teacher.

Nobody warned Maggie about Bo-Wad.

Sometimes in the past when Willow Lane special school had a substitute bus driver, my brother's best friend would ride past his own house and end up at ours. Then he got off the bus with Stevie and they entered the kitchen together yelling, "Cool Bo-Wad!"

On this crispy cool day, I saw it happen from the barn where I was fixing my old bike for Stevie. I watched the unfamiliar bus driver open the door and let both boys tumble down the steps and land on the dirt by our mailbox.

Arm in arm, they stumbled up the driveway like two soccer players trying to steal the ball from each other, only there was no ball. For the life of me, I don't know why the two clumsiest kids on Earth insisted on walking with their arms locked together. They clomped up the porch steps, giggling.

That's when I decided to go help Maggie with her official introduction to Bo-Wad. As I stepped into the kitchen, they were drinking huge glugs of water from plastic cups, choking, and splattering their shirts with exploding dribbles. Stevie stopped long enough to sneeze all over Maggie's arm.

Most wimpy people would be bothered by Stevie's big sneezes, but Maggie didn't even flinch. She wiped it off with a dish towel and tossed it on the washer where Sock Mountain used to be. "Do you know this guy?" she asked me. "Is he the famous Bo-Wad?"

"Yes."

"Does his mother know he's here?"

"Probably not. We have his phone number somewhere."

Maggie picked up our telephone notebook and started to page through it. "Hmmm. Is it spelled 'W-A-D'?"

Dad walked into the room, stripped a homemade first aid patch off his neck, and set it on the table. "Maggie, I can't wear all this stuff when I work. It gets caught on tractor knobs." Then he saw the little boys. "Oh, Bo-Wad. Haven't seen you in a while. Must be a new bus driver today?" His eyes crinkled as he broke into a welcoming grin.

Bo-Wad, of course, pushed his droopy lips into the famous lopsided smile that spread wide across his thin face. Bo-Wad loved my dad.

"I can't seem to find a phone number for Bo-Wad." Maggie was thumbing through the notebook.

Dad took it from her. "The first time Bo-Wad showed up here I had a terrible time figuring out his name. Thank goodness, the school was still open, so I called there for help."

Bo-Wad grabbed Maggie's sleeve and said, "Shevie shpishals."

"What?" she asked.

"Shpishals. Me and Shevie shpishals."

Stevie pulled Bo-Wad away from Maggie and dragged him down the hall, probably to play with the cool trucks in the living room.

Dad put his finger on something in the notebook. "Okay, Maggie." He smiled as he closed the book on his finger. "Here's the bet. I'll do the dishes tonight if you can tell me Bo-Wad's real name."

Maggie shifted her gaze to me. "Do you know it?" she asked.

"Yes. But I'm not telling. We men have to stick together." I winked at Dad.

He winked back.

"Okay, I get three tries." She stood up straight.

I knew by now that she liked challenges.

"Bo Watson," she guessed.

"No." I said.

"Bo Wadsworth?"

"No."

"Am I close?"

"No."

"Alexander Abernathy."

Dad opened the book and showed her the name. "Joe White."

"Joe White?" She rolled her eyes.

"Bo-Wad, Joe White. Plain as the nose on your face." Dad handed her the book. "Can we invite Bo-Wad for dinner?"

"Of course," she said. "It's your house."

It was kind of funny, Dad asking her for permission in his own house. But then again, she was the cook.

While Dad was on the phone, Stevie and Bo-Wad came out of Maggie's room. Stevie's fist was clenched around a piece of silky blue material that draped down his arm.

"Hey, you guys shouldn't go in Maggie's room," I said.

Ignoring me, Stevie held the blue clothing up to Maggie. It looked like a nightgown or something. I probably shouldn't be staring at it.

"Shevie shpishals," Bo-Wad pleaded.

Maggie took it from him. "What are you doing with my slip?"

I turned away, feeling my face grow hot.

"Shevie shpishals," Bo-Wad repeated. "Peas, Shevie shpishals."

"Is there an interpreter in this house?" Maggie nudged me, so I turned back around.

"Shpishals," Bo-Wad repeated.

She put her hand on Stevie's head. "Tell me what your friend is saying."

Stevie grinned. "Spindles. He want. Spindles for me."

"Spindles," Maggie repeated. She lowered the slip so the boys could touch it. "Show me spindles."

Stevie picked at one of the elastic straps.

"So, you want some spindles? You'll have spindles. I'll get right on it after supper." She draped the slip over the back of a chair and walked to the sink. "Meanwhile, go play cool trucks."

"Spindles now."

"No, I'll do spindles after supper."

"Okay."

Satisfied, the two little boys went down the hall to their trucks.

Turning from the phone, Dad bumped into the chair with the shiny blue material. "What the?" His face got red.

"William," Maggie said. "Your mission is to figure out what exactly a 'shpishal' is, or in the other language—'spindle'. And to tell me what it has to do with my slip."

Dad eyed Maggie for a moment. "Sometimes I think I'm going crazy around here." He walked down the hall.

"That makes two of us," she said to his back.

I tried not to look at the slip on the chair as I helped Maggie set the table with an extra plate for our guest, Bo-Wad. We weren't used to having lady underwear sitting in the house, and I didn't know how to act around it.

I heard Dad discussing shpishals and spindles with the little boys in the living room, but it didn't sound like he was getting anywhere. I did tell Maggie that "Shevie" was Bo-Wad's word for "Stevie." Other than that, I had no information.

Once we got settled around the dinner table, Maggie gave Bo-Wad a tender look, which he returned with one of his heart-warmer smiles, so big his eyes squeezed all the way shut. She asked him if he wanted to take off his sweater. It was toasty in the kitchen from all the cooking, and his face had a pink glow.

He nodded.

Since I was sitting beside him, I unzipped his sweater, pulled it down off his shoulders, and hung it on the back of his chair. Underneath his sweater he wore a plain white shirt and bright blue suspenders. He lovingly ran his fingers along his suspenders before he picked up his spoon.

"Hey!" I shouted. "Spindles!"

Maggie's raised her hands. "Ahhhh," she said. "And after supper, for the simple sacrifice of one old slip and four safety pins, we will have Shevie shpishals." Then she looked at Dad, who was wearing a funny half-smile.

She palmed her forehead. "I can't believe I just said that."

"And with such excitement in your voice," he added.

For some reason, her face reddened. "Yes, definitely—I'm going crazy in this house."

Things at home were going along okay. Dad and I were getting used to having Maggie around. Her cooking alone made it worth having a lady helper in the house. But school was making my stomach hurt. And to make matters worse, it was parent-teacher conference time. In previous years, Stevie and had I stayed with Uncle Ned and Aunt Nelda while Dad went alone to meet the teacher. Ned and Nelda were the closest thing we had to grandparents, and I always had fun playing chess and eating cookies at their farmhouse on the other side of the walnut grove. Afterwards, Dad would come home looking as if someone, my teacher, had stomped all over him.

For some reason, though, after all these years Dad decided to bring me along to the conference, and Maggie and Stevie, since Nelda had a headache and couldn't watch him. Dad said he wanted this conference to be a team effort. Personally, I think he was tired of being told by my teachers that his son was hopeless. Maybe having me and the sarge along would make my teacher behave nicer.

First of all, Maggie made us get cleaned up, even Dad. She'd mended one of his shirts and ironed it, explaining that he should save it and only wear it off the farm. She'd even polished up a pair of old shoes she'd found at the bottom of a closet. I was there when he tried to jam his feet into them. After failing, he carefully wrapped them in newspaper and returned them to the closet before telling Maggie, "I appreciate your efforts to spruce me up, but those shoes were my father's, and they're two sizes too small for me. I'll keep them nice so Luke can grow into them someday. Then your shoe polishing efforts won't go to waste."

"Okay, William," is all she said.

When we got into the truck she suggested we say a prayer, which made me a little nervous. Did she expect a bad thing to happen at the conference?

Before I could absorb that thought, Dad agreed to say the prayer. I was surprised at that. Dad hadn't been much of a religious man since Mom died. But lately, Maggie had been leaving her woman Bible study stuff sitting on the kitchen table, and when she wasn't looking, Dad peeked in it.

In fact, yesterday I'd caught him sitting there with the Bible wide open, and he was bent over reading it, sort of like Eddie did when he was using his eyes to gobble up the Hardy Boys books, trying to figure out the mystery.

Now, sitting beside Maggie in the truck, Dad cleared his throat.

This must be some kind of a test to see if Dad was the man after God's own heart, and she was plotting to catch him. I held my breath to see what Dad would say.

He took a deep breath and closed his eyes. "Heavenly Father, help us have a good conference. Give us wisdom so we can learn some ways to help Luke with his schooling." He paused for a moment before ending it. "May cool heads prevail. Amen."

"May cool heads prevail?" Maggie asked quietly. "Do you usually have fights with teachers?"

"Me?" Dad shook his head. "Nooooo."

She pointed at me. "Him?"

"Nope," Dad said with a grin.

We all knew whose head needed to be cool, and she sighed. "You think you're so funny."

When we arrived at my school, Miss Finch had a file folder all ready with my name on it.

Dad introduced her to Maggie right off. "This is Maggie Bowman. She's our cook and housekeeper, and she often helps Luke with his schoolwork. So, we brought her along. This is a team effort."

Miss Finch had pulled her blonde hair back in a bun, trying to look older, I suppose—since conference day meant meeting with grown-ups. Even with her hair like this, I thought she looked pretty and I wished I could be one of the students who pleased her.

Everyone sat down except for Stevie, who stood beside Maggie, leaning against her and patting her huge stomach. "Cool tummy," he said.

She put her arm around him and gave him a squeeze.

He grinned at her, and a warm feeling passed through me.

Miss Finch took a deep breath and spoke to Maggie. "Nice to finally meet you—after the notes you've been sending."

Notes? What notes?

Then my teacher turned to Dad. "It's not customary for children to be present at the conference."

Maggie jumped right in. "That was actually my idea. Maybe Luke should know everything."

Everything? Maybe not. Maybe I wanted to be playing chess with Uncle Ned and listening to his funny stories about the old days.

Miss Finch continued. "I have all the things here you requested, Mrs. Bowman." She opened the folder. "Here are the two tests you asked about. One is history, and the other is science. As you can see, both are multiple choice tests. I find they are easy to grade, and most students can manage them."

"And Luke?" Dad had hope in his voice.

"D and an F. With these kinds of grades, I don't see how we can promote Luke to sixth grade at the end of the year."

"Oh." Dad clammed up.

My heart did a nosedive to the bottom of my shoes. I had to pass. I always go to school with Eddie and the other kids in my class. I had to stay with them. How awful it would be to get left behind with those kids who were now grubby fourth graders! Plus, next year was sixth grade nature camp. I had to pass.

Miss Finch continued. "He seems so smart when we discuss things in class, but when it comes to the seatwork, he, um…"

I really didn't like coming to my own school conference. I wanted to run for the door. "Would you like me to take Stevie to the playground?" I offered.

"No," Dad said without taking his eyes off the teacher. "What were you saying about his seatwork?"

"It's not acceptable."

"What specifically?"

"Reading, writing, spelling, and math."

Dad looked like someone had smacked him in the face with a board. Probably Miss Finch's answers were sending his heart down to his shoes too.

She continued. "He needs to study more and write neatly."

I hung my head, wanting to just disappear.

Maggie scooted forward to examine the test Miss Finch held out, and Stevie moved with her.

With a big sigh, Dad stared over her shoulder.

I had no desire to see it. I knew what it looked like.

"This is the history test about our country's first settlers," Miss Finch said.

Maggie squinted up at the fluorescent lights, then focused on the paper again.

Dad's eyes opened wide. "Luke knows this stuff. Why did he write the wrong answers? Look, he wrote *d* instead of *b*. Sometimes he gets those mixed up."

My chin drooped down farther on my chest and a big silent sigh washed through me.

"He knows all about the settlers," Dad argued. "I read it to him. We discussed it."

"You read it to him?" Miss Finch bristled.

This was not going well. I sprang to my feet. "I need to go to the bathroom."

"No, you don't," Dad snapped.

I sat down. I didn't dare say anything to Dad about cool heads prevailing.

"He knows these answers." Breathing deeply, Dad took the paper and turned to me. "Luke, did the Dutch settle in Canada, New York, Florida, or Virginia?"

"New York."

"See?" Dad asked me the next question, which I answered correctly, and so on. When we had finished the test, I'd answered every question correctly but one.

Miss Finch seemed confused. "Luke, why didn't you write the correct answers on the test?"

Maggie looked at Miss Finch. "Can't you tell he has trouble with letter reversals, and these lights?" She pointed up at the ceiling. "They bounce the words all over the page."

"Cool lights," Stevie said, and sneezed.

Without missing a beat, Maggie pulled a handkerchief out of her purse and wiped her arm, then Stevie's face.

"What about the lights?" Miss Finch scrunched her forehead.

Maggie answered. "The lights in this room flicker unmercifully. It causes the letters on the page to run together like ants."

How did she know that?

"Don't you notice how Luke moves his head over the page to put it in a shadow? Don't you notice how his words run together when he writes—without spaces between them?"

I did that?

"And his *d*'s, *b*'s…his backwards 3s. Don't you notice that?" Maggie's voice was getting stronger, like she was going to stand up and preach, or maybe punch Miss Finch in the face.

"Yes, he's been stubborn about fixing those."

Stubborn?

"Stubborn?" Maggie sat up straight. "Stubborn?! Just picture in your head that you see the circles in those letters, but the stick parts are unclear. Is the stick on the right or left? How hard would this test be for you then?" Maggie waved my paper in front of Miss Finch's face. "What if you knew the information, but you couldn't manage the words on the page?"

Then Maggie did it—she sprang to her feet, knocking Stevie against Dad.

Her voice got louder. "Would you be able to finish on time? Would your answers be correct? What if the test made you panic, and after you filled in your answers, you couldn't tell what you wrote because it looked like…like…Japanese?" She slurped in a big breath. "How frustrating would that be, especially if you knew the information backwards and forwards and upside-down?"

Miss Finch was tongue-tied for the first time all year. Her face faded to a deathly white.

"Luke is a smart kid," Maggie declared. "He takes care of his brother. He cooks, he engineers complicated ramp systems. Why…he invents things!" She inhaled. "I see he got a *D-* on the bones test for science." She pointed to the paper sticking out of Miss Finch's folder. "Luke can name all those bones! Isn't there another way to measure his knowledge besides this kind of test?" Her face was bright red, and the veins stuck out on her neck as she slapped my history test down on the table.

Miss Finch, Dad, Stevie and I sat like big-eyed frogs, our mouths gaping.

Maggie turned to me, then to Miss Finch, then to Dad. "Oh, dear." She moved her hand to her chest. "I'm so sorry." Sitting down, she put her arm around Stevie. "Are you okay, sweetie? Did I scare you?"

He leaned lovingly against her.

Without speaking, Miss Finch quickly shoved my tests into the folder.

Dad broke the silence. "Well, Miss Finch. Is there anything else?"

"No. That'll be all." She looked a little, well, shocked. This was probably the most violent parent-teacher conference she'd ever experienced.

"We'll be going then." Dad extended his hand to Miss Finch, who shook it. "Thank you for your time."

"Sorry," Maggie apologized. "I got carried away."

Miss Finch only nodded as she took a small step back.

As we walked to the parking lot, Maggie mumbled. "I behaved badly, didn't I? It was probably a mistake to take me to the teacher conference."

Dad was in his own thought-world, so Maggie continued. "Looking at those tests, looking at her. I got so angry."

While I was getting Stevie settled in the middle of the seat with me, Dad helped Maggie climb up into the truck. Then he walked around to his side and slid in behind the wheel.

Maggie looked straight ahead as the truck bumped down the road.

"Well, Sarge," Dad finally said. "You sure whipped Miss Finch into shape."

"Be quiet," she snapped.

"How did you know about the lights?" I asked her.

She glanced at me. "Sometimes I have a similar problem."

"What?" Dad asked.

Maggie continued. "Fluorescent lights are the worst."

I spoke up. "I always thought that stuff with the letters happened to everybody. I didn't know some people see words that hold still. Dad, do your words hold still?"

"Yes, they do, son."

Maggie reached her arm around me and gave me a squeeze. "It's okay, Luke."

Maggie, the sarge, had a reading problem like mine? That's why she had written an *L* on my hand? But she was smart, and bossy, and she was no wimp, that's for sure.

My spirits lifted.

Dad turned the corner and headed us toward Frosty's Freeze. "I think we need to celebrate Sarge's victory over Miss Finch."

"Great idea, Dad."

"Best school conference I've ever been to," he said. "It never hurts to have a good fighter in your corner. What do you think, Luke? Ready for some ice cream?"

"Cool ice cream!" Stevie shouted.

I was ready to eat ice cream. I was ready to take the world by storm. I was ready to name all the bones in the world and all the Jamestown facts that ever existed.

"Cool ice cream," Maggie said. "Even though we'll need to hire a crane to get me out of this truck one more time."

We didn't need a crane. With the help of my dad and me, we got her out. And while I sat in my chair licking the thick, gooey chocolate syrup off my spoon, I felt a glimmer of hope. I still couldn't read or write any better than I did this morning. But as my Dad and Maggie sat side by side, discussing kids and school and teachers, and cows and tractors—I could tell, as I had done many times before, by the attentive way Dad listened to Maggie, that he thought she was really, really smart.

Maggie, whose words wiggled on the page—like mine.

FIVE

Maggie throws a rock.

'd never experienced a winter with females in the house before. Our previous women-people usually quit before the cold weather set in. Dad thought maybe it was because they liked our house when the summer breezes blew through it, carrying the scents of lilacs and peonies from the yard. He said one thing he knew about ladies was that they liked flowers. So, we just figured that's why the helpers lasted longer during mild weather.

Usually, when winter came, we had to hole up in the house, shut the windows, and lose the outdoor blossomy smell. Then, with our lady-people gone, Dad would take Stevie and me out to the barn with him while he milked cows and worked on tractors. He would poke up the fire in the barn woodstove, and we would play with our toy trucks and airplanes out there. Sometimes I helped Dad with the milking.

After everything was done, we all three walked to the house, which was cold because our furnace didn't work very well. We'd start up the fire in the Franklin stove in the living room and heat a can of something in the kitchen. Soon, our downstairs would be all cozy, and we would one by one land on the nearest bed or couch to sleep.

That was back in the old days.

Now, with Sarge in the house, Dad insisted that I bring in plenty of wood every morning before school. Before he went to bed every night, he made sure there was a good stack near the porch so I could get to it easily. When my school day was over, I returned to a house that was toasty-warm, not just from the woodstove, but another kind of warm from stew cooking and apple pie in the oven.

The sounds were nice, too, like when Stevie hummed as he colored at the kitchen table while the washer chugged away in the nook by the back door. It stayed cozy like this all evening while I did my homework at the table and we ate our supper.

Some nights Dad joined me at the kitchen table with his homework, as he called it, which was a result of Maggie after she'd caught him peeking at her Bible study book.

On that night he'd been sitting beside me at the table while I copied my spelling words. He hunched over Maggie's Bible study booklet, his eyes gobbling up the words like he was a starved man at a stolen feast. He didn't see her come up from behind.

"What are you doing?" she asked him.

He jumped up to a standing position, and I sat up straight. Boy, was he in trouble!

"I was just reading about David," he said.

"Were you reading my answers?" she accused.

"No," he croaked. "I mean, well, not on purpose. I was reading all the other parts, and sometimes your answers were there too. But I'm actually past where you are, and now I have to fill in the answers myself."

"In my book?"

"No. I answer them in my head." His face was a weird shade of dark red.

She stared at him for a moment.

"Sorry, Maggie." He handed her the book and escaped out the back door.

The next Wednesday, a fresh new copy of *A Man After God's Own Heart* showed up on the kitchen table alongside Dad's old Bible Maggie had found when she was cleaning under his bed. "If your dad can't go to church, then the church'll have to come to him," she told me.

I didn't know why anyone would want to do homework on purpose, but Dad told me later that even though he had been mad at God for a long time, something about Maggie's Bible study book tasted like a mug of hot cocoa on a cold day. Very confusing. While I was pounding my brain to get math problems lined up, Dad was sitting across from me getting cocoa. Some things just didn't seem fair.

The best part of my days was late at night after Dad read my schoolbooks to me—even though Miss Finch didn't like it—and I got tucked in under the soft quilt Maggie had made for my birthday on December 5. Somehow she'd learned that I liked dogs, and she'd found quilt material with pictures of hunting dogs and German shepherds like Rin Tin Tin. Some kids might think it was a bit childish, but I didn't care.

Maggie had turned into a very different person than what I had thought on that first day. Still bossy, but it didn't matter anymore.

I lay under my warm dog quilt and listened to the night sounds of our house. I listened to dishes clunking in the kitchen while Maggie put things away. Sometimes I heard Dad scoot a chair to the table so he could drink coffee and finish his Bible homework. In my bed, I closed my eyes and let my mind wander off as I heard two voices—my dad's, sort of a deep rumble like an old car driving on the brick street in the middle of town, and Maggie's voice, strong, yet gentle.

Maybe it was Maggie's voice that made our house feel so warm. Or maybe, it was just Maggie.

When an envelope came in the mail for her with a return address from Hank Coleman, I began to worry. Why would she be getting mail from a man in Richmond? Who was he—her boyfriend? Was he rich? Was she going to leave us and go marry him? Did he have kids? Was she going to go take care of them?

I kept thinking of her Bible study book, *A Man after God's Own Heart*. Was Hank Coleman one of those?

She didn't talk about the envelope when she picked it up off the table, just smiled and carried it to her room. What did that mean? I worried he was someone who would take her away from us just when I was getting used to having her around. After all, it was winter. Maybe, like all the other lady helpers, she was going to move on.

It bothered me all afternoon. Finally, I asked, "Who's the letter from?"

"A friend of mine," she said. "You would like him." Obviously, she liked him.

"A lot? Do you like him a lot?"

She pressed her hand to her heart. "Yes, very much."

A sadness came over me then, and I didn't want to ask more questions. Not only did I have to worry about school, but now this?

As time marched on, though, Maggie, her stomach all pooched out with a baby inside, stayed. My fears scooted under the rug, and life ran smooth and calm—for a while.

Then Elizabeth started spending Tuesdays and Thursdays with us. Mostly I didn't want her to come. At school, Eddie and I stayed as far away from girls as possible. I think, like Dad, we didn't understand them.

Even though I didn't really want Elizabeth to come to our house, she was a female, and she was smart. After she got to know us, maybe she could give us some ideas about how to keep a woman, or at least, Maggie.

The first day Elizabeth got off the bus with me, I didn't know what to do with her. I figured she would go inside and do girl stuff with Maggie. Instead, she wanted to see cows and tractors in the barn with me. Then she wanted to find out if I could throw a rock over the barn, which I could, and did. Dad, who heard us, came out and threw a rock over the barn too. Elizabeth tried several times, but her rock hit the roof and rolled back toward us.

"Girls!" I said, rolling my eyes. "Skinny little noodle-arms."

"Oh, shut up," she growled, pulling a glob of blonde hair away from her thin face.

Maggie, who had been flapping a rug over the porch rail, came marching down the steps. "What did you say, Luke?" She stopped beside me. "Did you say *girls!* Like…girls can't throw?" She glared at Dad for a moment.

"I didn't say anything." He held his hands up. "I'm innocent."

She turned back to me.

"Yeah, girls can't throw." My voice kind of quivered at the end. I was beginning to think that maybe I shouldn't have said that.

Maggie held her hand out to Elizabeth. "I'll take that rock."

Elizabeth gave it to her.

"Okay, Luke," she said. "What's the bet?"

"Huh?"

"What'll you give me if I can throw this rock over the barn?"

Oh, no.

A chuckle rumbled out of Dad.

I looked at Maggie. How could she wind up and throw a rock with her big belly in the way?

Elizabeth spoke up. "Dishes. He'll wash dishes."

"Hey, that sounds good." Maggie glanced at me. "Okay?"

"What do I get if you *don't* get the rock over the barn?" I asked.

"You *won't* have to do dishes."

"Okay." I winked at Dad, but I was nervous on the inside. After all, Maggie was the one who had easily popped open the stuck door and wheeled the unmovable motorcycle out into the living room. Maybe I was in trouble. Maggie faced the barn. "How many tries do I get?"

"Three," Elizabeth volunteered. She wasn't helping much.

"One," Dad said.

"One," I repeated. My heart was beginning to sink into my shoes.

Maggie took a step back, put her hands together like a pitcher on the mound at Wrigley Field, and flung the rock.

Washing dishes for Maggie was different than how I'd done it before. Well, actually, I hadn't done *that* many dishes. In the old days, Dad and I would fill the sink with hot soapy water, set the plates in there, and leave them until the next day. When we needed dishes, we rinsed them, wiped them off, and used them fresh and damp.

Maggie gave me dishwashing *lessons*. "First," she said, "you wash the glasses because they're the cleanest to start with. They don't get the water all dirty like other dishes, and the water is still clean so it won't smudge up the glasses."

She went on to silverware, then plates and bowls, then pots and pans. She showed me how to set them in an organized way on the dish drainer, and that I must stop halfway through the process to dry the first ones so there would be room for the pots and pans.

She taught me some science too. "Use the hottest rinse water you can stand. Hot water evaporates quicker than cool water, and the dishes are already partly dry when you get out the dish towel."

I didn't really *want* this lesson in dishwashing, but I got it anyway, because Maggie's one and only throw cleared the barn like a sparrow with the wind under its wings.

I didn't say it, but I would much rather have Maggie give me *throwing* lessons.

The next evening Maggie carefully lowered herself into a kitchen chair and propped her feet up on the bench. She'd been quiet during dinner.

I wondered if she was sick or something.

"You've been doing that homework for a long time," she said.

"I'm trying to work harder at this stuff, like Miss Finch said." I stuck my English paper inside the book and slammed it shut.

"Do you think it's helping?" Dad stood at the sink, trying to scrub the grease out of his calluses with a stiff brush.

"Maybe. After I do my homework, I go over it again to find mistakes." Somehow, I wasn't being successful. I'd find only one or two mistakes. Then at school Miss Finch found a bunch more, marking them with her bright red pen. My papers always came home looking like they'd been stabbed to death.

Sighing, Maggie set her ring on the table.

"Why'd you take off your ring?" I asked.

"It pinches. I think my fingers are swollen." She wiggled them.

It was shiny gold, with a row of three small diamonds. "It's nice," I said, picking it up.

"Thanks." Her eyes seemed sort of wet.

"Where'd you get it?" I asked.

"From Ted. It's my wedding band." A tear escaped.

I shouldn't have asked where she got it.

"Today would've been our anniversary."

No wonder she was sad. All of a sudden, my stomach was sinking.

Dad's scrubbing stopped. "Why didn't you say something? You could've taken the day off."

"No, I wanted today to just be normal, you know—busy."

No one spoke for a moment.

She touched the ring. "It didn't work. I've been struggling all day."

Dad turned off the faucet. "How many years would this anniversary be?"

"Three."

I didn't know what to say, and Dad didn't seem to either. He just stood there looking at her, the pain in his eyes. Even though it had been four years since my mom died, Dad still had a hard time on their anniversary. One year on that day he dug a patch of dirt behind the barn and threw a handful of wildflower seeds on it. Every year he added to it, expanding its borders, adding more seeds—until recently. I guess it was big enough, a mass of colorful blooms waving in the summer breeze behind the barn where nobody could see it. I told him it was beautiful. He said he hated it. He should've planted flowers for Mom when she was alive.

One night I'd found him facing the kitchen window, slumped forward with his hands over his face. I remember asking him if he was praying. He shook his head and told me to go back to bed. I'd stopped in the doorway for a second and looked back. He stood straight, facing the night sky, his shoulders rising and falling with each deep breath.

Later he told me that the morning before Mom died, he'd been complaining because she wanted to buy a pair of shoes she'd seen at Montgomery Ward. The last thing he said to her as she walked out the door was, "How many shoes do you need, anyway?" That was the day she was in a car accident. He spent the next two days at the hospital with her while Aunt Nelda took care of us. Mom didn't regain consciousness, and Dad never had a chance to tell her he was sorry. He told me his last words to her should've been, 'I love you. Buy all the shoes you want.'"

Now Maggie slid her foot off the bench and pushed herself up out of the chair. "I need some fresh air." With tears streaming down her cheeks, she grabbed her coat and walked out the back door.

Dad and I went to the window and watched her stop at the fence, looking out over the moonlit meadow as her large stomach rested against the wooden slats.

"It's not a good day for her, is it?" I said.

"No, and she probably didn't want to take off the ring her husband gave her. It's just another reminder that he's gone."

She covered her face with her hands, and my heart broke inside of me. "Dad, we gotta do something."

"People have to grieve, son." Sighing, he scratched his chin. "I never quite know what to do when a woman cries."

"Maybe you should go hug her. That's what you do when Stevie cries."

"Nice idea, but she might just slug me."

"Huh?"

He set his hand on my shoulder. "A man just doesn't go up to a lady who isn't his wife or his sister or mom and give her a hug, especially when she's the sarge."

I didn't want to watch Maggie cry, so I turned away from the window. The ring rested, shiny and small, on the kitchen table. "Dad, maybe she can wear the ring around her neck on a chain. Don't we have one somewhere, maybe in that little blue box in your room?"

"I'll go look."

I put my books away while Dad rustled around in his room. He'd told me recently that it was harder to find his stuff than it used to because Maggie kept rearranging things to make our house more efficient. In a few minutes, he came out, chain in hand. "I forgot we had this." He handed it to me.

I fiddled with the clasp and in a jiffy, fixed it up with the ring.

We went to the window again and looked out. Stevie was leaning against Maggie, his head against her side, their arms twined around each other.

"I guess she's getting her hug after all," I said.

"Yeah, from a man she'd never slug."

It was during Elizabeth's fourth day at our house that she brought up the subject of Mr. Romeo. We were sitting at the kitchen table doing our homework, writing the list of presidents we needed to memorize, which was turning out like I'd feared. She kept fixing my words, making me erase them and rewrite them correctly, and she was getting on my nerves. Mostly, I wanted to pass fifth grade, but second-to-mostly, I wanted Elizabeth to stop bugging me. So, I decided to get away from her. I pushed my chair back and stood.

"Where are you going?" she asked.

"I need a break. I'll go see what Dad's doing."

"I'll come too."

Oh, great. She was the one I need a break *from*.

"Maggie's nice, isn't she?" Elizabeth said as we walked across the yard.

"Yeah, I suppose, in a bossy kind of way." Of course Maggie was nice.

We stopped outside the barn door and looked in. Between the tractors, we could see a straight shot of my dad as he sat at his desk, scrambling his black hair with his pen while he stared down at his papers.

"Do you suppose your dad is in love with her?" Elizabeth asked.

"What?" I screeched. "He's only known her for a few months. Besides, did you look at her stomach lately?"

"Like she swallowed a globe," Elizabeth said.

We watched Dad tip his chair back, stretch his arms, yawn, nearly fall over backwards before catching himself, then continue to examine his papers. When Dad had his mind on something, he had his mind on it good, which is probably why he was always accidently clobbering himself.

"Really, Luke. Maggie will have the baby, and then she'll be thin and pretty. Men will flock around, asking her out on dates and stuff. She's so nice, and she's like creative."

I tried to imagine Maggie without the stomach bulge. I tried to imagine men asking her out on dates. I remembered the day she received the letter from Hank Coleman, how it brought such a smile to her face. And I thought of the polite, well-dressed man I'd seen at church last week when Maggie talked me into going with her. He introduced himself to me as Keith Sanders, the brother of Bonnie, one of Maggie's quilt club friends. "That's ridiculous, Elizabeth." But I wasn't as sure as I wanted to be.

Inside the barn, Dad looked at the calendar on the wall. "I hate bills," he announced to his desk as he accidentally poked his cheek with the pen. "Ow." Groaning, he clutched his face.

"Your dad needs to brush up on his woman-winning skills so he can compete with the other men—is all I'm saying," Elizabeth said. "He's not exactly Mr. Romeo."

"Mr. Romeo?"

"You need to tell him to get his act together and become charming, otherwise you're going to lose Maggie for sure. Trust me. I know these things."

"He doesn't have any woman-winning skills. The guy grew up with no mom or sisters to learn from. He says he's woman-illiterate." Even though I wanted Elizabeth to help us, I wasn't in the mood to change my good dad into a mushy romance person. "He's just who he is."

"What about your mom? How did he get her to marry him?"

"Blind luck. That's what he says."

Elizabeth sighed. "Well, Luke. You guys obviously like Maggie. Don't you want to keep her?"

I turned and looked at the kitchen window, knowing that oatmeal cookies were baking in the oven. I saw Maggie at the sink, her lips moving like she was talking to someone, probably Stevie, like she talked to me all the time.

"Yeah, I want to keep her." *Definitely.*

"I can help," she offered. "I'll observe your dad—you know, kinda like he's my science project. Then I'll teach him how to win her heart."

"I don't think anybody's going to win the sarge's heart unless she wants him to."

"I don't think you should call her Sarge." Elizabeth pressed her long fingers against her chin, staring analytically at my dad, his hair sticking out like a wind-bent awning over his forehead.

Yes, he could probably use some help.

"So, Luke, do I have your permission?"

"For what?"

"Permission for me to help your dad win Maggie's heart so you guys can keep her."

"Uh…okay. You can try." It wasn't what I had in mind, but it was as good a plan as any, just as long as she didn't fix him too much.

Elizabeth spent the first part of dinner staring at Dad. She watched him as he ate his food, chewing contentedly. He'd probably done some hair combing before dinner, because his hair wasn't sticking out quite as bad as before. He'd scrubbed most of the oil out of the creases in his hands, making them red and raw. I decided he looked pretty good right now. I wondered what Maggie thought.

Elizabeth was frowning at him.

I wondered what she saw that was wrong. Was it the way his shirt collar stuck up crookedly on one side? Was it the scratch on his nose?

Dad and Maggie glanced at each other with raised eyebrows as if to say, *What's with Elizabeth?*

Finally, Stevie spoke up. "How-come you look at my daddy?"

Elizabeth stared down at her plate. "No, I wasn't doing anything."

"Uh-huh," Stevie said.

Scowling, she glanced up, and Dad caught her eye.

"Elizabeth, if you have a question to ask me, go ahead. I have nothing to hide," he said.

Her eyes flitted my way, then returned to Dad. "Sir, why didn't you have a mother?"

"What?" Dad focused on me for a second.

I wondered if my cheeks were getting red.

He turned back to Elizabeth. "My mother died when I was born. Someone found her collapsed on the street and brought her to the hospital, but she didn't make it."

I knew I'd probably heard this story a long time ago, but I didn't remember it now. Elizabeth's eyes were open wide. I suppose mine were too.

"What was her name?" Maggie asked.

He smiled sadly. "Jane Doe."

"Oh, dear." Maggie set down her fork and put her hand on her chest.

"Jane Doe?" Elizabeth asked. "Then why isn't your name William Doe?"

I wondered the same thing.

Maggie was strangely silent.

Dad answered the question. "Jane Doe is what the people write on documents if they don't know who the woman really is. If an unidentified man shows up dead, they call him John Doe."

I felt sick. I wished Elizabeth hadn't asked the question. It was a dumb idea to give her permission to be Dad's woman-winner scientist.

"Then your father raised you?" Elizabeth asked.

Maggie jumped in. "Sweetie, if they didn't know who the mom was, they wouldn't know how to find the daddy."

"Wow," Elizabeth said, apparently recovering from her stupid questions.

"Where did you get your name?" Maggie asked Dad.

"Somebody named me while I was at St. Peter's Orphanage in Fort Wayne. Don't know why they picked that name."

We were silent for a few moments while I tried to grasp the idea of my dad being an orphan.

Finally, Maggie found her voice. "So, William, how did you end up here?"

He gave her a soft smile. "When I was eight, the Bradleys adopted me." Then his eyes went to a faraway place. "Soon after I came here, my new mother, Pansy, became very sick. I sat with her in what is now Maggie's room, reading to her while Dad milked cows and worked outside." Dad pushed his hair off his forehead, revealing a fresh cut.

Maggie's eyes lit on it for a second. She would probably get out her first aid kit after supper.

Dad spoke in a serious tone. "One day when she was asleep, I came out here to watch for my father." He pointed to the window, framed by new yellow sunflower curtains. "I stood there looking out and saw him bringing in the cows—winding along the path to the windmill and across to the barn. When I went back to check on Mom—she was gone."

"Where'd she go?" I asked.

Dad answered, a hint of sadness in his voice. "Heaven. She died."

"Oh," Elizabeth said quietly.

Something inside of me sank. My dad found her—dead? In this very house?

Maggie's eyes teared up. "What'd you do?"

"I just stood there for a while—in shock, I guess. Even though we knew she was going to die." He shook his head. "Eventually, I pulled myself together and went to get Dad."

What would I have done? Screamed. I would've screamed.

Dad took a deep breath. "I lived here with Dad until he died of a heart attack. Named my first son after him, Luke Bradley." He tousled my hair. "He left me this farm and his beloved cows. Then Stevie was born, and later Ramona died in a car accident."

Ramona was my mom. Sometimes I can barely remember her, but for some reason when I'm near a person who smells like Aqua-Net hair spray, it brings her back to me.

Elizabeth's eyes were as big as pancakes.

"I decided to stay on this farm where Stevie can always be happy—away from people who stare at him, or tease him, or...whatever." He exchanged a smile with my brother, who probably didn't understand everything he'd just heard, which was okay. After stabbing a blob of potatoes, Dad looked around the quiet table. "I seem to have everyone's attention tonight." He grinned at Elizabeth. "Are you glad you asked your question?"

"Uhhh..."

He gave her a gentle, reassuring smile. "Anyway, I decided to take care of Dad's cows until the last one is gone. As each cow passes on, I'll add tractor space in the barn. I don't mind the cows. I don't mind milking these last ones by hand like he did."

I sat there, trying to take it all in. With one ten-minute conversation two females, Elizabeth and Maggie, had extracted a whole new world of information from my own dad whom I had known all of my life.

SIX

*If I had known about this beforehand, I would've had
a panic-embarrassment nervous breakdown and a
stomachache. Then I would've run away from home.*

Christmas week came, and we still had Maggie in the house.
The kitchen was the place to be. Thankfully, she seemed to
think that holidays were a time to bake, and cookies flowed
out of our oven. I helped her decorate them before we drove into town
to deliver them to her Bible study friends and the pastor at her church.

Because school was out, I spent most of my time helping her with
chores. Dad told me I should because, well…her big belly got in the
way when she tried to bend down, and she was tired all the time. So
I did a lot of lifting and carrying, and wiping up the floor after Stevie
dropped his food.

Dad also told me that Maggie was probably staying busy so she
wouldn't dwell on how sad she felt because she was spending Christmas without her husband. He said he liked it when he came in from
the barn, and I was chatting away with Maggie and Stevie while we
decorated cookies. Maybe we were helping keep her mind off her loss.

Stevie really took Maggie's mind off her troubles when he licked the
top of the colored sugar shaker. While I got Stevie sidetracked with his
bag of pennies, Maggie emptied the sugar shaker, washed it, dried it,
and reloaded it. "I've always wanted to lick the sugar shaker myself,"
she commented as we started to work again. I thought it was funny, so

I started giggling, and she joined in. Maggie's eyes loaded up with tears of laughter that somehow shifted into the other kind of tears—the kind that made her lip quiver. Overcome with a deep look of sadness, she slipped out of the kitchen and went to her room. With a heavy heart, I finished decorating, parked the sugar shaker on a high shelf, and ran out to the barn for advice.

Dad explained that sometimes I needed to just let her be sad. "It's all part of her mourning, son. You just need to let her go off alone and deal with her sorrow."

I wondered why he knew so much about taking care of someone who lost her husband, and then I remembered. He probably went through the same kind of sadness after my mom died. Watching Maggie's grief, I was beginning to realize that my dad had gone through the same thing, only I had been too young to understand it. I remember the Saturday nights when I was in bed. I could hear the radio in the kitchen pulling twangy music up from the hills of Tennessee with Eddy Arnold singing "If I had the wings like an angel, over these prison walls I would fly. And I'd fly to the arms of my darling, and there I'd be willing to die." Sometimes the next morning I would find an empty Old Crow liquor bottle in the trash, and Dad would be asleep on the couch like a dead dog, his long arm flopped down to the floor.

Now this year, Dad brought down the box of my mother's special Christmas decorations. With Elizabeth's help, we pulled out each one and hung it carefully on the tree while Maggie sat in the recliner chair and watched. Thankfully, Stevie was at Bo-Wad's house so we could decorate the tree without having things go crashing to the ground like the "cool tree" did last year, with Stevie under it.

"There's a date on this decoration," Elizabeth said, holding up a homemade wooden baby rattle with a red bow. "It says, 'Ramona's first Christmas.'"

"That's right," Dad said. "Luke's grandmother made that the year his mom was born."

"My mom's name was Ramona," I explained.

Elizabeth hung the rattle beside a little wooden candy cane.

"What a nice idea," Maggie commented. She took a sip of cocoa.

Elizabeth was staring back and forth from Maggie to my dad like she often did, probably wondering if they were falling in love yet.

"What's this?" I asked as I pulled a heart-shaped ornament out of the box.

"That one's from our wedding year." Dad took a deep breath.

"Oh." A new loneliness was hitting my gut. I wished I could talk to my mother, to hear the story of every ornament. I was missing her for the first time in a long while. All of a sudden, Christmas was getting hard.

I pulled out a different heart, a blue one.

Dad took it from me. "This one represents the year she became the mother of her first son."

Me.

A thick glob was forming in my throat. I was afraid to talk.

"How many of these are there?" Elizabeth asked as she hung the hearts side by side.

"Twenty-seven." Dad stood. "It's time for me to go get Stevie." And he was gone.

Maggie struggled herself out of the chair and went to her own room.

Elizabeth and I hung the remaining ornaments in silence, which was unusual for her. Then we stood back and admired the tree.

"I think it's a wonderful tradition," she finally said.

"What is?"

"Having a decoration that represents each year of someone's life since birth."

I nodded.

"Too bad it's too late for us to start. We've already been alive too long." The tree lights sparkled as they reflected off her glasses.

An idea popped into my head. "Hey, I know someone who can start on the yearly ornaments."

"Who?"

I glanced around to make sure the sarge was still in the other room. "Maggie's baby."

"You can't do that. It's not even born yet," she whispered.

"Yes, I can. And I want you to help me. You're good at crafts."

She stood, thinking for a moment, staring at the tree, her eyes moving along the rows of decorations, probably trying to get an idea or two. So, I let her contemplate while I carried the empty box into my dad's room and shoved it into the closet.

We sat in the living room, our stomachs full of warm biscuits with sausage and gravy. Maggie said we needed to have a Christmas breakfast, one that was warm and filling and fast. After she cooked it and we ate it, Dad made her sit down with her coffee while we cleaned up the dishes.

Now, as we waited to open our presents, my belly felt good, not like the old days when Dad and Stevie and I went straight from bed to tearing open our presents while our stomachs growled like angry bears in a cave. I decided I liked eating first, and I liked sitting at the table with all of us together, Stevie swinging his legs because they didn't touch the floor.

Besides Christmas breakfast, Dad had another new and different thing in store for us. Maggie asked him to read the Christmas story out of the Bible. I started to protest, but Dad held up his hand. "Luke, I should've been doing this all along. This year, we'll start a new tradition."

I reluctantly closed my mouth.

"Luke, I'm reading out of your book of the Bible." He winked at me. "Huh?"

"Luke, chapter two."

"Oh, I get it." There was a book of the Bible named after me.

I sat back and listened to Dad read the story of Mary and Joseph and the baby, Jesus. Maggie placed her hands on her huge stomach. I never saw a belly so big. She must've been thinking about her baby who would be born any day now. I'd never thought about it before, but Mary probably had a big tummy while she traveled to Bethlehem.

Stevie snuggled against Dad as he continued, reading about the angels who rejoiced, and the shepherds who went to see the newborn king. I didn't really know what all the fuss was about. But I sat and listened anyway, hoping that each sentence was the last so we could tear into our gifts.

I was especially curious about the big wrapped box behind the tree. It looked the right size to be a Lionel train set, one that Dad and I had stared at long and hard the day after he'd been paid for the fixed motorcycle. If this box held a train, Dad would probably play with it, too, just like he did with my racecar set last year.

Eventually, Dad finished the story, and he said that this year we would open our gifts one at a time.

I groaned. He and Maggie must've planned our Christmas morning together—with new rules.

Maggie was first. I held my breath as she unwrapped her gift from Stevie and me. She stared at it with some kind of wonder, I think. Lifting it in the air, she examined the white lace that Elizabeth had wrapped and glued around the wooden clothespin body, trying to cover it up as much as possible. The wood underneath was painted a dark blackish shade of purple because Stevie would have it no other way. I thought Elizabeth was going to have a heart attack when she first saw it.

I'd added the paperclip halo that poked out of its head and the wings from our pink feather duster.

Maggie glanced at Dad, whose eyes were big.

"Cool angel," Stevie said.

Her lip twitched. "Oh, of course." She focused back on it and smiled warmly at my brother. "Cool angel."

"We made it," I offered.

Her eyebrows went up. "I see." For some reason, I thought she was trying to not look at Dad, who had his hand over his mouth.

Stevie ran to her and hugged her tightly. "For you."

As she cuddled him against her side, she winked at me. Then she held the angel out in front of her. "Why is there a 'B' on its chest?"

"*B* for baby," I said.

"What?" she asked.

I knew I was going to have to explain. "We thought that since your baby is the only one who is young enough, we'd start doing the yearly ornament tradition with him, like my grandma did for my mom."

"Oh." She brought the angel to her chest. "What a precious idea."

Something inside of me swelled up. I'd been afraid she wouldn't want a dark purple angel, but now—I think she liked it.

She turned to Dad. "William, do you think you could put the angel on top of the tree?"

He moved our aluminum star down a few branches, then hung the angel by its paperclip halo on top.

After that, we got to the serious business of opening the big box, a Lionel train set, complete with tracks, cars, and little gray pills that made smoke come out of its smokestack.

After we opened the rest of the presents and cleaned up the torn paper, Maggie excused herself and took a nap. Dad, Stevie, and I spent the rest of the morning setting up the train in the living room—beneath the watchful eyes of a purple angel with a *B* on its chest.

This had to be the best Christmas ever.

A few days later we had a snowstorm so bad the drifts rose above the windowsill in Dad's bedroom, and flakes continued to fly.

Dad did what he always did when it snowed like this. First, he reminded us of Ned's cousin George, who had walked from his house to his barn in a blizzard one night in 1941. Uncle George thought he was returning to the house, but he actually went the wrong way, and he froze to death about six hundred feet away in a field. The moral of the story was: Don't go outside and walk at night in blizzards.

I'd heard the story a hundred times, but maybe it was the first time for Stevie and Maggie. Anyway, Stevie didn't like to go out in the cold, and Maggie said she didn't have the energy to walk as far as the door. So, I think the story was wasted on them.

Dad brought the lanterns in from the barn and filled them with kerosene while I loaded the woodbox by the Franklin stove in the living room. Last year, when it got below zero, our furnace didn't work right and our house got pretty cold. It was okay for us bachelor guys, wandering around the house with our coats on, but Dad said that as long as we sheltered a woman in delicate condition, she needed to stay toasty warm. The Franklin stove did a better job than our furnace anyway.

Maggie didn't help with any of this. She leaned back in the recliner chair and tried to get comfortable, moving sideways, then shifting to straighten up, then sliding to the other side. She told me she felt like she was carrying a bowling ball all day long, one that kicked and punched. As I set the last chunk of oak in the woodbox I looked at her and tried to imagine what that would be like. I decided it wouldn't be much fun.

As the evening wore on, we looked outside from time to time. The snow continued to blast through the air, swishing about before it landed. Dad's window was almost covered now by a slanted drift, and past it everything was covered in a thick blanket of white—the road, the mailbox, and miles of fields. We wouldn't be going anywhere for a while.

Stevie and I pulled out the marble contraption while Dad looked for a book in his room. "We'll start *The Prince and the Pauper*," he announced as he tossed the dog-eared book onto the couch. He'd read it a million times. Often, I wondered why I hadn't inherited my dad's gift of reading. "Hot chocolate, anyone?"

"Me!" Stevie waved his hand.

"Me too," I added.

Dad stopped by Maggie, who lay on her side in the recliner chair.

"Not right now," she said, looking up at him. "But thank you."

Dad lowered his eyebrows, reminding me of the day Stevie and I both came down with chicken pox. "Are you okay?" he asked her.

She sighed. "Could you help me out of this chair? I'm afraid if I try it myself, I'll end up like Humpty Dumpty—eggshells all over the floor."

"Well, we can't have that." He pushed the recliner chair up straight, then took her hand and pulled her out. That's how she got out of chairs these days, with help from one of us.

Dad walked into the kitchen, and Maggie went into the bathroom.

Stevie and I enjoyed the cocoa while we rolled marbles near the Franklin stove, thankful for the way it made the living room so toasty warm.

Dad brought down our blankets and closed the door to the steps. "We'll all sleep downstairs," he said. "Too cold up there." He opened the doors to all the downstairs rooms, letting the heat spread through.

Then he sat on the couch and picked up *The Prince and the Pauper*.

Maggie walked from the bathroom to her bedroom. I heard her fiddling around near her dresser.

"We'll wait for her," Dad said.

She stepped into the living room, but she didn't sit down. "William?"

He looked up from the book. "Yes?"

"I think we should talk."

"Huh?"

"My contractions seem to be getting regular."

He jumped off the couch. "Holy mackerel! Contractions? When did that start?"

"I'm not sure. In fact, I wasn't sure at all, but in the last hour or two..."

"I'll call the doctor."

Hopping up, I followed Dad into the kitchen, where he grabbed the phone and plastered it against his ear but didn't speak. He just stood there, his brow furrowed.

Maggie came beside me, waiting.

"Hey, go sit down," he told her.

"I'm okay. They're about seven minutes apart. We have plenty of time. I feel like standing."

He clicked the phone receiver twice, then held the phone to his head again.

"What are seven minutes apart?" I asked.

"The contractions," she answered.

"What are contractions?"

Maggie put her arm around me. "Contractions are the signal that the baby will come soon."

I probably didn't really want to know that. "What do you mean by soon? Do you mean this week?"

"Maybe tonight."

A jolt of fear hit me.

I looked at Dad, still holding the phone against his ear. I think if he pushed the phone any harder, it would smash into his brain.

"Is he there?" Maggie asked Dad.

He hung up. "The phone's deader'n a doornail. Must be a line down somewhere."

"Oh, boy," Maggie muttered.

Dad put his hand on my shoulder. "Your job, Luke, is to check the phone every now and then. See if it works." He rolled his eyes. "As if phone men would be out climbing poles tonight."

"Okay," I said, swallowing hard.

He turned to Maggie. "What's my job, Sarge?"

As she looked up at him, her lip quivered.

Dad moved his hand from my shoulder to hers. "I'll be the sarge tonight. First, we'll get you comfortable in your room."

"I haven't been comfortable since before Halloween."

He led her out of the kitchen.

I picked up the phone. No dial tone. A chill ran up my spine. How were we going to do this? How could Maggie have a baby—without a doctor? I looked out the window at the swirling snow.

Dad got Maggie settled in her room, then went to the bookshelf in his room.

I followed him there. "What are you doing?" I asked.

"Looking for the first-aid manual." After tossing a handful of books on his bed, he continued to rummage through a stack on the floor. "Ah, good." He sat on the bed. "I think there's a chapter in here somewhere about delivering babies."

"You're going to deliver a baby?" My stomach did a flip flop. "Tonight?"

He stopped turning the pages. "Perhaps you would like to do it?"

"Dad, we need to call a helicopter. Let's get her to a hospital."

He raised his eyebrows. "Call a helicopter with what? A dead phone?

And did you ever hear of a helicopter that flies in blizzards at night?"

I was getting really, really scared.

He leaned over the book, scanning the table of contents.

What if Maggie died—like Dad's mother? "Did you ever deliver a baby before?" I asked.

"Yes, several."

I let out a whoosh of relief. "Really? When?"

Stopping his search, he turned to me. "Cow babies, Luke."

"Ohhh." My heart sank.

"I don't know if that helps or not." Dad tossed the book on the floor. "This isn't the right one."

Down on his knees, he rustled through a bottom shelf, and soon lifted a dictionary-sized ancient black book titled *Riley's First Aid Manual.* As he gave it a shake; dust showered the floor. "This is it. Come with me."

When we turned around, Stevie was standing in the doorway, his face full of questions.

Dad put his arm around the little guy. "Okay, Stevie, can you put your pajamas on by yourself tonight?"

My brother nodded.

"Go ahead, then. Maggie set 'em on the steps."

As my brother padded away, Dad turned to me. "You might need to tuck him in tonight."

"I'll help wherever I can."

He squeezed my shoulder. "I know you will. Let's go check on Maggie and have a planning meeting."

She lay on her side with a frightened look on her face. "Six minutes." She put her watch on the little table beside the bed.

Something thumped in the hall. Stevie was probably bumping the walls while he got dressed.

Dad sat at the foot of the bed, first-aid book in hand. "Okay," he said. "Here's the plan."

"Do you need me for this?" I asked. "Maybe I should go help Stevie."

"He's okay. I hear him squirreling around."

Maggie spoke. "He lies down to get dressed. Looks like a turtle on his back."

"I taught him that," Dad said. "Otherwise, he loses his balance when his foot gets stuck in the pantleg. If he doesn't lie down first, he crashes into the walls and furniture."

Why were they talking about that at a time like this? I was getting more nervous every minute.

Maggie squeezed her eyes shut and held her breath.

"Another contraction?" Dad asked.

She nodded.

My chest tightened. Man, I wanted to get out of there. "I don't want to deliver any babies," I croaked.

"Relax, Luke." Dad dog-eared the page in the book. "Your job is to be in charge of your brother."

"Oh, whew." I could handle that.

"Put him in my bed. Give him extra blankets and leave the door open so the living room heat goes in there."

Stevie arrived beside me. He looked real proud of himself, even though his pajama top was inside out.

Maggie kissed him. "I have a feeling that when you wake up in the morning, there will be a baby in the house."

That thought put a fresh blast of panic into me.

She continued. "Say your prayers with Luke tonight. You get to sleep in your daddy's room."

"Cool Daddy." Stevie planted a slurpy kiss on Maggie's cheek. His eyes looked serious. Sometimes I think Stevie can sense when something's not right. After he kissed Dad, I was ready to scoot him out of there.

"Come check with me after you tuck him in," Dad said.

"Okay." But I didn't really think anything was okay. The snow was piling up around us, and we needed a doctor.

"Keep the fire going. You'll probably need to add wood in an hour or so. Check with me first."

"Sure, Dad."

Stevie was his usual little cooperative self. After I checked the dead phone one more time, we sat on the floor in front of the Franklin stove and wrapped Dad's old raggedy quilt around us. I opened the door to the stove so we could see the fire dancing inside, keeping us toasty, and I told him stories.

It felt like we were sitting around a campfire, only it was winter with a blizzard outside, and the stories I told weren't the scary kind. They were about the explorers my class had studied. Then I pointed to Stevie's bones and named them so he could get a head start in school. I wondered if kids learned about bones at Willow Lane special school.

He fell asleep by the time I got to his fibula, so I shut the stove door so no sparks would land on the rug. I half-dragged, half-walked Stevie into Dad's room and laid him on the bed. That's when I realized the little guy had fallen asleep before he said his prayers. So, I prayed for both of us.

Meanwhile, Dad's voice had droned on while he read to Maggie from the old medical book. Then he walked around the house, gathering gear, I suppose—baby blankets, towels, and stuff. I heard the teapot whistle go off in the kitchen, and Dad took care of that too.

He was in Maggie's room now, talking with her. I couldn't hear their words, which was okay. I didn't want to learn stuff about birthing babies. I wondered if Dad really knew what he was doing, and if human babies and calves are born enough alike for him to know what to do in a pinch, and if the book was too old to give good information on how to deliver a baby. I was wondering these things when Dad called out, "Luke, come here."

Oh, no. I walked into the room.

"It'll probably be a few hours before the baby comes, so I'm going to run out to the barn and get the cows settled for the night. It'll take me about thirty minutes to get my chores done, and I'll hurry back."

"Thirty minutes?" My throat tightened. "What about the storm?"

"Don't worry, son. You stay in the house with Maggie. If she needs me right away, just shout into the intercom. I'll come running."

Thank goodness for the intercom.

I followed him to the kitchen and stood while he put on his coat and boots.

"Dad?"

"Yes, son?"

"Do babies ever come real fast—you know, zippedy doo-dah before you're ready for them?"

He was thoughtful for a moment. "That won't happen. Her contractions are still six minutes apart. I predict the baby will come after midnight sometime."

"But what if the baby doesn't wait 'til then? What if he decides to come right now?"

"If he decides to come right away, Maggie will know, and she'll tell you to get me." Dad pulled a stocking cap down over his head. "Your face is all scrunched up like a prune. Relax, Luke. We're okay. I'll be back in thirty minutes. I'm just in the barn. I'm not in China."

I tried to relax my face so he'd think I wasn't worried, but I knew he wasn't fooled because he smiled and tousled my hair.

"Son, call me on the intercom to check in if that'll make you feel better."

"Okay." For sure.

He swung the door open, and we looked out into dark night. He flicked on the porch light which instantly exposed whitewashed flakes, swirling with eerie silence like tiny ghosts. Then a gust of wind howled across the yard, whipping its icy chill at our faces.

Dad flicked on the yard lights. They glimmered against masses of sparkling snowflakes, leading the way to the barn. He stepped out into the knee-high snow on the porch. "Wow, look at that drift. It's like a mountain in front of the barn. I'll have to walk around to the far side and climb over the Dutch door." He grabbed the shovel by the porch and headed out. "I'll hurry."

I couldn't be still while I waited. I had to do something. Maggie's door was open, so I took her a glass of water.

"Thanks, Luke." She took a sip and smiled at me. "I'm doing fine. Sit down. Tell me a story."

I told her about Eddie's goofy dog, Lucky, who could catch a stick in mid-air, and Elizabeth's poodle, FiFi, who was totally worthless, but cute in a nervous sort of way.

Maggie seemed calm, so I left.

Stevie slept like a little teapot in Dad's bed so I went to the basement and fetched an armload of firewood. I stopped in the kitchen and flipped the intercom button. "Hi, Dad. Everybody's okay here. When are you coming back?"

He answered, "I'm almost done. Five minutes."

I grabbed a bucket, filled it with snow from the porch, and carried it into the living room. I remember once, when I was little, Dad and I made snow sculptures in front of the fire until the snow turned to slush. I could do that while I waited.

I checked on Stevie again and forced myself to go back to Maggie's room.

She lay stiffly on her back, beads of sweat glistening on her face. "Things are moving along faster than I expected," she said.

"What things?"

"Please get your dad in here."

"Okay!" I bolted toward the door—just in time to watch the lights flicker like butterfly wings, then die...out.

Complete darkness.

"Oh, no!" I turned to Maggie and could see nothing in the pure black of the room. "No electricity!"

"Oh, boy," Maggie groaned. Her voice sounded shaky.

My hands shook as I fumbled against the wall and felt my way down the hall to the intercom. I flipped the switch. Dead. No electricity!

SEVEN

Time flies when you're having a panic attack.

In complete darkness, I moved along the wall to the pantry and found the kerosene lamp I knew was sitting on the shelf—with the matches beside it. After lighting the lamp, I found the other two close by and lit them, too, carrying them one at a time to the kitchen table.

As I set the last one in place, I realized something about my dad. He was in a pitch-dark barn in a blizzard. I knew there was a flashlight out there on his workbench, but Stevie had played with it this morning, and he forgot to turn it off. It was probably dead. Did Dad have fresh batteries out there? How would he find his way out of the barn through all those tractors? How would he find his way to the house? What if he had been outside the barn when the lights went out? Should I put a lamp on the porch to guide him?

I picked one up, opened the door and held it out. A gust of wind whipped across the porch and into the open glass chimney, extinguishing the flame. I shut the door.

I relit the lamp and set it on the counter so some of the light would shine out the kitchen window. I knew it was not enough. Its pathetic flame would barely poke into the blanket of flying snow outside.

First, I would take a lamp to Maggie. Then I would decide what to do about Dad.

Maggie smiled weakly. "We'll need more light. Are there more lamps?"

"Yes," I said. "I'll be right back." I returned quickly and set a second lamp on the dresser near the foot of her bed.

"Where's your dad?" she asked.

"I don't know. It's dark out. He's either in the barn or outside the barn." In the flickering light, I could see sweat rolling down her cheek, or was it tears? "The blizzard is thick and it's pitch black out there. I need to help him find the house." I was scared to death.

"Be still." She closed her eyes for a moment and whispered something—a prayer?

Well, we needed it.

She opened her eyes. "I'll keep praying."

"Good."

"Luke, don't leave the porch unless you have a rope around your waist, and first tie it to the house."

"I know. I'll tie it to the porch post."

"Good," she said.

"What about you?" I asked.

"Don't worry about me."

I wasn't sure if she meant that or not, but I left. I stumbled up the dark stairs and dug Stevie's Woody-whistle-pipe out of the toybox.

Back in the kitchen, I threw open the back door, cringing as an icy gust hit me full in the face. I put the pipe to my lips and I blew out into the wind, hoping that its high pitch could cut through the storm.

I stopped long enough to put on my coat before stepping outside, kicking snow as I reached the edge of the porch, and blew the pipe over and over. I wondered if the wall of flying snow muffled sound like it muffled light.

Back inside, I decided to get organized. First, I went down the hall to check on Maggie.

"William?" she asked.

"Not yet."

"Go blow that pipe."

As I returned to the kitchen I thought about my dad, and how his mom died when she gave birth to him.

Oh, please, God. Don't let me think about that now.

Then I remembered how when Dad was a boy he had left his adoptive mom lying in the very same room where Maggie was now, and when he returned she was dead.

Hot tears boiled into my eyes and rolled down my cheeks.

No tears now! They'll freeze to my face.

Swiping them away, I grabbed the kerosene lantern and carried it to the porch, holding it up to light the way—until the wind doused it. I blew the pipe again, long and hard. Then I stopped. All was still.

No light, no sound.

Nothing.

Please God, don't let my dad die out here!

I blew the pipe again. After a few minutes I returned to the kitchen, relit the lamp, and ran to Maggie's room.

She was shivering.

I hustled upstairs to my room in the pitch dark, yanked the dog quilt off my bed, and scrambled down the steps. The quilt flowed behind me as I whipped it into the air and brought it down over Maggie.

"Thanks, Luke."

I ran to the Franklin stove and shoved a chunk of wood inside.

What if she died like Dad's mom did in that very room? What if my dad was freezing to death out in the blizzard? How could I take care of Stevie—and a baby?

I found a long piece of clothesline in the pantry and tied one end around Stevie's pipe. Carrying it outside, I tied the other end securely to the porch post. After wrapping the end near the pipe around my waist twice and my arm four times, I headed out into the blizzard, blowing on the pipe and hoping I was walking toward the barn.

Eventually, I brushed against something solid, the barn. Feeling along the side, I came to the window. The inside of the barn was as pitch dark as the outside. I tried to walk around back but my clothesline stopped me, tight against my waist.

I banged on the window.

No answer.

I pulled my sleeve down over my fist and crashed it through the window, breaking glass into the barn.

"Dad!" I screamed. "Dad!"

No answer. He wasn't in the barn. He was outside, somewhere—wandering.

I sucked in a breath of icy air. The inside of my nose was frozen stiff. I shut my eyes to keep out the chilling wind. I kept blowing the pipe, trying to not think about my dad out lost, maybe in a field like Ned's cousin George, a frozen dead guy to be found the next day.

I wondered what George looked like when they found him.

"I can't stand this!" I shouted. "I can't stand this anymore!" I swung the whistle to my lips.

I don't know how long I blew. I just know it seemed like forever. I stopped to rest, frozen like an ice cube near the barn, and knew that I would not last much longer.

Maggie might need me.

I blew the pipe once more, my eyes shut, fighting the freezing wind, fighting tears.

Then I stopped. My fingers were numb, my toes were numb, my face was stiff.

I grabbed the clothesline and pulled myself to the house, banging my shins against the porch steps in the darkness.

Inside at last, I welcomed the warmth as I threw off my wet gloves and yanked off my loose boots. Leaving snow dumplings all over the kitchen, I stumbled into the living room, the clothesline still wrapped around me and the whistle pipe hanging from my arm.

I cried while I stood before the crackling fire. I would warm up for five minutes…no, two minutes. Then I would go out again.

"William?" Maggie called out.

"Not yet. I'm going back out."

She groaned, sending a new chill up my spine.

I wasn't even close to being warm, but I knew I couldn't wait. I found a pair of dry mittens, Maggie's, and headed out the door again. My feet were still frozen, but it didn't matter. Nothing mattered. Nothing but my dad.

I put the pipe to my lips.

This time I marched down the steps, plowed through the snow, and headed straight out—anywhere. I tried to brush my frozen-wet cheek with my thick mitten, but it only felt worse, scratchy.

I blew the pipe.

I shouted.

I screamed.

The numbness crawled from finger to finger with a freezer-burn ache. My toes clenched together, trying to get warm. The inside of my nose was dry and stiff like cardboard. I tried not to think of my dad wandering around in the blizzard, lost, looking for landmarks, surrounded by a mass of flakes blocking his view of…darkness. Would he find something? The trough? The porch? The fence? The mailbox? The mailbox was too far. He would die by the mailbox.

I really needed my dad. He was kind, and strong, and he took care of us. A sob broke out of me and my body shook. I bent down, folded over at the waist, holding my stomach and sobbing, tears filling my eyes, making them cold.

I wasn't helping anyone like this. I needed to stand up and fight for my dad.

I drew myself tall and blew the pipe again. Then I stopped for a second, dropping my hand to my side, my head hunched down to escape the biting wind. I needed an idea, something new to try.

Maggie was inside praying. Maybe I should pray. What should I say? Now I lay me down to sleep…No. When Maggie prayed, she just talked to God like He was sitting right next to her, listening. Where was God now when I needed him the most? I looked up into the dark, my face peppered with fresh bits of cold dots, numbing my cheeks. I blinked away the iciness that touched my eyes, then closed them.

I shoved my face down into my jacket and took a deep breath of what I hoped was body-warmed air. I blinked away the tears that threatened to freeze my face, then stood straight again, frustration and anger rolling up through me in rising waves. "God, I need some help here!" Ducking down for another breath, I rose up again. "I don't deliver babies! I'm just a kid! We need a grown-up here right now! We need my dad! I'm just a kid!

"I... don't!

"Know!

"Howwww!

"Toooooo!

"Deliverrrrr!

"Babiesssss!"

Then I let out the biggest, longest scream of my life. It shot out of me like a lion's roar. In fact, it was blasting out so hard I almost threw up.

Something bumped my arm. I opened my eyes wide to see a movement in the darkness. The hovering presence of a snowman the size of my dad stood before me.

Relief overwhelmed me, bringing me to my knees. Fresh, warm tears jumped into my eyes as I wrapped my arms around his legs.

It was too cold to talk.

We followed the clothesline to the porch, up the steps, and into the kitchen. Dad dropped the shovel by the door as he shut it behind us. He shook off piles of snow and tried to get his coat off. Our hands were both too frozen to work our buttons. We were two dead-thumbed, wind-thrashed snowmen, struck silent by awful thoughts of what might have been.

I unwound the pipe and clothesline.

Dad wiggled his reddened fingers. Finally, he spoke. "I climbed over the Dutch door at the back of the barn. I went around the far side so I could walk along the shorter drifts there. As I took off toward the house, the lights went out. Absolutely black. No sound but wind. I stopped in my tracks. Lost my sense of direction completely. I stopped and I listened. Nothing. So, I took a step toward what I thought was the house. Then I heard some noise behind me. First a pipe, which sounded like the wind. I stopped and listened. More pipish sounds, and I took a few steps toward them." His face was red, chapped. "Then a big loud voice shouted about not delivering babies, and a big screaming roar. I followed that sound to you." Flopping down on the chair, he tried to kick off his boots. They didn't budge. "Luke, how is Maggie doing? How far apart are her contractions now?"

I stood. "She needs you right away."

He lurched off his seat and ran down the hall, his coat flapping, and his boots sloshing snow blobs at the wall.

The hour that followed was like a blur in my head. I remember Dad asking me to melt snow in the kitchen. Our water pump was electric, so our faucets didn't work. I heated snow-water in the kitchen, two pots full, then gathered several armloads of firewood from the cellar and carried it to the living room. While I was doing this, Dad walked back and forth between Maggie's room and the kitchen, which is where we both stopped. He sat down and pulled off his boots.

"Is Maggie sleeping?" I asked.

He shook his head. "No. She's…in labor."

"Does that hurt?"

"Yes."

I didn't want to know that Maggie was hurting. I shouldn't have asked.

Dad stood and went into his room where Stevie lay sleeping, so I stretched out on the couch near the Franklin Stove.

The warmth made me drowsy, the softness of the couch like a nest, comforting after my frozen night out in the snow, my worries about dad now at rest.

A low moan came from Maggie's room, cutting into my contentment. I sat up.

Dad came out of his room, now dressed in dry clothes.

She moaned again.

He picked up the living room lantern and took off toward her room, leaving me in the dark with only the soft red of embers in the belly of the Franklin stove.

I set a fresh log on top of the embers and secured the door like my dad taught me to do long ago, even before our fire flood that happened in our kitchen. Now I was surrounded by complete blackness, the kind that no matter where you looked—there was nothing. I lay down again, enjoying the smell of woodsmoke, the crackling of the fire, knowing that my dad was nearby—safe. A long sigh passed through my body. Fresh tears threatened to bubble into my eyes. I didn't want to think about the close call we'd had outside, my dad and me. I didn't want to remember trudging through the cold snow, leaving Maggie alone in the house, praying.

Another moan came from the bedroom. It dug into my heart, pushing more tears out of me. I brushed them aside. Maggie had been praying for me when I was outside; I needed to pray for her now. So I did. And then I let my heavy eyelids slide down.

I didn't sleep well that night. I dreamt of someone, a woman, Maggie—moaning, and I couldn't find her in the snow. I dreamt of my dad trying to soothe her with his voice, but I couldn't understand his words because the cold wind was howling around him. He was lost with Maggie, both of them together, and I couldn't find them. The moaning got louder, merging into another sound, louder, groaning like someone trying to push a truck up a hill, harder and harder. Dad's voice was gone now, lost in the blizzard. I shivered, pulling my covers up to my chin, which didn't help. I was still too cold. We were all freezing to death. I cried out, waking myself. I opened my eyes but saw only darkness.

Silence.

I looked around at nothing but black. I remembered now. I was in the living room on our couch by the woodstove, and I wasn't warm enough. The fire had gone down.

I heard a sound like a lamb bleating, shaky, new. Oh, wait. It was a baby. I sat up, wishing I could go see what was happening in Maggie's room, but not moving. Dad said he'd come get me when it was time to see the baby.

A door squeaked. I recognized the shuffling of Stevie's feet coming toward me, and his hand touched my knee. "Daddy?" he asked.

"Not Daddy," I said. "Luke." I pulled him onto the couch and wrapped my blanket around us both to get us warm. We sat like this for a while, Stevie leaning against me, breathing with his mouth open because his nose was stuffed up. There were no other sounds coming from Maggie's room. I sat and waited.

Dad's heavy feet came into the living room. His lantern spread its soft glow around us, casting shadows across the living room. He added wood to the stove and stood beside us a moment, the lantern wavering slightly. "You guys okay?"

"Yeah." I yawned. "What about Maggie?"

"She's a trooper. Baby's a girl."

Stevie stretched his arms. "Daddy, guess what?"

"What, buddy?"

"I go bassetbaw."

Dad reached over and tousled my brother's hair. "Good to know." Then he left, taking his lantern with him. I didn't need light anyway. Stevie and I leaned to the side like two trees toppling in the forest until we lay flat on the couch, wrapped together in my blanket.

The next thing I remember was Dad nudging my arm. "Luke," he said. "Luke."

When I opened my eyes, I saw that Stevie was in a sleeping bag on the floor, and Dad's rollaway bed was in the living room—with Maggie peacefully asleep on it. Dad was sitting in the big chair, leaning toward me. We were all circled around the crackling Franklin stove like it was a campfire, welcoming us into its warmth.

In the soft glow of the stove, I could see that Dad's cheeks were red—chapped, probably from being out in the icy cold last night. I put my hand to my own face as if it could tell by feel if I was red, too.

"Luke."

I yawned. "What?"

"I need you to milk the cows."

"Why?"

"I'm staying here. I'm not leaving Maggie."

"What time is it?"

"Daybreak. Past my regular cow-milking time." Dad's voice had never sounded so tired. He rubbed the whiskery stubble on his chin.

"Can't you go?" I asked.

"No, son." After a glance at Maggie, he furrowed his brow. "Not this morning."

"Is there enough daylight to find the barn?" My eyes slid shut.

"Yes. And the snow has stopped."

I relaxed against my pillow.

He pushed my arm again. "Sit up, Luke."

I opened my eyes and sat up.

"Look down."

I did. There, between the couch and Maggie was a drawer from Dad's dresser. In it was a little baby, asleep.

"It's a girl, Alice, named after Maggie's grandmother," he said.

The baby was tucked tightly in a yellow blanket. Her face was round and pink, and her eyes were shut. Dark fuzz stuck out from beneath the little cap that covered her head.

"She has fuzzy hair," I said. "And fat cheeks."

"Hey, that's what she said about you."

"Huh?"

"My attempt at humor, son. Wake up."

I swung my legs off the couch, being careful not to bump the drawer.

I don't remember ever being this tired before. I usually hop right out of bed in the mornings, but today was different. There were anvils in my feet, and my body wanted to just tip to the side and plop back down on the couch. I walked into the kitchen and stared out the window.

A giant snow-pillow fight had taken place in our yard, leaving mounds of white fluff, polished smooth and decorated with long, knuckled finger-shadows from leafless trees. Past the barn, dawn spread across the field and up the hill, etching its way through the black walnut grove. After everything that had happened last night, I could hardly believe the fresh snow still appeared beautiful to me.

I turned from the window to face my dad in the light from the window. He looked like he'd been through a war, his face all roughed up from the cold, and his eyes dark and puffy. His hair was smack-flat on one side of his head and sticking out like rooster feathers on the other. I wondered what mine looked like.

My head felt all woozy. I knew that I was more tired than I was hungry or thirsty or any of the other things my body was crying out for.

"Eat something first." He poured me a bowl of cereal.

I didn't want to go out into the cold. "Do you think the cows can wait?"

"Cows don't wait."

"Maggie and the baby are sleeping. Maybe you could leave them long enough to milk the cows—or at least, help me?"

"I need to stay close to Maggie for a while yet. She seems kind of weak."

I frowned. "What's wrong with her?"

"Nothing, I guess. But I still don't want to leave her." He set the teakettle on a burner. "Dress in layers. Add a log and poke up the fire out there. Milk Peaches first. Then do Lady—don't let her kick you. I thought about coming to help you with Elsie if Maggie's doing okay, but I don't want to leave her just yet. Can you milk all three of 'em?"

The seriousness of Dad's voice reminded me again of his adoptive mom who died in the house. "I'll do all three. You stay here."

Our gloves were still wet from last night, scattered all over the kitchen in little puddles, so I put socks on my hands, matching ones— because of what Maggie was trying to teach us. As I stepped out onto the porch, the cold air slapped me in the face, jolting me awake. It took about ten minutes to fight through the snow drifts and get the fire poked up in the barn's wood burner.

I settled myself on the stool beside Peaches, reached under her, and began to milk in the weak light of the window I'd broken last night. The workbench beside it was covered with a bed of snow, a few jagged pieces of glass sticking out. With a sigh I rested my cheek against the cow's warm flank like I'd seen my dad do many times, and I closed my eyes. It had been a while since I'd helped with the milking.

Usually when I did this, Dad was nearby, his face against a different cow. He'd milked cows every morning since he was my age. It was a part of his life. He said it was his twice-a-day thinking time. Well, this morning I was too tired to think.

Peaches' fur was smooth, and her warmth reached out to me, lulling me while I squeezed the milk out with a rhythmic ting as it hit the bucket. It was probably splashing all over the place, but I didn't care. Peaches was warm, her milk was warm, and I knew that she would hold me up while I relaxed against her soft comforting side.

All was quiet on the homefront—for now.

EIGHT

The sarge takes charge.

When Miss Finch asked us to write an essay on "What I Did During Christmas Vacation," I wrote about how Eddie and I built a snow fort in our yard. Somehow, an essay that started out with *I saved my dad's life* just didn't seem very fifth-graderish. Besides, the memory of that night left a sinking feeling in my gut. I'd almost lost my dad.

And I didn't like to think about the two days that followed—the days without electricity. Maggie had rested near the crackling fire in the living room, with Dad hovering over her, giving her sugary tea and canned soup, trying to make her strong. The first day when she needed to go anywhere, he carried her. She didn't argue. The second day she said she could walk, so he helped her up and locked their arms together, staying beside her as they moved about the house. At one point I heard her say she felt like she was being escorted to a tea party. That was the first time he smiled since the blizzard.

I didn't want Maggie to be weak like that, and I didn't want Dad to be so worried.

While he was taking care of Maggie and the baby, who slept most of the time, I milked cows, carried wood, and cooked canned food. And every night I washed the dishes—glasses first, then silverware, then bowls, then pans. I used snow-water I brought in from the yard and heated on the stove. We even kept snow-water in the bathroom to pour into the back of the toilet so it would flush.

One day I found an old poultry scale in the barn. I cleaned off the dust and feathers so Maggie wouldn't know that the last thing it had weighed was a chicken. "Look what I found." I set it in the kitchen.

Dad got the baby and laid her on it. Alice weighed in at seven pounds even, including her diaper and blanket. When the scale wobbled beneath her, she jerked her arms out, startled, and took to wailing like we were killing her.

Dad picked her up quick and held her close, rubbing her back and saying, "There, there, there," until she quieted down. Then he handed her to me so he could go tell Maggie how much her daughter weighed, and that a female's hate relationship with a scale started at day two.

I remember sitting in the kitchen chair with Alice looking up at me like she couldn't quite figure out what I was. I decided it was pretty amazing to know someone who'd only been born two days ago. She was soft and little, and smelled like talcum powder. Babies are something special.

On the third day, our electricity returned and the telephone started up again. Dr. Reber came to the house, told us Alice was as healthy as could be, and that Maggie was a bit anemic, whatever that means, but would probably strengthen up in the days ahead. He gave Maggie some pills to take, told Dad to continue letting her rest and give her lots of fluids, and to report to him within forty-eight hours if she didn't perk up.

Before Dr. Reber left, he took me aside and shook my hand. "Maggie told me what all you did the night of the blizzard," he said. "You acted brilliantly, Luke." And he was out the door.

Brilliantly. That was a new one.

Then good old Uncle Ned and Aunt Nelda arrived, bringing groceries. First, they fussed over baby Alice. While they were doing that, Dad leaned back in the recliner chair and immediately fell asleep.

"I'll bet he's exhausted," Aunt Nelda said as she laid a blanket over him.

More than that, I think he finally felt like Maggie was safe.

Aunt Nelda tied an apron around her thick middle and got busy in the kitchen while Uncle Ned went outside to get the last bag of groceries from the truck. After I set up the chess board for him and me, I rested my head on the table. That's the last thing I remember until I woke up the next day in my bed upstairs under a pile of warm blankets.

Dr. Reber was right, Maggie perked up—gradually. It was almost a month before she was in full force, being the sarge again. Little by little, things got back to normal. School was in session, Elizabeth was coming to our house again, Stevie and I set up a Popsicle stick airport in the living room, and Dad returned to his cows and tractors. I was no longer the milking assistant and cook helper.

There were two main differences.

One, there was a baby in the house, a sweet fuzz-head who everyone liked to hold. Sometimes I sat beside Dad and watched Alice make faces. We called one the pouty-mouth face and another the scrunchy face. Dad said I used to make faces like that when I was a baby.

Sometimes she stretched her arms up, clenching her little fists around my finger and squirming all over. Sometimes she grunted, and sometimes she made us all say, "PU!"

That's when we gave her to Maggie.

The other difference was Maggie. She was turning into a normal looking lady, one without a bowling ball for a stomach. When she went to church now, she dressed in different clothes, and she was looking like the pretty ladies in the Sears Roebuck catalog. This got me worrying again about Mr. Coleman, the man who sent those letters from Richmond—and Keith Sanders, the friendly guy at church that Elizabeth kept telling me about.

Meanwhile, I failed my presidents test. Miss Finch mostly couldn't read my writing, and when she could, the names were spelled wrong.

My mid-January semester report card came home with two Fs, four Ds, one C and two As. My As were in Conduct and gym class. I was right on track for repeating fifth grade. I'd tried everything I knew. There was nothing left. Every day when I showed up at school and saw

Eddie and my other friends—and the obnoxious fourth graders who might move up and join me next year in fifth grade—my heart did a nosedive to the bottom of my shoes.

Elizabeth started coming to the house even when it wasn't her regular time. She wanted to help with the baby, she said. Maggie taught Elizabeth how to give Alice a bath and change her diapers. Sometimes I helped too, but mostly I stayed away during the diaper changing lessons. Babies can be smelly.

When Alice was asleep, Elizabeth wandered around and found other things to do, like play chess with me. The first time we played, I beat her in six minutes flat, so she wanted to play again.

I beat her again.

"How did you learn to play chess so well?" she asked while I lined up my pawns.

"Uncle Ned and I have tournaments sometimes, just the two of us."

"Who's Uncle Ned?" Elizabeth was twirling her long blonde strands around her ear.

I knew she was trying to get me to notice the new barrette thingies she got for Christmas, but I decided to make her work a little harder before I said anything about them. "Uncle Ned is Dad's uncle. You've met him. He lives up the hill past the walnut grove."

She sighed and let her hair drop down over her ear. "So, Luke, how come you're so good at chess and not at other stuff?"

"What other stuff?" The words slipped out of my mouth before I could suck them back in. I knew what other stuff.

"Never mind." Maybe she wanted to suck in her words too.

Sometimes I felt like there were five big letters stamped on my forehead—S-T-U-D-I-P.

"Let's play again. This time I'll be black. Maybe it's lucky." Elizabeth pushed her glasses up on her nose while I fixed her queen and king. She had them on the wrong side of each other.

"They're backwards," I said. "They should face mine across the board."

"We're backwards," she said.

"What?"

"We're backwards. You and me."

"What do you mean?"

"I'm good at school, and you aren't. You're good at chess, and I'm not. You're good at sports, and I'm not. Everything you are, I'm the opposite. Everything I am, you're the opposite."

So what if we were opposite? I focused on the chess board. "I'll let you start this time."

She took a deep breath. "Maybe you can teach me basketball."

"Huh? Why?"

"I'm tall. My dad wants me to play in a girl's league. He thinks I'll become a star." She sighed.

"That sounds like fun."

"I hate basketball. It messes up my fingernails, and it's smelly."

This from a person who came to my house to change stinky diapers.

A plan was forming in my head. "I'll make you a trade."

"Like what?"

"I'll teach you basketball if you can help me get better grades." I decided not to point out that she was already forcing school-help on me whether I wanted it or not.

Her eyebrows lifted. "Oh?"

"And we won't tell anyone. I can surprise Miss Finch with good grades, and you can surprise your dad by being a basketball star."

"Okay." She sat up brightly. "Every day when I come here, we'll have an hour of schoolwork for you and an hour of basketball for me."

"We'd better do the basketball first, before it gets dark."

"That makes sense." She shoved her chess pieces off the board. "Let's start right now."

I should tell you that our basketball hoop is a real, actual basket—a round, wood-slatted bushel basket with the bottom cut out. I discovered it in the barn loft one day. I cleaned it up, hammered out the bottom, and Dad nailed it to the side of our barn at regulation basketball height. At first, we tried using a real basketball with it, but the weight of the ball smashed up the basket, and now it was missing half of the splintered wood slats. Then we switched to a lighter, rubbery bouncy ball—much better.

Before I introduced Elizabeth to her first lesson, we had to stomp the snow flat in front of the barn. Then we were ready to play. Well, sort of. I soon realized that some people have very little control of their arms and legs. Elizabeth's basketball technique looked a lot like a spider trying to catch a fly without the help of a web.

The ball slipped out of her hands when she dribbled, and we had to chase it around the yard. Finally, I pointed her at the barn so the ball would bounce back at her when she bungled it. Once when I threw her the ball, it smacked her right in the face, and her cheek turned bright red.

I wanted to stop then, but she said, "No way. I'm gonna get this if it kills me. My dad wants a basketball player, and I'm it." She clenched her jaw and picked up the ball. "I hate this! I hate not being good at something!"

I knew what she meant, but what was I supposed to do with her now?

"Okay," Elizabeth said. "Next!"

"Next…what?"

"Shooting lessons! That's what!" She stared at the basket, lifted the ball into position, and gave it a wobbly push. She had the strength to throw ping pong balls.

In spite of all this, we kept at it for the whole hour in the slippery snow. She made a basket near the end of our session and acted like it was Christmas or something. She said it was the first basket of her life. Imagine that! Personally, I'd say it was an accidental basket, but I didn't point that out.

I was glad the hour was up because honestly, I was worn out from thinking about how to change her from a daddy-long-legs spider to a basketball star. I had my work cut out for me.

Next, we got our books and settled in the kitchen where Stevie was playing pennies at the other end of the table. He said pennies were his homework. Cool pennies. He jiggled them in his little cloth bag for a while, then lined them up in rows.

Maggie was at the stove. Her homemade meaty vegetable soup filled the room with its tomato-beefy smell, warming me before I even had a chance to taste it.

I looked at Elizabeth, who had opened both of our language books and was staring at hers, twirling her stringy blonde hair. Instead of using up our brains' energy to do a language lesson, I wished we could come up with an idea to keep Maggie in the house forever.

"Which of us should read?" my friend asked without looking up.

I was sure she knew, like everyone else, that I'm a terrible reader. I guess she was just being polite. "You."

"Okay." She read the introduction about verbs, which I already knew from listening in class.

Dad stepped into the room and sniffed. "Ahh, vegetable soup." He saw Elizabeth and me, rubbed his chin, and exchanged a glance with Maggie before walking on to the living room. Sometimes I felt like he and Maggie talked without words. They just used their eyes, sending a silent message over my head.

"Okay," Elizabeth announced, "We're supposed to find each verb and write it down."

That was easy enough.

"Do you need help with the first one?" she asked.

"I understand verbs." Sometimes Elizabeth's help wasn't all it was cracked up to be. I wanted to punch her, but instead, I took a deep breath.

"Why aren't you doing anything?" she asked.

"I'm thinking."

"About what?"

"I'm thinking about you, and how bossy you are."

She tapped her pencil on my hand. "Hey, I'm helping you, bratface."

"Hey, I didn't call you names when you were out there bobbling the basketball."

"I wasn't bobbling it."

"Hey, bobbling. Cool verb," I said.

Stevie jiggled his penny bag. "Cool verb!"

I looked at the first sentence. *The frog jumped into the pond.* I wrote *jumped* on my paper. So far, so good. Second sentence: Sam brouphed, draug…something. Wait. *Sam brouted his money to the store.* Brought! I smacked my forehead with my hand. Got it! I wrote it down.

Maggie was hovering over my shoulder.

I covered my paper with my hand.

"Let me see." Elizabeth lifted my fingers. "You just wrote *droput*. What is that?"

Maggie answered for me. "He means *brought*."

"But he spelled it all wrong. Luke, maybe we should work on spelling. What grade did you get in that?"

"F!" I snapped.

"Oh, I…uh…I won't tell anyone."

"If you do, I'll break your face." A rush of heat shot up the back of my neck. School was so easy for her, and I hated the way she was staring at me like I was pitiful.

Maggie picked up my pen and grabbed my hand. "Luke, if you write the *L* on…"

"What *L*?" Elizabeth asked.

I yanked my hand away.

Elizabeth didn't need to know about that, for Pete's sake! She already knew I was stupid enough. I slammed my book shut.

"Luke," Elizabeth said in her helpful voice. "Do you want to work on spelling words?"

"That sounds like a good plan," Maggie said.

Just what I needed—more schoolwork.

Elizabeth and Maggie were ganging up on me. I didn't want to do any of it, verbs, spelling words…

That's when I heard someone else behind me, gently nudging Maggie to the side. I felt my dad's strong hand on my shoulder. He pulled me away from the table, collected our jackets, flipped on the outside light, and ushered me toward the barn. Without speaking, he shoved the basketball into my hands and said my favorite words, "One-on-

one. First to ten."

We battled it out in the yard for a long time—with me trying to figure out ways to throw the ball up without hitting his arms, which seemed longer than Frankenstein's. I had to work on timing the ball just right to get around him, and sometimes I succeeded in breaking loose. I ran him around the snow-flattened court to make him tired.

Then he started to cheat, like he always does. When Stevie and I were smaller, our basketball games always ended the same way. Dad would stop and shout, "I've had enough of you varmints buzzing around me like bees!" He'd wrap his big old arms around us, ball and all, and scoop us off the ground, wrestling with us until he shot the last basket. Then he would drop to the ground and lie there like he was dying of exhaustion.

Tonight was no exception. He shouted, "I've had enough of you, you varmint, buzzing around me like a bee!" And he grabbed me, ball and all.

While I wrestled him, he managed to pry the ball out of my hands, and with me plastered against his side, he tried to shoot the ball. His last four throws, with me clawing at his arms, didn't even loop above the basket. They smashed into the side of it, and wood splinters fell everywhere. Finally, he made the shot.

He flopped down on the ground and lay there, panting. "That's not as easy as it used to be. You're getting too big."

I picked up the ball. "You won, but you cheated, so it doesn't count."

"You always say that."

I sat down beside him on the cold snow.

"Feel better?" he said.

I smiled. "Yeah, but we're going to need a new basket. We just killed that one."

"Maybe we can use the clothesbasket on the washer. Maggie'll never miss it." Right now, it was loaded to the brim with everybody's clean socks.

I laughed. "Yeah, or the new one she bought for Stevie's toys."

"With her own money."

"How about the red one?"

"It's full of quilting stuff right now. She'll never give it up for basket-ball." He sighed. "Females. They just don't get it. You had two of them in there, trying to help you with your homework. They just want to fix you...us. They're ruthless."

I knew exactly what he meant.

"Maggie, besides following me around smacking first-aid patches on my head—she wants to spiff me up in new clothes, and fatten me up, and this weekend she wants to give all of us haircuts."

Right now, I was angry at Maggie. She had no right to talk about my reading problems in front of Elizabeth. "Why are they so bossy, anyway?"

"You're asking me to explain women? You might as well ask me to fly an airplane to Mars."

"Blindfolded."

He laughed. "And when it comes to Maggie, well..." A smile flickered across his lips. "I wish I knew."

"Knew what?"

"Just..." He looked at me like he had something important to say, but he shut his mouth tight and shook his head. "Nothing."

I wondered what was on his mind about Maggie, but I knew I could never force words out of Dad's mouth when he didn't want to talk, so I let it go.

I lay beside him and felt the cold crisp evening air against my cheeks. I didn't really feel like I'd played a game as much as I'd been hugged.

Dad elbowed me. "Do you suppose Maggie and Elizabeth are upset because I yanked you out of there in the middle of their homework ambush?" I saw worry lines cross his face.

"I don't know, Dad."

He sighed. "I'm probably in trouble with the sarge."

I wished he hadn't said that. "She won't leave us, will she? I mean, if she gets really mad at you?"

He clenched his jaw.

"She's different from our other lady-helper people, Dad. I was okay when they left us, but I don't want her to go."

"I know exactly what you mean." A sad sigh escaped him. "I'd say Maggie's the best thing that ever happened to us."

"She's almost kinda like having a mother." I'd never put Maggie together with that word before, *mother*—maybe because when you have a mother, and you lose her it leaves a big hollow valley in your gut.

Dad turned to me, his eyebrows furrowed. "She's the sarge, son. If she wants to stay, she'll stay. And when she wants to leave, she'll leave."

We both lay in sad stillness, soft cloud-puffs rising from our mouths as we breathed softly into the cool air. I was trying to think of a sure-fire way to keep Maggie, but nothing came into my head.

Dad was silent.

"Maybe you can think of a way to keep her," I suggested.

"I'm not good at that. Women are a mystery I'll never solve." I could tell by his voice that our discussion was sending his heart down to his shoes.

"Did you understand Mom?"

"No."

"How'd you get her to marry you if you didn't understand her?"

"You don't have to understand someone to love them."

"Did she understand you?"

"Mostly."

Maggie stuck her head out the door. "Dinner's ready."

Standing, we swatted the snow clots off our clothes.

"Let's stick together," Dad said. "And let me do the talking."

"What're you gonna say?"

"I don't know. Something'll come to me."

We walked together into the kitchen, and Dad didn't say anything. I figured he was trying to get a handle on the mood in there before he spoke. I heard Elizabeth in the living room singing to Alice.

Maggie helped me take off my jacket and hung it on the peg. "Luke," she said.

"What?"

"School was terrible for me. I hated it, and I don't want you to feel the same kind of misery I felt. So in my exuberance to help you do school-work, I tend to get carried away. I was insensitive to your feelings."

I looked at Dad.

He had nothing to give, no words.

She continued. "Elizabeth and I made a rule. Here it is—only one of us can help you at a time. No ganging up on you. And you call the shots. We can give you ideas, but you choose the plan of attack. It's better if you have some control."

That sounded like a major improvement. "Okay."

Dad remained silent.

"Will you forgive me, Luke?" Maggie asked.

I turned to her, eye-to-eye. "Sure."

Relief flowed across her face, and I received my second hug of the evening.

Dad never did think of anything to say, but it didn't matter.

"So, Dad. What's that about anyway?" I asked.

"Huh?" He looked up from his Bible study book on the table. "What?"

"Dad. What's that about—*A Man After God's Own Heart*?"

"It's about David."

"David who?"

"The Bible David. The one from David and Goliath."

"Who?"

"David and Goliath. Oh, come on. You know, the boy who slew the giant and later became the king of Israel."

"What's—slew?"

"Killed."

"He killed a giant? How?"

"Don't you remember the story from Sunday school?"

"I was pretty young when we quit going to church, Dad. I don't remember much besides Stevie's loud singing and how he sneezed all over Mrs. Adams that one time."

Dad covered his face and groaned. "I have done you such a disservice."

I didn't want him to feel bad. "It's okay, Dad." I patted his arm.

"No, it's not okay." He sighed. "We need to make some changes around here. You need to start going to church with Maggie."

"I did. Twice."

"No, I mean regularly."

"Wait, Dad. Just me? What about you?"

"Stevie doesn't do well in church. You know that."

"But…"

Maggie walked into the room and pulled a pot out of the cupboard. "How's the studying going?" she asked.

I groaned.

Dad turned to her. "Maggie, I'm having trouble with King David being a man after God's own heart. I don't get it."

She set the pot on the counter.

I wondered what she was going to make in the pot. Possibly noodles for spaghetti? My stomach began to growl.

Maggie was standing over Dad, looking down at his workbook page.

Dad spoke. "David saw Bathsheba on her roof taking a…" Noticing me, he paused, then looked at Maggie. "You know. He stole his neighbor's wife, then sent her husband, Uriah, to the front line of battle so he would get killed—while David was loafing at home with…" He glanced at me again, then at Maggie.

She nodded. "Right. I know."

"How could he do that?" I asked. "Isn't it against the law?"

"Luke, he was the king. He could do whatever he wanted."

"Well, who voted him into office?"

Dad and Maggie gave each other one of those crinkle eye glances I wasn't supposed to see.

I took a breath. "So what happened? Did the Urima guy get killed in battle?"

"Uriah," Dad answered. "And yes, he got killed."

"Wow. That's awful."

"Exactly." Dad continued. "So, Maggie, how could God call David, 'a man after My own heart' when he did such an evil thing?"

I set down my pencil. Dad's homework was way more interesting than mine.

Maggie held the pot in the sink and rinsed it out. "David's friend, Nathan, told him how wrong he'd been. Then David realized he was guilty. He fell on his face before God, totally humiliated and sorry, and he asked for forgiveness."

"Did God forgive him?" I asked.

"Yes, God forgives sinners. That's what He does," she said.

Dad, worry lines across his forehead, focused on his book, tapping his pencil beside it.

"Then what did David do?" I asked Maggie.

"After he repented, he changed."

"So that's why he's called a man after God's own heart—because he repented, and he changed?" I asked.

"Seems kind of simple." Dad was scratching his chin. "But still, not easy. How did David forgive…himself?"

Maggie had stopped messing with the pot and stood facing him, a look of concern on her face. "You'll figure it out, William. I know you will."

He sighed.

I realized that this had become one of those grown-up conversations that sailed over my head. I'd lost what they were talking about.

He shifted in his chair and focused on me. "How are you doing with your assignment, Luke?"

"Dad, let's trade homework."

Elizabeth wasn't there the day the sarge made me stay outside after school. I stood on the porch, begging to come in out of the cold, and she said, "Go to the barn with your dad. No men allowed until supper except for Stevie."

"Why not?"

"None of your beeswax, unless you want to come in and do kitchen work."

I was insulted, but I left. I would stay out of her way, whatever it was she was doing.

The familiar scents of motor oil, hay, and cows greeted me. Picking my way through the tractors, I plopped down at Dad's desk, pushed his receipts to the side, and arranged my books and papers. "What's the sarge doing in there?" I asked.

Dad stepped from behind a huge tire. "Where?"

"The kitchen. She won't let me go in."

"Haven't been over there all day." He put his hand on the fresh new first-aid patch taped over his left ear. "When she brought my lunch out, I accidentally let her see my latest injury. Nurse Sarge is back in business."

He grinned.

I guess we were both glad the sarge was back in business, even if she had locked me out of the kitchen.

By the time I finished struggling through my homework, Dad was putting away his tools. We walked to the house together.

Maggie let us enter this time, and right away I knew we were in for no ordinary meal. There was a white tablecloth on the table with cloth napkins and glowing candles. I felt like I was in a fancy restaurant instead of our farmhouse kitchen.

"Go wash up," Maggie instructed. "Be quiet about it. The baby's asleep."

Stevie put his hands over his mouth to cover a giggle.

Dad and I tiptoed down the hall to the bathroom.

Maggie had Dad and me sit at the two ends of the table, with her on one side and Stevie across from her. She was wearing a new dress with an apron over it, and Stevie had on a clean shirt.

Maggie stretched out her arms and said, "Give me your hands, you two."

I slid my hand across the table and joined hers, palms together. Her hands were buttery smooth, probably because she used the pink lotion on the windowsill every night after her kitchen work was done. Dad held up his big mitts, scrubbed as clean as he could get them, but still permanently stained from years of tractor grease etched into his thick callouses and scars. "These?"

She cleared her throat. "Yes, William. A man who works hard should never be ashamed of his rough hands."

Dad brought his hands down and reached toward her, carefully wrapping his long fingers loosely around hers, like he was afraid his tough skin might bother her—as if she was a delicate lady instead of the sarge.

Stevie joined us on the other side so we were a full circle, connected. His almond shaped eyes were all crinkly-giggly.

"Okay." She took a deep breath. "We're going to say grace."

As we bowed our heads, I caught Dad studying her, his eyes lingering like when he read a favorite book he couldn't put down. He saw me, lowered his head, and shut his eyes.

"Okay," she said again. "Father in heaven, thank you for these two fine men who took such good care of Alice and me on the night of her birth, and in the days that followed. Amen."

Something warm and comfortable filled me as we raised our heads, a hush around us.

"This is a special dinner to honor my two heroes," Maggie said. "Stevie is my assistant." She gave him a wink, bringing a wide smile to his face while he slid off his chair.

I took a deep breath as the idea soaked in—this dinner was about me and my dad, heroes.

Dad's fingers went to his napkin.

"Don't touch that," Maggie whispered.

His eyes quizzed hers.

"I mean it."

He put his hands on his lap.

Stevie walked around the table, slid my folded napkin out from under my fork, gave it a shake, and set it on my lap, carefully smoothing out any wrinkles and making sure the corners lay flat against my stomach and legs. "Cool napkin," he said.

Then he did the same for Dad.

After fixing Maggie's napkin, he sat down and took care of his own.

I had a feeling that Maggie had kept him busy all afternoon practicing cool napkins. I wondered if, in the future, we would ever again be able to just grab our napkins and start eating.

First, Maggie served us hot rolls and homemade cheese potato soup. I'd never tasted anything like it before, thick and rich like sending a warm, flowing, cheese-filled blanket down into your cold empty stomach. She followed it with pork chops and green beans, two of Dad's favorites.

I don't remember everything we talked about at the table, but I know we talked—well, mostly, Dad and Maggie did. They talked about David in the Bible and how he sinned, and how God's big desire is to forgive people for their sins. It seemed like lately Dad wanted to hear about God's forgiveness again and again. While their discussion went on, I was enjoying every perfect bite. It felt terrific to be honored in such a way—with food. And I could tell by the way Dad was looking at Maggie, he must be feeling that way too because he kind of glowed.

Stevie and Maggie served the special dessert, peach pie and ice cream. When it was over, Dad helped Maggie do the dishes while I went into the living room.

For a while I played with Alice, who was now awake. She smiled at me twice—big, toothless smiles. Then I helped Stevie finish putting away his Popsicle sticks and metal airplanes in the box I'd given him for Christmas.

I went up to my room, flopped down on my bed, and listened to the sounds downstairs. Stevie sang "cool bubbles" in the bathtub with the door open so Maggie could keep an eye on him. Dad's rocking chair creaked in the living room as he sang "baby-baby-baby" to Alice in a funny, high-pitched voice. I think sometimes he forgot that other people could hear him.

Maggie's footsteps were moving—in the bathroom, in the kitchen, in the living room—circling around, making our house run like a comfortable, people-caring machine.

I thought back to the old days before she came. I remembered lying on my bed next to Dad while he read to me from *Treasure Island* and noticing there was peanut butter in his hair from my pillow. I remembered spaghetti fossils in our pans, and I remembered babysitting Stevie day in and day out, making sure he didn't try to cook on the stove like he did that terrible day when I couldn't get Dad to wake up.

And I remembered those nights, too, when my dad stood in the kitchen, staring out the window at the moon. In the dim light, he'd look so sad, his shoulders drooping. When I asked him what was wrong, and he said, "Nothing." But in those days, I'd catch him being sad other times, too, when he probably thought no one was watching. And sometimes he seemed angry, his hands fisted, his lips clenched.

I suppose if a guy didn't have a mother, and he didn't have a wife—and his kids were losers—he would have good reason to stand at a window and look sad. Back then, I didn't realize what we were missing.

But now I knew. I knew tonight when Maggie stretched out her hands to join us all together before she thanked God for us. Before this, we'd never had a woman in the house who knew how to whip us into shape.

Before this, we'd never had a Maggie.

NINE

*This is how a man named Hank, a hoop, and
a dog brought syrup-difity into my life.*

Wednesday was Maggie's day off, and she usually went to town. First, she went to her quilt ladies' Bible study with people like Elizabeth's mom and a friend named Bonnie whose brother, Keith, smiled a lot when he talked to Maggie at church on Sundays—at least that's what Elizabeth said. Elizabeth was kinda like a spy, trying to make sure nobody tried to steal Maggie away from us.

After the Wednesday lady gathering, Maggie usually cashed her paycheck, put some money in the bank, and went shopping with the rest. Sometimes she brought home stuff like new dishtowels or curtains and treats for us. My favorite was the flat square bubblegum that came with the baseball cards, which she always asked to sniff after I opened them. She said fresh bubblegum was her favorite smell—before it gets chewed.

One Wednesday afternoon, just as Elizabeth and I finished a long, noisy memorizing session on states and capitals, Maggie walked into the kitchen carrying a big sack from Woolworths.

"Did you buy us something?" I asked.

"Yes, underwear." She went to her room, bag in hand, and shut the door.

Underwear wasn't what I was hoping for.

I glanced at Elizabeth who had organized our math papers and was now trying to untangle a chunk of blonde hair from her glasses.

I wondered if she was pretending like she hadn't just heard the word, *underwear*.

She pointed at my work. "The reason you're doing so bad at long division is because your columns get mixed up. Look, the numbers in your tens column are curving over under the ones column."

I was still having mixed feelings about the homework-basketball trade.

"I brought you something." Elizabeth pulled out a stack of graph paper with squares the size of dice. "Use this instead of regular lined paper. Maybe it'll help."

"Do you sit at home and think about this stuff?"

"No, not really." She frowned at me. "But last night I was trying to design my own cross-stitch pattern on graph paper, and this idea just flew into my head about you and your crooked lines."

"Thanks." I yanked the sheet out of her hand. If she put half as much effort into practicing lay-ups as she did fixing me, she'd be hitting the basket instead of the barn wall, Dad's truck, and the window Dad had just replaced after I broke it during the blizzard.

"You can write the numbers in the columns," she said, setting her finger on the first square of the graph paper. "It'll help line 'em up. Try it."

I shifted my brain away from yesterday's basketball disaster and carefully wrote my first long division problem, one number per square.

Dad burst in from outside and set his coffee thermos on the counter. He walked down the hall, his big boots clomping on the wooden boards, and knocked on Maggie's door. "I saw you carry in a sack. What'd you buy?"

Dad was going to be disappointed. No treats this time. She bought underwear.

Maggie opened her door. "My, you're nosy."

He laughed. "Yes, I am."

"Do you think I bought something for you? More bubblegum?"

"Maybe. What'd you buy?"

"Underwear."

Elizabeth flinched.

"Underwear?" Dad asked.

Did they have to keep saying *underwear* in front of Elizabeth, for Pete's sake?

"I bought new underwear for everybody." Maggie shoved a package at his chest. "Here's yours."

Dad's neck got red just then, but he took a big breath and kept right on talking. "You're not supposed to use your money on us. It's your paycheck for working so hard. Spending it on the house is bad enough, but why are you buying us underwear?"

"I'm the one who washes all those old raggedy things you guys wear around here. It's time. Trust me."

Elizabeth was completely still as her eyes drilled down into her math book.

I didn't know what to do.

"Well, let me pay you back," Dad said to Maggie.

"No. Consider it a gift to you."

"Really, Maggie…"

"William, if you protest one more time, I'm going to smack you. Here, take these packages for the boys."

"Who gets the ones with the sailboats on them?"

"Stevie."

"Maybe I wanted some like that."

"They don't make that kind for grown-ups, so quit whining."

"Okay, Sarge." Dad turned and walked toward his room and Maggie went back into hers.

After a deep breath, Elizabeth sat up and leaned toward me. "Your family is weird. Your dad calls Maggie, Sarge."

"I know. He always calls her that. Besides, we're not really a family."

"Well, whatever you are."

Whatever we were—I liked. It was fun to hear Maggie and Dad argue about sailboat underwear, and I liked having a baby in the house who smiled at me. At night it felt good to lie under my dog quilt across the room from Stevie and know he'd been tucked in with clean pajamas and fresh kisses on his cheeks.

I returned my attention to copying the first math problem, trying to keep the numbers in the squares so they lined up straight this time. I hated to admit it, but I think it helped. Maybe Elizabeth was a genius. "Do you think Miss Finch will mind if I use graph paper?"

"If it helps you, she'll be glad," Elizabeth answered as she erased one of my numbers and changed it to a different, probably correct one. She blew on the paper, then looked at me. "Well, at least, I'd be glad if I was the teacher. I would be thankful for anything that can help a kid like you."

Like me?

Elizabeth was focused on her page, squinting as she wrote her neat numbers on the regular lined paper. I tried to imagine what it would be like to be a schoolkid like her. I couldn't do it.

One sunny March Saturday morning was different from all the others. Maggie loaded Alice and me into Dad's truck and drove us all the way to Richmond to visit her aunt. Dad and Stevie stayed home to work on tractors.

When we got to town, Aunt Joyce, a chubby grandmotherly lady, grabbed up Alice like she was a sugar pie donut. Then she turned to me, and the next thing I knew she was hugging me like I was a sugar pie donut even though I'd never met her before. There I was, blinking, my face smashed into her soft apron that smelled like homemade bread.

"Oh, Maggie," she said as she let me go, "Hank Coleman said he'll be home this morning before he goes to pick up Pat. If you run over there now, I'll keep the baby. Land sakes, what a cutie."

I stepped away from Aunt Joyce. She'd said Hank Colemen. Hank Coleman? The guy who wrote letters to Maggie? A sad feeling dropped into the pit of my stomach.

"Okay." Maggie grabbed her sweater. "Come on, Luke."

"Me?" Why would she want me to go with her to see Hank Coleman?

Maggie and Aunt Joyce exchanged a glance that said they knew something I didn't.

"Why are we going there?" I asked, trying to hide my anger.

"Just wait." Maggie led me to the truck. "What's bothering you, Luke?"

"Nothing." I shook my head. "Who's Hank Coleman, anyway? Isn't he the guy who writes to you?"

"Yes, he's been doing a favor for me." She climbed eagerly into the truck. "You'll like him."

I doubted that, but obviously, she liked him. I wondered what the favor was, but I didn't ask. I was too worried about him stealing her from us.

We drove down a street where leafless maple trees lined both sides like giant soldiers standing at attention. We parked in front of a red brick two-story house with white columns on the front. Mr. Coleman must be rich.

Whatever his bank account, he turned out to be a friendly, loud guy who hugged Maggie the minute she walked into the big clean living room.

I wanted to sock him.

Then he turned to me. "So, is this the famous young man who rescues people in blizzards?"

I was embarrassed, but I nodded. How did he know that? When had Maggie talked to him? Maybe she did more on her days off than go to Bible study and shopping.

While Maggie was trying to sit on the couch, a little fluffy black dog tore into the room and was going nuts around her ankles, jumping up and down and banging into the coffee table. "Oh, my little Bosco," she said as she hugged him and petted him.

Maggie and Mr. Coleman shared a dog? I took a long, deep, sad breath. I hated being here. I wanted to just run out the door.

After the dog was done attacking Maggie with all his joy, he ran to me, so I sat on the floor while he pressed his happy whiskered face against me. I held him close and petted him, hoping to make the heavy glob in my chest go away.

The man brought in some lemonade and sat down on a chair near Maggie. I stayed on the floor and wished I could just play with the dog and not worry about Maggie and Mr. Coleman.

He asked Maggie a lot of questions. He wanted to know if William Bradley was good to her, if she needed money, and how baby Alice was doing.

I was glad she gave him good answers. Yes, Dad was good to her, she didn't need money, and the baby was a blessing.

I wondered if Maggie thought Mr. Coleman was good-looking. He was kinda big, and about my dad's age, I suppose. I tried to compare him and Dad to decide who would win if there was a contest to see which guy was the most handsome. Dad was taller and thinner, and his clothes weren't as new, but other than that, I couldn't tell. It's hard to judge those things about your own father.

While they talked about some people I didn't know, I looked around the room, enjoying the smell of furniture polish. Nobody seemed to be here besides us. On the piano there were several framed pictures of people, a baby, and two men holding fish.

I got up to examine the last photo up close. I recognized Mr. Coleman as the guy with the huge fish—while the other man, who looked somehow familiar, held a tiny one. Both men had a crooked little twist to their lips, like Eddie and I might have when we're trying to hold in the giggles.

Then I realized who the second man was—Maggie's husband, Ted, looking very alive. Something stabbed in me.

Before, when I'd seen Ted's fireman picture on Maggie's dresser, I thought of him as just a face, not someone with twinkling eyes who had fun with his friends. A lump rose in my throat as I turned away from the picture and tried to shake off this new sad feeling.

Mr. Coleman was handing Maggie a large manila envelope. "This is the material we talked about last week. Read the introduction first."

She'd talked to him last week? My neck bristled.

"Just take your time with it. Let me know if it helps. Then we can discuss a plan." He glanced at me then, like I was somehow involved. His eyes seemed kind, but I looked away. "I'll get the traveling dog hotel." He stood and disappeared into another room.

Maggie picked up her purse and the envelope.

"What's a dog hotel?" I asked her.

"You'll see."

The man returned, carrying a large box with two rows of quarter-sized holes in the side. "Come here, Bosco."

The little black dog jumped into his arms.

"What kind of a dog is that?" I asked, trying to be polite.

"The best kind, a mutt. We think he's a cross between a cocker spaniel and a poodle."

"Called a cockapoo," Maggie added.

"He's supposed to look like a curly haired cocker spaniel, be smart like a poodle, and not shed." Mr. Coleman laughed. "As you can see..." he held up the squirming dog, "he looks like a long-haired dachshund that's been in a hurricane, and he sheds all over the place. He barks at cats until they come toward him, then he runs away."

Maggie smiled. "And once he got into Ted's bag of blueberry muffins and hid them all over the house like they were Easter eggs." She turned to Mr. Coleman. "Remember that?"

He laughed again as he put the dog in the box and closed the top, arranging the flaps so they stayed together. Lifting it, he turned to Maggie. "Lead the way, my dear."

My dear? Just what exactly was going on here?

"What are you doing?" I asked. "Where's the dog going?"

Grinning, Hank Coleman winked at Maggie.

Anger boiled in me, but I kept my mouth shut. I wanted Dad to be proud of me.

We went outside and waited while Mr. Coleman put the dog hotel in the bed of the truck. I climbed into the passenger seat while the guy gave Maggie another big hug, one that made tears spring into her eyes.

We were going to lose her for sure. Something inside of me ached.

Then he let her go.

She got in on the other side, put her purse and the envelope on the floor, and started the truck.

"There's an awful lot of hugging going on around here," I complained.

She sniffed.

"What are we doing with his dog?"

"Bosco's my dog," she said. "I didn't know if I should bring him when I first came to your house, so I parked him here. Now he's coming home with us."

"A dog?" My spirits brightened. "What about Dad? Does he know?"

"Yes, he does. I gave William a list this morning. He and Stevie are going into town today to buy dog food."

"Really? Dad knows? And it's okay?"

"Yes, it's okay."

"And Stevie knows?"

"Yes."

"Stevie loves dogs." A dog, for us! "Why didn't you tell me about this before?"

"I like surprises."

"Wow! Good one!" Then my spirits fell as I remembered Mr. Coleman winking at Maggie, calling her *my dear,* and hugging her twice. And that last one was a doozy. I wondered if he was in love with Maggie, but I was afraid to ask.

She hummed a little tune as we rode down the street.

Was she so happy because of the hug? Why hadn't I paid closer attention to her and Mr. Coleman's conversation instead of petting the dog and looking at pictures? Finally, I couldn't stand it any longer. "Is he…uh…?"

"Spit it out," she said.

"Is that guy married or anything?"

"Do you mean Hank?" She glanced at me. "Why do you ask?"

"I just wondered."

"He's married to Pat."

Hank Coleman was married. Relief poured over me.

"Didn't you hear us talk about her?" Maggie asked.

"I don't know. Where was she?"

"She's visiting her sister in Ft. Wayne this week—with their baby son who's named after my Ted." Maggie's lip quivered as she drove.

Her Ted. Before today I hadn't really thought that much about Maggie's marriage. It's almost like she just showed up last September out of nowhere.

I sat back and tried to imagine Maggie with her husband, Hank's fishing buddy. "So, was Mr. Coleman your husband's best friend?" I asked.

"No. I was his best friend." She smiled sadly.

She'd lost her best friend. Another stab hit me in the gut.

"Actually, Hank and Ted were great friends ever since high school. Did you see the fishing picture on the piano?"

"Yep." I let out a heavy sigh. "Is Mr. Coleman a fireman too?"

"No, he's a college professor. He's doing research that might help kids who struggle with reading."

Like me.

"That envelope on the floor has something for you to try. It has to do with your eyes and light." She continued. "I sent Hank some of your school papers to look at, and I told him about how you hold your head over your books to shade the page."

She what?

"Besides the problems with lights, he wonders if you might have some dyslexia. He wants to work with you sometime, maybe next summer."

Anger rose in me. "Why would you do that? Why would you send him my stuff?"

She glanced at me. "What's wrong? I'm trying to help you."

"Now he knows I'm stupid."

"You're not stupid."

Right! I turned to the window, tears welling in my eyes. "I've already got enough people trying to help me." None of it was working, anyway.

We stopped at a railroad crossing and waited for a train to trudge across our path, both of us stuck in our own silence while the ground rumbled beneath us.

When the train was gone, Maggie shifted gears, and we bumped over the tracks. "I'm sorry, Luke," she said. "I should've asked you first."

My anger dribbled away as we moved along the smooth highway. I decided to change the subject. "What was your husband like?"

"Umm…" She took a deep breath. "Well, he was a good man—strong and kind. Had curly hair and dimples like Alice." Maggie stared at the road while she talked. "They're so much alike, yet she'll never meet him on this earth." She cleared her throat. "He liked baseball and kids, and every Saturday he cooked hamburgers on the grill, even in the winter."

Her face seemed locked in sadness while we drove on down the road. I figured she was done talking for now or she would've said more. I wished I could do something to make her feel better about losing her good husband. We were silent during the rest of the drive. I guess she was remembering Ted, and I was wondering what it would be like to know him when he was alive, fishing and laughing with his friend.

And I wondered what I could do make her happy again.

After we returned to Aunt Joyce's house, I found out why we'd brought Dad's truck instead of Maggie's car. First, we carried several boxes of baby stuff, clothes, a typewriter, and a portable television with a handle on top to the truck bed. Then, with the three of us hoisting it, we lifted a real basketball hoop and backboard off the garage floor and loaded it.

"There," Maggie said, after we settled it in place and she rearranged some of the other items.

"Whose hoop is this?" I asked.

"Mine," she said. "Never had a good place to put it since high school."

"Yours?"

Aunt Joyce laughed. "Land sakes, Maggie practiced for hours on that thing. She could beat anyone playing one-on-one."

Part of me was surprised that Maggie, who was short for a grown-up and female besides, was good at basketball. The other part of me remembered the easy flight of a rock over our barn.

Aunt Joyce continued. "Did she tell you she was the starting point guard for her high school team?"

"Your school had a girls' basketball team?" I asked.

"Nope."

"Huh?"

Aunt Joyce talked away. "No girls' team. So, the boys' coach recruited her, and she earned the starting point guard position. Wow, was she fun to watch. Quicker than a slice of lightning, weaving around those tall boys. She broke a record for steals in one game. They just didn't see her coming."

"Okay, Aunt Joyce. That's enough." Maggie turned to me. "Luke, we'll put the basketball hoop over the barn door. Your dad already measured. He thought you would enjoy an actual real basketball hoop." She patted it. "A lot better than having this thing sit in a dark old garage."

I swelled with excitement, beaming at her. "Thanks!" I couldn't wait to get home and start shooting. "Man, I'm going to save up for a real basketball."

"Your dad is buying one today." She grinned. "I put it on his list."

This was better than Christmas! And to top it off, I no longer had to worry about Mr. Coleman stealing Maggie out from under my nose. And…she must be planning to stay. After all, she was hanging her basketball hoop on our barn.

"I can just hear Stevie saying, 'Cool basketball,'" I said.

"I don't even know if he can say basketball."

Aunt Joyce helped us get Alice situated in the truck, and we drove off, the smiley lady waving until we were out of sight.

All in all, it had been a totally unpredictable day in the best possible way. I remember Dad saying a word once that described a day like this. It was…serruptiv…I turned to Maggie. "What's the word that means something happens that you didn't expect, and it's really good?"

"Uuhh—"

"Serruptivity?" I asked.

"Oh, wait. I think I know what you mean. Something like that."

"Syrup-difity?"

"Can't think of it. Give me a minute." She shifted the gears and turned out to the main road.

We moved along at a quick pace, lapping up the miles, carrying home a real basketball hoop and a dog. What a day!

Alice nodded off to sleep.

"Luke?" Maggie said. "Don't tell your dad the hoop was mine, at least not right away."

"Why not?"

She grinned. "I think I'll challenge him to a game of one-on-one."

"Oh, I get it, a challenge like you gave me the day you stood there and acted all girlie, and then sent that rock flying over the barn."

She laughed, her eyes crinkling. "Hmmm. I wonder what kind of a bet I can make. What kind of a deal."

I couldn't help but grin, too—and the word came to me. "Serendipity."

TEN

I almost blew it when I called her Aunt Bee.

W hat's that in your hand?" Elizabeth whispered. When Miss Finch had rearranged the classroom, she placed Elizabeth beside me, probably because she knew Elizabeth was good at quietly helping me, which was okay most of the time.

I opened my fingers. "I found Miss Finch's watch on the floor."

"Aren't you going to give it to her?"

"Yeah, but after I fix it. The little clasp dealie broke." I was in the middle of bending paper clips into an invention that would allow Miss Finch to actually open and close it to get it on and off her wrist.

"That's a pretty fancy piece of paper clip."

"Fancy doesn't count. It has to work." I glanced past her and saw Miss Finch busily scribbling something on the chalkboard, so I motioned to Elizabeth. "Stick out your arm."

She did, and I slid the watch on her skinny wrist and fastened the paper clip clasp.

"Wow, it's even adjustable," she said.

"Shh." I unclasped it and put it inside my desk for now.

Elizabeth continued to whisper. "Do you remember that man at church who talks to Maggie all the time?"

"What man?"

"Keith Sanders."

"Yeah, maybe. What about him?"

"I think he likes Maggie."

"Everybody likes Maggie."

She rolled her eyes. "No, I mean—romantically."

My stomach tightened. I had just gotten things settled in my mind about Mr. Coleman, and now Elizabeth was making me worry about another man who could take Maggie away from us, including her cute baby, dog, and basketball hoop. My heart was falling down into my shoes.

Elizabeth kept yapping. "I found out some things about Keith Sanders. He's a dentist, which means he's probably rich. He drives a red sports car convertible and he wears suits, and his clothes and stuff match. And he has clean fingernails."

She was comparing him to my Dad, which made me angry.

"And he always finds Maggie after church and talks to her."

I wondered what it would be like to have a woman-person in your house who you knew would stay. "Let's change the subject." I slammed my language book shut and shoved it into my desk.

"Okay." Elizabeth put her book away too. "Hey, what did you get on your math test?"

Oh, brother—a much better topic, grades. "C this time." Actually, C-.

"Good." Normally, Elizabeth wasn't such a talker in class, but she kept watching me like she had more to say.

"Why are you looking at me?" I asked.

"I went to the spring basketball tryouts yesterday."

"How did you do?"

"I don't know yet. But I think maybe I made the team."

Boy, that team must be really, really desperate if she maybe made it.

"I used that spin move you showed me. The coach said it was creative."

Creative?

I glanced around to see if Miss Finch was watching us. She was sharpening a pencil.

Elizabeth kept talking. "I don't know if that's a good thing or a bad thing—creative, in basketball anyway." She leaned toward me. "What do you think he meant?"

I turned back to Elizabeth. In her case, in her version of the spin move? Goofy? Uncontrolled? Unmanageable like the strands of hair that were tangled in her glasses right now?

"Now you're staring at me," she snapped.

"Creative. He just meant creative."

Miss Finch cleared her throat. "Okay, everyone, get ready to do page 123 in math. I'll pass out paper while you find the page. Don't forget to keep your decimal points lined up in columns."

After opening my math book, I took a sheet of graph paper out of my folder. Miss Finch let me use graph paper all the time now for math. I just kept my own supply.

Elizabeth nudged my arm. "The tryout was fun. Maybe I like basketball."

"Good."

After Miss Finch finished passing out the regular schoolwork paper, she came to my desk, opened my graph paper folder, and pulled out two sheets. "I'll pay you back later," she whispered. Then she gave one to Michael Luckritz and the other to Kathleen Olds.

I glanced at Elizabeth, and her eyes met mine for a half second. She had seen it, too, and a little smile tweaked the edge of her mouth.

Elizabeth—creative, in the best possible way.

"I wonder who does the whistling for that theme song?" Maggie asked, shifting gently without waking Stevie who was curled on the couch between us, his birthday quilt tucked under his arm. She'd given it to him at dinner. After examining the pictures of trucks and airplanes, he'd followed her around all evening with eyes of love, clutching the gift to his chest. Past Maggie, Dad sat in the rocking chair, holding the baby.

"I'll bet it's Andy Griffith whistling," I said. "That's what it sounds like to me."

One reason I liked *The Andy Griffith Show* on Maggie's television was because the family was like us with no mom. Instead of Aunt Bee, we had Maggie.

She ruffled my hair. "I guess I'd better put Stevie to bed. He's all worn out from cool bassitball."

Dad stood up and turned off the television. "That Barney Fife makes me laugh my head off." He glanced at Maggie. "Where do I put Miss Alice? In her crib? She's half asleep."

"I'll take her." As Maggie slid off her seat, Stevie leaned to the side and plopped down on the couch without waking up.

"I'll be back to wash the pudding off Stevie's face before we get him to bed." Maggie eased the baby out of Dad's arms and into hers.

"You know what?" I said to Maggie. "You're just like Aunt Bee."

Maggie looked startled. "I am? You mean chubby and with an old-fashioned hair-bun? And when she gets flustered, she waves her hands and says, 'Oh, my!'"

I gasped. "No! Not at all." I looked straight at Maggie. "I mean you take care of us, like Aunt Bee takes care of Sheriff Taylor and Opie. And you cook good."

Maggie laughed. "Okay, I get it. Thanks, Luke." She carried the baby to her bedroom.

Dad rolled his eyes. "Close call, Luke. You almost joined me in my specialty—saying the wrong things to the ladies." He picked his book up off the floor. "It's dangerous to have two of us in the same house, you know. Maybe we should ask the sarge to give you some instruction before it's too late. You know, 'how to talk to a female' lessons, or something."

Yikes, he was starting to sound like Elizabeth!

He continued. "I want you to get married someday and have grand-children for me to play with."

"Oh, Dad. That is so yuck."

He laughed and opened his book.

I supposed I might get married someday, if I could find somebody who could throw a ball like Maggie. But right now, I didn't even want to think about girls.

I wandered down the hall and peered into Maggie's room.

She was on her way out, shutting the door behind her. "Shhh." Her brown eyes sparkled.

"Maggie, I really didn't mean the hair-bun, chubby part of Aunt Bee, I meant the good stuff."

Maggie patted my head. "I know, sweetie. I was just giving you a hard time."

I started to go to church with Maggie for two reasons. First, Dad wanted me to learn all the Bible stuff I'd been missing. Second, Elizabeth told me I needed to keep an eye on Keith Sanders and make sure he wasn't flirting with Maggie. But one March Sunday morning my throat felt scratchy, so Maggie said I should stay home. Hopefully, Elizabeth would be at church to keep an eye on things.

Dad and I helped Maggie load the baby into the car.

"William, you might want to check Luke's temperature," she said to him. "I don't think he's got a fever, but you never know."

Dad pressed his big hand to my forehead. "Seems fine."

"I could've done that," she said.

He chuckled, and she rolled up the window and drove down the driveway. We watched her turn out to the road and drive off. Then Dad let out a big sigh.

I wondered if he wished he could go to church with her instead of staying home with Stevie all the time and doing their own personal church service, which I hadn't been around to attend because I always had to go with Maggie.

Dad walked over to the porch steps and sat down on the top one. "Church will come to order," he announced. He turned sideways and stretched his long legs out across the porch. Stevie, who had been playing with a little blue car on the bannister, settled beside me on the porch, both of us leaning our backs against the house like Dad was doing.

The late morning sun was sending its soft glow over the farm, melting the last touches of snow, turning them into juicy white blobs. Twittering birds hopped around in the brown grass. This was my kind of church.

"Sing a song, Daddy," Stevie said right off.

Dad had already warned me that when he started porch church with Stevie, they always sang. "We start with 'Amazing Grace,'" Dad told me. "Feel free to join in."

"I'll just listen."

Dad started the song in his steady, gravelly voice. "Amazing grace, how sweet the sound."

"Amazing grapes! Amazing grapes, like meeeee!" Stevie shouted. Elsie, who was leaning against the windmill that pumped water into the trough, let out a big long moooo. Then my brother lowered his voice into a low, sing-songy version of the same words, over and over. Sometimes he was singing about amazing grapes, and sometimes he was singing about cool bassitball go-go-go.

Dad let my brother continue alone for a few moments, then stopped him. We both applauded so Stevie stood up, bowed, and sat down again.

I could see how this wouldn't fit too well with real church.

"Maggie memorized all the verses to 'Amazing Grace,'" I said.

"I know. She made me do it too." Smiling, Dad shook his head.

"She made you memorize song verses?"

He rolled his eyes. "It was a suggestion in her workbook. We had a contest to see who could recite all six verses first."

"Really? Wow, Maggie and her competitions."

"I know." He ran his hand through his hair. "She drives me crazy sometimes."

"So who won?"

"Who do you think?" He pointed his thumb at his chest.

"You?"

"Yessiree, dude, you don't see me doing extra dish duty around here."

I laughed.

Stevie crawled to the other end of the porch, stretched out on his stomach, reached under the bannister rail and pulled out a toy truck.

"Now it's time for my solo," Dad said.

What?

"Listen up, son. I'll sing you a couple of the verses." He took a deep breath.

I sat quietly while he sang.

"Amazing grace, how sweet the sound, That saved a wretch like me; I once was lost, and now am found, Was blind, but now I see.

"Through many dangers, toils, and snares, I have already come; 'Tis grace has brought me safe thus far, And grace will lead me home."

Dad stopped while Stevie, on his hands and knees, pushed his little truck past us and launched it down the steps, ending up in the dirt beside the porch. "Daddy, I go barn?"

"No, buddy. Stay here where I can keep an eye on you." He gave my brother's shoulder a gentle squeeze, then released him to go sit by his truck.

"Good song, Dad," I said. "Is church over?"

He glanced at Stevie, who was making a rock fence around his toy truck. Then he turned to me. "It's pretty nice out here today. How are you feeling, anyway?"

"Not too bad. I think my throat is kinda better. Maybe the fresh air's good for it.

He chuckled.

"Do you give a sermon at porch church?" I asked.

"Oh, so now I'm the preacher?"

"You know, after the songs and the offering, there's a really longg-gggg sermon about sin and stuff." I held my hand over my mouth and yawned really big.

"I'm afraid I haven't prepared a sermon for today." He chuckled, then turned to me. "So, what does Maggie's preacher say about sin and stuff?"

Stevie was pushing his toy car along the bottom step.

I answered Dad's question. "The pastor says everybody sins—even him. He kept saying, 'For all have sinned and come short of the glory of God,' over and over. He must've really wanted us to remember that."

Dad nudged me with his elbow. "Apparently it worked."

"It sounded all hopeless until he said Jesus died to pay the price for everybody's sins."

Dad scratched his chin.

Elsie let out another big long moooo.

Stevie lifted his head, turned toward the cow, and answered. "Moooooo-moooooo!"

That's when Dad started to tickle me. This went on for a few minutes, with Stevie joining in because he probably needed some tickling too.

Afterward, we all lay on our backs on the porch, tickle-tuckered out, as Dad put it, listening to the chirping of birds up near the rain gutter somewhere.

Like I said before, this was my kind of church.

"So, Luke," Dad said. "What else did Maggie's preacher say?"

"He had some black paper ripped up into blob shapes, and he said we can take our sins and sorrows to the cross. Then he carried the blobs over and laid them at the foot of the cross behind his pulpit. He said, 'Let Jesus take care of them for you.'"

"Hmm." Dad scratched his chin. "Then what did he say?"

"I don't know." I took a deep breath. "Alice started to do her squirmy-wormy thing, and she was drooling all over my arm. So Maggie took her, and I helped find the bottle in the diaper bag. After that I watched the old lady next to me doodle cat faces all over her bulletin, and then pretty soon church was over."

"Sorry I missed all that." Dad looked out over our meadow. "Church was never that exciting when I used to go."

All the while, the birds chirped around us, the cows mooed softly, and Stevie made rumbly car noises along the banister. Dad broke the silence. "Okay, for our sermon today I'll tell you the story of David, the man after God's own heart."

I settled beside him, but my feet didn't reach nearly as far as his did. I wondered if I would ever be as tall as him. I yawned again, openly, no hand.

"So you're bored already, and I haven't even started yet."

"Whoops."

"David was the boy who killed the giant, Goliath."

"I know, Dad. Elizabeth told me the whole story. She said he had some stones that he put in a sling, and he swung it around and hit Goliath in the forehead where his helmet wasn't covering anything. She actually has a picture of it in her Bible."

"Really."

"So we made a sling out of rubber bands and a hanky, and we went outside and slung rocks at stuff."

"What stuff?"

"Birds, trees. Just so you know, we couldn't hit anything. It was very awkward. Well, we did hit the house once."

Dad stiffened up. "Break anything?"

Thankfully not. "No."

"Good." He relaxed.

"Elizabeth said that David was a shepherd boy, so he probably practiced for hours while he was out watching a bunch of sheep eating grass. She said he was probably bored out of his brains."

Dad grinned.

"I wonder if he ever used the sheep as target practice. Their thick wool would probably protect them. What do you think, Dad?"

He laughed. "I really don't know about that. Don't you try it on any of our animals."

"I won't."

"It's interesting how in the story God used a boy to do a man's job."

"Hmm." I liked that thought—a boy like me having victory over a giant.

Dad rubbed my head. "It's a lot like you practicing your schoolwork with Elizabeth, over and over. That's a good way for you to slay the schoolwork giant."

"Yuck, schoolwork." I sat up straight. "Hey, Dad, what's your giant?"

His smile dropped. "I have several giants. One of them is guilt..." His voice trailed off as he glanced at me. "And another giant isn't a what. It's a who." He sighed.

"Who?"

"Church is over." Dad stood up, stretched, picked up his books, and walked into the house.

I knew who the who was. Maggie.

"So," Maggie said as we sat down to our traditional Sunday lunch that Dad had fixed. "How are you feeling, Luke?"

She had changed into her comfortable clothes and put the baby down for a nap while Dad cooked hotdogs and beans and I got out the plates. Because half of the table was loaded up with Maggie's sewing machine and quilt squares, we sat scrunched at the other end with Dad and Maggie on one side across from Stevie and me.

"I feel better," I said. "And no fever. Dad took my temperature."

"Good." She used a knife to spread mustard on her hotdog bun. "Elizabeth came and sat with us this morning, helped with the baby."

Good. I could always count on Elizabeth to take care of business, like keeping an eye out for that too-friendly Keith Sanders. "Who else was there?" I asked as casually as possible.

"Just the usual people."

"Bonnie?" I asked.

"Yes, and her husband."

What about her brother, Keith? Did he sit near you? "Who else?" I pressed.

She turned to me. "Mr. and Mrs. Sawyer, Amelia Michelson, Rick Dahl, and the Breidenbachs with their baby twins, Mindy and Cindy. And Doris Jones and everybody in that family except for the puppy and the horse."

"Oh."

"Eddie's older sister came with the Gills."

"That's nice."

"Enough?"

I nodded, even though I still hadn't heard the name I didn't want to hear.

She sat up straight. "Do I need to take a lie detector test? Am I on trial here? Yes, I really went to church. I didn't go to Rocky's Beer Bar."

I clammed up.

Dad cleared his throat. "What did the pastor preach on?"

"Oh, boy." She set her fork down. "You, too?"

His eyes crinkled into a smile. "I'm pretty sure you didn't go to Rocky's Beer Bar. Alice would've told me."

Maggie poured a puddle of ketchup on her plate. "Pastor Nicholson divided the 23rd Psalm into sections and said a bit about each part. It was really good. Just what I needed." She patted her chest. "Right here."

Dad sighed. "I wish I could've heard it."

"You should try coming to church. Maybe Stevie will do better now. He's older. And I'll sit by him and catch his sneezes before they hit the pews. I've always got clean diapers in my bag."

I wondered what she would use to stop his singing.

"I don't think Stevie and I are ready yet, Maggie," Dad said. "Let me think on it."

I wished he would decide to go. I wished we could all climb into Maggie's car and drive to church and sit together like a family. That would keep Keith Sanders away. "Maybe Bo Wad's mom could babysit him," I volunteered.

"They spend Sundays in Connersville with her parents," Dad said.

"Oh."

Maggie dipped her hot dog in the ketchup and took a bite. "Mmmm. You guys are such great cooks. This is my favorite meal of the week."

"You always say that," I said.

"It's my favorite meal because somebody else cooks it. On Sundays I feel like I'm the queen." She took a forkful of beans, smiled at Dad, and popped it in her mouth. "Yummy."

"I'm quite an impressive cook," he said. "Opening bean cans takes a lot of practice."

She laughed. "How was home church this morning?"

"There was singing," I said.

"Cool singing?" She winked at Stevie.

"Yeah! Cool singing." He choked on his hotdog and sprayed it all over his lap.

Dad got off his chair and helped Stevie get cleaned up. "Okay, buddy?" Dad cut the rest of my brother's hotdog into pieces.

"Good job, Daddy."

Maggie turned to Stevie. "Did you sing Amazing Grapes?"

The kid smiled so hard his eyes almost got buried in his cheeks.

"How do you know about that?" I asked her.

"He sings it for me."

I finished chewing my bite of warm, mustard-drenched hot-dog. "Stevie got really loud when he got to 'that saved a wrench like meeeeeee.' Elsie was out by the windmill, and she mooed along with him."

Stevie went, "Moooo."

Maggie's smile widened. "A wrench like me? That's so cute."

"Huh?" I set down my hot dog.

Dad and Maggie gave each other a quick grown-up glance, one that said they knew something I didn't.

"What?" I asked Dad.

"Wretch, son. Not wrench. 'That saved a wretch like me.' The word *wretch* means a miserable person."

"Oh." I guess that made more sense. Jesus died for miserable people, not tractor tools.

Dad smiled. "The man who wrote that song, John Newton, transported slaves on a ship. That's how he earned a living, as a slave trader. He was a horrible, miserable person."

"And we sing his song in church?"

"He changed. He finally realized that God would forgive him even though he was a horrible, miserable wretch."

"Like David," I said.

"Yes, like me, at least I'm trying." His voice had become quiet.

He probably didn't mean to say it aloud. I could usually tell when he was thinking about the day my mom died, and how before she left the house she and Dad had been arguing about shoes. Once he told me about all the guilt that piled on his shoulders, guilt about the argument, and his attitude that morning, and about the fact that he hadn't been a very good husband. And some other things, too, things he said he didn't want to talk about.

Maggie must've already heard Dad's story, because otherwise she'd be asking him about it now. She slid her small smooth hand sideways and laid it on top of Dad's big calloused one. Dad looked at her. "Sometimes it just hits me all over again."

"I know."

Stevie and I were quiet, well except for his hotdog chomping.

Dad talked to Maggie like we weren't in the room. "Maybe later you can tell me what the pastor said about the 23rd Psalm."

"Sure." She moved her hand back to her side.

"Hey, Dad. How did you know about that slave trader who wrote 'Amazing Grace'?" I asked.

"Read it in a book."

If only. If only I could read books like Dad did. I sighed.

Maggie and Dad got to talking about church while I focused on my food. At one point I looked around the table. There was Maggie, listening to Dad, quietly sending a smile my way. Beside me, Stevie hummed while he chased his slippery hotdog chunks across his plate with a spoon. Dad paused with his fork poised above his Campbell's pork and beans, and grinned at each one of us. "I'm so thankful for all of you," was all he said.

Porch church and hot dogs. It doesn't get any better than that.

The map was almost as wide as my desk. The USA, all fifty states, including the two new ones, blank, waiting for me to write names and capitals. I looked around the room at the other kids, their pencils scratching, knowing that this was the test everyone must pass in order to go into sixth grade.

I knew them all, every state and capital, even the two new ones—Alaska and Hawaii. Elizabeth and I had made a huge map in the wide open empty side of the barn. My great-grandparents' old butter churn was Maine, the broken rabbit hutch was Florida, an empty rusted toolbox was Washington, and a splintered barrel was the southern tip of

California. Then we took sharp sticks and drew us a lumpy, bumpy, sort of accurate map of the states.

When that was done, Elizabeth brought out her states junk bucket, as she called it. We spent the first day pulling things out of her bucket and setting them in place. She set the apple in Maryland so we could remember "An-APPLE-us, Maryland." On Lincoln, Nebraska, we set a penny, Lincoln side up, and on Little Rock, Arkansas, we actually put a little rock. I found an old Christmas card with Santa Claus on it, and we set it in New Mexico for SANTA Fe, and so on. My favorite was the two sticks we put on Michigan so we could play-fight to remember Battle Creek, Michigan. Then Elizabeth spoiled it all by looking in her book and seeing that Battle Creek was just a town in Michigan, and not the capital. Lansing wasn't near as much fun, even though I told her it sounded like Sir Lancelot, and he was a sword-fighter guy.

Two weeks of playing "states" every day had paid off. I could name them forwards, backwards, in my sleep and in the shower last night. Yet, Miss Finch had just spoken words that were like a knife, twisting into my gut. She'd said, spelling counts.

I'd known all along that spelling counted, but now reality was sinking in. My chest tightened.

I picked up my pencil and looked down at empty Minnesota, needing me to squeeze the words into the tall shape of the state. A tear dropped on Montana, and I quickly wiped my eye. Surely, I didn't want to be remembered as Luke Bradley, the boy who cried while he was flunking his fifth-grade states test.

But I know every state, every capital.

Spelling counts—and you have to fit the words into the state shapes, except for the small East Coast states, clustered like tiny lopsided puddles, each connected to a line for me to write on. How could I tell which line went with which state? How could I be sure my *b*'s weren't *d*'s?

I was clenching my pencil so hard, my fingers ached. I loosened my grip, then drew an *L* on my left hand.

What good did that do?

I sucked in a deep breath, lowered my head, and began to write.

"Dad, you need to go to church with us next week." I leaned across the latest tractor to join our collection. It seemed that when the spring thaw came this year, tractors sprouted out of the neighbors' fields and rolled right into our barn. Dad and Uncle Ned had spent the last two months building a roof alongside the barn so Dad could store two more tractors without letting them sit in the rain. Today, the spaces were all full.

Dad stood tall on the other side of a small red tractor, set a screwdriver on the metal seat, and looked around the barn, surveying the scene. "Luke, maybe someday you can help me with this."

"Fixing tractors?"

"Sure. Why not? You're good at gizmos and inventions and fixing things."

I'd never thought of it that way before.

"When someone brings me a tractor, I find the problem, fix it, and return it as good as new." He grinned. "Gives me satisfaction when the customer drives off down the lane, like I've given him back an old friend. Ever feel like that?"

I remembered Miss Finch thanking me after her watch was secure on her wrist once again, held tight by my paper clip invention.

Dad's eyes were on me, his eyes crinkling.

"Dad, you're trying to distract me. I said you need to go to church with us."

He picked up the screwdriver and scraped something on his side of the tractor. "So you think I need church-going religion now? What about Stevie's singing and sneezing? And who's going to stay home and cook the famous Sunday lunch hotdogs if I'm at church?"

"Dad, all you do is open the package and drop the dogs in a pot of water. How long does that take?" I was getting frustrated. This was important. "Dad, when I go to church with Maggie there's a guy who always talks to her."

The scraping stopped. "What guy?"

"His name is Keith. Maybe he's rich."

"Keith Sanders? Bonnie's brother?"

"Yes."

"He's a good man, son. What makes you think he's rich?"

"You should see his car. It's a red T-bird convertible."

After a moment of silence, Dad took a deep breath. "Luke, Maggie's a friendly person. She's nice to everyone—rich people, poor people, you, me, and even guys with red convertibles."

"One time he sat with her at the end of our row." It made my stomach hurt just to think about it.

Dad wiped his face with his handkerchief.

"Last week at the potluck the guy looked all around until he found her. You should've seen him. He came walking over to her with a look on his face like Stevie gets when he spots the Tonka Trucks at Woolworth's."

Dad rubbed his grease-stained pantleg and sighed. "It's bound to happen sooner or later, son. We can't keep Maggie forever."

"Why not?" My heart was sinking down into my shoes.

"Well, Luke, think about it. She's pretty, she's spunky, she's a catch. Any man would fall in love with her the minute he saw her."

"We can't let that happen."

"We don't have a choice," he said. "What do you want me to do, lock her in the cellar?"

"Maybe you could marry her so we can keep her."

He chuckled then and bent down to his work. "Ahh, it sounds so easy."

"Really, Dad."

"Women don't like me. When it comes to females, I'm out of my league."

"Mom liked you."

"Yeah, but she always said I was clueless." He tapped something on his side of the tractor.

"So why did she marry you?"

"She loved me. I think maybe she thought she could fix me." He continued to tap.

"So how could somebody fix you?" I asked. "We need to get started on this right away."

"I don't have a clue. Remember? Clueless?"

"Well, what exactly don't you understand about women? Maybe we can fix just that part of you. Maybe if you understood women, then the rest would fall into place."

"So you think you can fix me so I'll understand women?"

"Yeah. What don't you understand?" An idea popped into my head. "Elizabeth will help us. She's an expert at this kind of stuff."

"She is?" He peered over the tractor again. "You mean like knowing why they get their nails done all the time. When your mother lived at home with her mom and sister, they all marched to the beauty parlor and got their fingernails done. Anyway, when we were married, she still wanted to do that."

"So, why not?"

"It costs money. I needed milking machines. I'm a dairy farmer. I had six cows back then. All I did was milk cows." Dad sighed. "Which should we have—milking machines or fingernail appointments?"

"That's a stupid question. Milking machines."

"You're a guy, like me. We think milking machines. They think—fingernail appointments."

This was not making sense.

Maggie strolled into the barn. "In a few minutes I'm taking Elizabeth to her Girl Scout meeting, then I'll stop at Stevie's school and look through the shoe pile with Bo-Wad's mom. Those two guys must have a matching pair somewhere. Did you know that Stevie came home wearing two right shoes today?"

Dad and I were silent. In the old days, we just stuck any two shoes on him every morning and hoped for the best.

Maggie continued. "Luke. What shoes did Stevie have on today when he left for school? Did you notice?"

I shrugged.

She sighed. "Okay, then. Anyway, I have Stevie and the baby with me. There's a pot of soup on the stove. Luke, will you stir it in a few minutes? It should just simmer. Leave the lid tipped so steam can escape."

"Okay."

"Then stay inside so you can keep an eye on it."

"Sure."

She smiled at me, her warm chocolate eyes making my heart melt. We really needed to keep her.

"Maggie?" I asked.

"Yes."

"Which would you rather have, a fingernail appointment or a milking machine?"

"The fingernail appointment sounds nice. Haven't had one of those since forever."

"See?" Dad said.

"What's this about?" she asked.

"Nothing." Dad sighed.

I glanced at Maggie. "Dad would rather have a milking machine than a fingernail appointment. He says that with my mom, she wanted fingernail appointments instead of milking machines."

"Really?"

"That's probably why she told him he was clueless."

"I think we've heard enough on this subject," Dad snapped.

Maggie put her hands on her hips and looked at Dad. "William, do you need milking machines?"

"I've always needed milking machines."

Her gaze wandered over to the cows. "You could probably get the milking done a lot faster with machines."

"Yes, but I'm okay this way now, with only three cows left..."

"You could set aside more time for the tractors. You're getting famous for your repair work. I heard someone recommend you to a farmer at the grocery store just yesterday." She looked back at Dad. "Why didn't you ever get milking machines?"

"They never fit my budget."

She scratched her temple. "Maybe we can cut back somewhere else. Let's see. I could use the money Elizabeth's parents pay me. I could put half into a milking machine fund. Or, maybe you could not pay me for a few weeks…"

"No, Maggie. You're at the top of the budget. I'm a man of my word."

Maggie's eyes latched onto dad for a moment, then she looked down at her fingernails. They were clipped short and scratched up with a bandage on her left pinky. She walked out of the barn.

"Go stir the pot," Dad told me.

I scrambled to the barn door and stopped, looking back at Dad. He stood by the window, watching Maggie.

"Dad?"

He turned to me.

"This is what it feels like in normal families, isn't it—having a mom and dad, both taking care of everybody?"

"I suppose so." He smiled sadly. "Kind of like a parent partnership."

"I like it."

"Me, too, son. Let's enjoy it while it lasts." He tossed his screwdriver at his tool box. It missed the mark, bouncing off the open lid and landing on the shelf. Dad shook his head. "I need to take a break. Why don't you go ask Maggie if she'd like us to keep Alice so she can run her errands without lugging a baby along."

"Thomas Edison's teacher said he was so addled that he'd never learn anything." Elizabeth set her glass in the sink.

"What do you mean by addled?" I asked, sliding the now empty cookie jar back on the counter.

"His brain didn't work like everybody else's." She went to the table and opened her history book. "He only went to regular school for three months. Then he got kicked out, and his mom had to teach him at home."

"I didn't know that." The genius who invented light bulbs and movies was bad at school? Sometimes Elizabeth knew just what to say.

Maggie stepped into the kitchen. "Okay, we need some team effort." She was wearing a pair of overalls that I think used to be my grandfather's. She had cuffed up the pantlegs so her pink tennis shoes poked out beneath them. "I've decided that Luke and I should milk the cows so William can keep working on his tractors. He needs to finish one tonight to make room for another one tomorrow."

My eyes widened. Maggie? Milk cows? Well, she could do everything else from throwing rocks to shooting baskets.

"Elizabeth, would you stay in the house with Alice and Stevie? You can call on the intercom if you need me."

Elizabeth smiled. "Sure."

Maggie turned to me. "Luke?"

"Okay."

While we walked across the yard and into the barn, I told Maggie about Thomas Edison. She said she wasn't surprised. Some people weren't properly appreciated until well past due.

Dad was standing at his bench, fiddling with his ratchet set. I could tell by the way he leaned his long body over the workbench that he was tired.

"Dad, we came to milk the cows so you can keep working on tractors," I announced.

"Hey, good." His eyes crinkled as he viewed Maggie in her overalls.

"My milking uniform," she said.

I'm not sure, but I think her face got kind of red for a second.

She cleared her throat. "Usher me to a cow. Give me a bucket and a stool."

Dad chuckled.

"I'll show her," I offered.

"Okay, I appreciate the help. Start her on Peaches."

Peaches had a sweet disposition. She would be a good starter cow.

Maggie proved to be a capable, strong-handed student. After a bit of a struggle, she soon had a steady rhythm of milk squirting into her clean metal bucket.

I picked up the other stool. "I'll start with Elsie," I told Dad.

"Good. Whose idea was this?"

"Maggie's."

Dad observed Maggie, bent forward on the short stool, her forehead resting against Peaches' side, her arms moving up and down. Dad's face seemed peaceful.

"I only hear one cow getting milked in here," she remarked into the side of her cow.

Dad gave me a wink. "The sarge has spoken."

ELEVEN

This is how taking Dad to church backfired.

I t didn't take much urging to talk Dad into going to church with us the next Sunday. He didn't announce he was going until that very morning. Maggie spent twenty minutes scrambling around, trying to find him a clean shirt while he searched for decent pants to wear.

"Next time, give me a day's notice, William," she said, walking into the kitchen with a wrinkled white shirt. "You don't exactly have church clothes just hanging around ready to put on. Boy, I know what to get you for your birthday, whenever it is." She handed me the baby so she could set up the ironing board.

"July 26," I volunteered from where I sat at the table. "His birthday is July 26."

"William, I don't even know how old you are. Can you believe that?" She yanked the ironing board into a standing position.

"Well, I don't know how old you are either." Dad raised his coffee cup to his lips.

"I guess I didn't put it on the application."

They both laughed.

The baby grabbed my nose in her fist.

"Ouch." I peeled her tight little fingers away. She squealed at me and scratched my ear with her sharp fingernails. "Ouch, you."

Maggie plugged in the iron. "We never even figured out whose cousin knows whose niece who knows each other that knows us."

Dad added, "Well, except we both knew the kangaroo."

"You guys are weird," I said.

Dad chuckled and kept talking. "In fact, Maggie, I'm wondering if you actually came to the wrong house last September. What if we don't know anyone who knows anyone who knows either one of us?"

Maggie stood up straight and faced Dad. "Why, all of a sudden today, do you want to go to church? What happened to porch church with mooing cows in the background?"

Dad glanced at me for help.

I spoke right up. "It was my idea. He needs religion."

Dad smiled and shrugged.

Maggie looked at both of us and sighed. "Somebody go find Stevie. And make sure his pants are on frontwards today."

We did manage to get to church on time. Maggie settled at one end of the short pew and Dad sat at the other end with Stevie and me between. Dad was armed with several big hankies, ready in hand for my brother's sneezes. On the ride there, Stevie had promised Dad he would only sing if he knew the song. Otherwise, he would just listen to the singing. That's when I started praying that the church would not sing, "Amazing grapes, how sweet the sound."

Maggie said, "I'm sure that Stevie's singing is beautiful music to God's ears."

That was probably true, but it wasn't God's ears I was worried about.

Keith Sanders came in late and sat in the back, but not before he sent a big grin in Maggie's direction. Somehow, I wished we'd pushed Dad and Maggie to one end of the pew so it looked like they were together. Even better, we should've put Dad on the outside, sorta like a bodyguard.

I thought he looked good in his ironed shirt and clean pants. Maggie had given us all haircuts last week, and after she finished she told each of us that we were handsome dudes. I'd asked Dad what a dude was, and he said, "A guy who works on a ranch." I don't know if Dad was really a handsome dude or not when comparing him to the other men around us. I just know I liked how he looked, tidy and content, with his arm across the back of the pew where Stevie sat. Dad sent me one of his eye-crinkling smiles.

I spied Elizabeth across the aisle, dressed in her favorite kind of prissy daisy stuff. She frowned, then pointed at Dad and Maggie as if to say, Why did you let them sit so far apart?

I was glad Elizabeth was on our team. Just like me, she wanted my dad to acquire lady-attracting skills and win Maggie's heart.

We managed to get through the music without causing too much of a ruckus. The first song had some of my favorite words in it. *I see the stars, I hear the rolling thunder, Thy power throughout the universe displayed.* Where had I heard these words before? They made a warm feeling pass through me, mingled with a deep sadness. *When through the woods and forest glades I wander, and hear the birds sing sweetly in the trees.* Nature. It was talking about nature. Tears welled up in my eyes. *And hear the brook, and feel the gentle breeze.* A man behind us belted out the words like he was in an opera. *Then sings my soul, my Savior, God to Thee. How great thou art...how great thou art...*I suddenly knew why this song made me feel peace and sadness all at the same time. My mother had sung it to me, and I'd stashed the memory in a faraway corner of my mind. She sang it to me when we looked out my bedroom window at night and saw the stars. A deep ache took over me. I glanced at Dad, detecting a bit of moisture in his eyes. He reached out and rubbed the back of my neck.

Stevie had turned around and stared at the man behind us, hypnotized, until Dad noticed and broke the spell by nudging my brother into the right direction, face forward. After a few deep breaths, Stevie broke into song, too, his low-pitched voice competing with the one behind us, both wavering like deep, fast-paced sirens. Later, Dad told me the word for that type of singing was called vibrato.

It was very hard to ignore.

"Basssss-it baw-baw, go-go-go," Stevie sang, his face glowing with joy, his arms outstretched. "Coooooollll, bassss-it bawwwwll..."

Suddenly…silence. Stevie went ramrod straight, his eyes wide and watery.

Dad was ready. Quick as a cat, he had the hanky over Stevie's face, ready for the explosion, which happened in a flash—a volcano, muffled by cotton, rumbling down our row from me to Maggie.

The song ended as my father finished mopping up Stevie's face, after which the boy boomed into the quiet room. "Good job, Daddy!"

I sensed the uncomfortable energy of the people around us, the sighing and squirming.

Maggie's arm went across my shoulder, and she gave me a warm squeeze. She was trying to make me feel better, I think. And she did. I liked our family row in church, and her being in it.

I didn't want to look at people staring at us, so I focused on my lap, then our feet. Maggie's to one side of mine, in her uncomfortable-looking tan colored pointy shoes. Then straight down, my sneakers dangled beside Stevie's, which didn't match. And his shoelaces were different colors and lengths—untied, of course.

Dad's shoes were speckled with straw and grease. I knew they held the aromas of our barn. I raised my head. His fingers were decorated with oil-stained creases that never washed out no matter how hard he scrubbed.

He gave me a smile that warmed me. Such a nice dad, and so not like a movie star.

Next to me, Maggie sat listening to the preacher. She was all fresh and clean in her pretty blue dress, her skin as smooth as cream.

She told me once that her faith had helped her get through the hard times after her husband died. I guess she was hungry to learn as much as she could about God. At least, that's what she looked like she was doing now instead of worrying like I was about other people in the room. Maggie was getting her feast.

I was getting nothing. Dad was at the wrong end of the pew. I had failed.

After church Keith Sanders hung around until we went outside. Then, in the fresh spring air, he approached us. Dad was talking to Dr.

Reber when Keith came our way, his eyes never wavering from Maggie, and he took her aside so he could talk to her alone. Finally, he left, which made me feel a little better.

Maggie walked over to Dad, who, with Alice under one arm, was pulling Stevie toward Maggie's car.

"William?" Maggie asked.

"What?"

She had a confused look on her face as she glanced at us. "Get into the car, everybody."

We climbed into the back seat.

"What?" Dad opened the door to the driver's side and slid in behind the wheel.

She sat down on the passenger side. "I think maybe Keith just asked me out on a date."

Both of their car doors remained open as Dad took a deep breath. "What do you mean, you think?"

"He asked if I would I like to join him and Bonnie and George for a cookout this afternoon."

Dad was silent, looking straight ahead. I couldn't tell if he was breathing.

"Is that a date?" she asked him.

"You don't know what a date is?" he growled.

"I was married to Ted, and then he died and I've been mourning. I don't even think about dates. Keith really caught me off guard. I'm not ready for this."

None of us in the back seat moved.

"Well, what did you say?" Dad asked.

"I said…I said…" She cleared her throat. "I said I would ask you."

"What? You mean—like I'm your father or something?"

"No. I don't know what I meant. Just…stupid words popped out of me. I was mouth-ka-bobbled."

"Duck! He coming!" Stevie screamed. He dove to the floor.

Keith strode to the car and bent down beside Maggie. "Are you coming? May I help you out?" He extended his hand.

Okay, Dad. Jump up and claim her! Say, "Get away from her, you woman-stealer! She's ours!"

Dad gave Maggie's shoulder a gentle nudge. "Go. Have a nice afternoon—adult conversation, no waterlogged hotdogs, no kid interruptions…Go. You deserve it."

She turned and stared right at him, eye-to-eye.

"Go. I mean it."

My heart sank down into the deepest pit ever. We were going to lose her. I knew it. Dad was just giving her up like he did those milk cans every morning when Crawford's Dairy truck pulled into the driveway.

I didn't cry, but my eyes fogged up as we drove home with Dad, alone and silent in the front seat. I didn't have the heart to climb up there and sit with him. I sat like a stone while the countryside whisked by.

When Maggie came home, Dad was half asleep on the recliner chair. Stevie was pulling trucks with strings up and down a ramp I'd made on the side of the porch steps. I was in the kitchen raiding the last piece of leftover pie. I decided that if Maggie was going to leave us, I would miss her pies, so I'd better eat all I could now.

She walked in, Alice asleep in her arms, and went to her room. In a few seconds she returned without the baby, sat down at the kitchen table, and kicked off her shoes. "Wrong shoes today. Ouch." She leaned back in the chair. "Why is the typewriter here?"

"I tried Elizabeth's typewriter experiment. I typed my four vocabulary words and a very short definition after Dad and I talked about them. It took forever." Pie was my reward.

"Did it help?"

"Maybe. Maybe not."

"That Elizabeth and her ideas." Maggie shook her head and smiled. "What was all the noise you two were making in the barn yesterday?"

"We were doing spelling, and she wanted me to shout the letters while I wrote them on the chalkboard, and to write the silent letters in pink."

"So the noise was you shouting letters?"

"No, it was us fighting about it."

Maggie laughed. "I think Elizabeth is more headstrong than I am." She glanced at me. "You do a nice job of putting up with us."

She had a way of making me feel good, even when the subject focused on Elizabeth and school. I wanted to keep Maggie always, right here in our house instead of somewhere with Keith Sanders.

"What's wrong, sweetie?"

Man, sometimes she could read my mind. "Nothing." Then I decided to flat-out speak what I had been wondering. "How was your date?"

"Uh...good. Relaxing."

I shrugged and took a bite of pie.

"Last piece?" she asked.

I nodded. "Do you want half?"

"No, I'm stuffed. We had cheeseburgers cooked out on a grill, potato salad, and all that. You know, picnic food. Very tasty." She patted her stomach. "I ate too much."

I took another bite. "Do you like him?"

"Keith? Sure. He's nice."

My heart fell down to my shoes.

She continued. "On the way home, we stopped by his house. It's all new. Guess what's in it."

She went to his house?

"An automatic dishwasher. You open it up like a big drawer and you stack the dishes inside. Push some buttons, and it washes everything. Later, you open it and the dishes are not only clean, but dried. You just put them away."

We were going to lose her for sure. It hit me like an anvil in the stomach. Not only was Mr. Sanders nice, he had a dishwasher.

"So, guess what I was thinking when he showed me the dishwasher."

"What?" I could hardly speak. I held my fork in mid-air.

"It seems unfair that a man with nobody in the house but him, has a dishwasher. And then us—we have a whole pile of people at every meal, and we don't have one." She looked over at our sink and laughed.

"Sometimes life is so backwards."

Plates were scattered like giant leaves on the counter. Dad's hotdog pan was still on the stove, plus the other pan for our cheese-dog experiment, and the glasses and silverware, ketchup and mustard splattered around.

Maggie stood and walked toward it, then stopped. "Better change first." As she headed down the hall, she hesitated and stared into the living room at Dad. With a sigh, she turned and went into her bedroom.

I finished the pie—with my eyes on the dirty dishes. A plan was forming in my mind. Maggie would have a dishwasher here, me. I would be the dishwasher, a living dishwasher. If she never had to do dishes here, maybe she wouldn't be attracted to Keith's dishwasher. I would do the glasses first and the pans last, just like Maggie showed me the day I lost the rock-throwing bet.

Something inside of me felt proud. I had devised a plan. Something inside of me still felt sad. Maggie was beginning to slip away from us. I would hold out as long as possible. And I would enlist my ally, Elizabeth, to work on a more vigorous plan of woman-improvement skills for my dad, while I did dishes.

Thankfully, Miss Finch folded my states test shut before she returned it to me. But all morning, every time I opened my desk to get a book, there it was, the folded test with the big red *F* inside and a place for my parent's signature. Before lunchtime, I shoved it under all my books and papers, but I knew it was still there, a buried reminder that I had failed again.

How could I get my dad to sign the test without feeling his disappointment? The further I'd pushed the paper down in my desk, the more it pestered me like a big horsefly buzzing around my head. I couldn't concentrate at all during the afternoon because of it, and Miss Finch scolded me twice for not paying attention. By the end of the day, I was so worthless I sat through the entire history lesson with my science book open in front of me. Luckily, Miss Finch was too busy helping Kathleen to notice.

Finally, I asked to go to the restroom where I stood before the mirror and took a deep breath. "Indianapolis, Indiana," I said. "Columbus, Ohio." I punched the wall. "Springfield, Illinois." I punched it hard again and again until my knuckles bled. "Harrisburg, Pennsylvania! Boise, Idaho!"

I bent over, clenching my hands in pain. "Ouch!" They stung as I rinsed them in the sink.

It wasn't fair. I knew the facts, but I'd failed the test.

The bell rang.

Eddie burst in. "What're you doing? Everybody's getting on the bus, and you're not ready yet."

"I'll walk home," I growled.

"Who's going to flick me on the ear so I know when I'm at my house?"

"Ask Paul."

"He doesn't do it right."

"I'm walking home. Don't wait for me." I stomped into a stall and shut the door.

"Okay. I get it, grouch." He left.

When things quieted in the hall I came out of the bathroom and headed back to class. Hopefully, no one would be there, and I could gather my stuff in private.

I lifted my desktop and dug down for the test. As I pulled it out from under my history book the test ripped. I yanked the stupid pieces out and crumpled them into a ball, stuffing them into my pocket. That's when I noticed I wasn't alone.

Miss Finch was standing in the doorway. "What are you doing to your test?"

My heart sank. "It ripped."

"Let me see."

I unwadded it and laid it on my desk, face down so I wouldn't have to look at the big red *F*.

"I'm disappointed in you, Luke," she said. "I can't even read half your answers. Your writing looks as if you're trying to hit a moving target." She flipped the wrinkled paper over. "Look at this mess."

My face felt hot, my throat tight. I swallowed hard and took a deep breath, knowing I needed to be respectful. "Sorry, Miss Finch."

After smoothing the mangled test, she folded it and handed it to me. "Maybe you should've practiced more."

More than the ten million hours Elizabeth and I had spent stomping around our big garden map, putting her stupid bucket props in place and shouting the names of states and capitals? I wanted to cry, or kick somebody, or…

"Go on home, now." Miss Finch's voice had a sadness to it, like I'd failed not just myself, but also her.

With a sigh, I shoved the paper into my pocket and trudged toward the hall, stopping in the doorway.

This just wasn't right. It wasn't right at all.

I heard Miss Finch move behind me, settling at her desk.

If I can go out in a freezing blizzard to blow on a whistle-pipe in the middle of the night, I can do this.

Reaching into my pocket, I pulled out the test and turned back to Miss Finch.

She lifted her head as I walked to her desk and spread the wrinkled map, right-side-up facing her, on top of her grade book. I stood up straight, took a deep breath and placed my finger on Washington state. "Washington," I said. "Olympia." I moved my finger down. "Salem, Oregon," then "Sacramento, California." Taking a quick breath, I continued. "Phoenix, Arizona," and moved all the way across the United States, naming every state and capital until I ended with "Tallahassee, Florida."

I wiped my face with my sleeve. "There."

Miss Finch was silent, her eyes huge.

Then I started with the presidents and named them all from George Washington to Dwight Eisenhower, each name louder than the one before as I swayed back and forth to Elizabeth's goofy "president song" that jingled in my head.

Right then, I hated my teacher. I hated school. "Flunked that one, too, Miss Finch!"

She took a deep breath. "I don't understand this, Luke."

"Me either!" Fire raging in me, I ran out the door, down the hall, and out into the rain.

It took me almost an hour to get to my mailbox at the end of our lane, and when I got there I stopped, soaked to the bone. The water, streaming down my face, had cooled me, and I was no longer angry—just sad. I was flunking fifth grade, pure and simple. There was nothing I could do. I knew all the facts, but that didn't matter because I couldn't pass the written tests.

I heard the rumble of Dad's truck coming from town, so I turned.

Stopping, he opened the door. "Where were you? I've been driving up and down the road, searching for you." He looked almost as miserable as I felt, only drier.

"I took the shortcut through Rich's woods." I climbed into the truck.

His eyes questioned mine. "What's going on with you?"

"I flunked my states test. You need to sign it, but I left it at school." I hung my head. "And I yelled at Miss Finch." Sitting like a stiff board, I fought tears while Dad stopped the truck in front of the barn.

He spoke quietly. "Just bring home the test, son. I'll sign it."

I turned toward the window so he couldn't see my face.

Slowly, he reached across the seat and touched my shoulder, rubbing it softly for a moment before he got out of the truck, leaving me alone to get myself straightened out before I went into our busy house.

In the weeks that followed, our lives went on as usual—with certain exceptions.

One was my new job—household dishwasher. Every evening after dinner I stayed in the kitchen with Maggie.

That first day when I told her to leave so I could do the dishes, she argued, but I stood my ground. Looking confused, she thanked me and left the room.

Now, it was a regular thing. Maggie would try to stay. I'd boot her out. Then I'd roll up my sleeves and fill the sink with hot soapy water.

Often, Stevie rolled up his sleeves too. While I carried the breakable dishes, he helped with pans and plastic bowls. All the while, he kept saying, "Cool dishes, cool dishes." There were times when the only thing that prevented people like me from bopping him on the head was the simple fact that he's always so cheerful. His deep little flat voice had a sing-songy rhythm to it as he said the words over and over.

So, I sang along with him. "Cool dishes, cool dishes, cool dishes."

"What?" Maggie said one evening as she walked into the kitchen. "Cool dishes?" She shook her head, grinning, and picked up the empty chicken platter. "Cool dishes, cool dishes, cool dishes," she sang as she carried it to the sink.

Stevie was laughing by now, so we all sang the words together.

Then I realized what was going on. "Maggie," I said. "We are doing the dishes for you tonight. Go rest."

"Oh, no. That's okay. I'll help." She carried the wet dishcloth to the table. "Cool dishcloth, cool dishcloth..."

"No, I mean it, Maggie. I'm doing the dishes."

Stevie marched across the floor with his hands full of spoons. "Cool dishes, cool dishes, cool dishes."

"Luke, you don't need to do this every night. It's my job."

"I'm doing the dishes. Go away."

She set the dishcloth on the table. "Okay. I don't get it, but I'll take it. Thanks. I'll go sort socks." She left.

Stevie lined the clean spoons in a row on the counter while I washed plates. "I go see Daddy." He sneezed on the spoons and left, dragging his quilt—with little dog Bosco close behind.

Back to that first night, it took me almost two hours to do the cool dishes, then I was up until ten o' clock reciting the preamble and doing decimal point problems on graph paper.

Even so, every night as time wore on, I pushed Maggie out of the kitchen. She looked at me with that "What is going on?" expression on her face. I'll tell you that she tried to do the dishes every evening, and

I sent her away every time.

The only good part about it was that after a week or so, I got quicker at it. Well, and Stevie continued to help me, along with his little cool dishes song, of course. Dad and Elizabeth pitched in sometimes, too, singing along with us. In fact, cool dishes became a regular event after each meal, with everyone helping except Maggie.

Another thing that happened during that time was our dreaded third quarter grades. Miss Finch told us to not open our report cards until we were at home with our parents. Elizabeth got off the bus with me that day, and we ran up the lane. Maggie wasn't in the house, so we checked the barn and found Dad standing beside a tractor, its side panel pulled open and his hands inside, clunking around with a metal tool.

"Dad, I'm home. Where's Maggie?"

"Grocery shopping. Did you get your report card?"

"Um, yeah." I hated the thought of opening it, sort of like it was a grenade.

"How'd you do this time?" He stared at something he was working on.

"I don't know yet. Miss Finch said we're supposed to look at it with a parent." That way the explosion would hit us both at the same time.

"Put it over there on my desk. We'll see it after I finish this."

I glanced at Elizabeth and took a deep miserable breath. I wished she wasn't here right now.

"Whoops." A big greasy bolt dropped on the ground and rolled toward me. "Can you get that, son?"

I picked it up and set it in his outstretched hand, then wiped my fingers with a rag while I listened to metal clonk against metal.

"Man, this is a mess," he said.

Elizabeth and I waited some more.

The clonking stopped, but he didn't turn away. "Son, you're just standing there staring at me, aren't you? I can feel your eyes boring into my back."

"Yeah."

"Do you want to know what the report card says?"

Not really.

Elizabeth nudged me with her elbow.

"I guess," I answered. Maybe there was a miracle inside, maybe not.

"Go ahead and take a peek."

Elizabeth stood beside me while I slowly slid it out of the envelope. I turned to her. "Don't tell anyone?"

"I won't."

By now, one thing I knew about Elizabeth was that she kept her word.

I took a deep breath and opened the report card, glancing down the column: D+, C, F, D, C-, C, and my regular two As in Conduct and Physical Education. No miracles, but I did better than last time. I'd raised my math grade to a C. The F was in science, land of multiple-choice tests. I had only one more grading period to go. I wondered if I could miraculously do well enough to be promoted at the end of the year.

Elizabeth's eyes were wide open like she was looking at the damage after a tornado. My bomb had hit an innocent bystander.

I smacked it shut.

"Luke, is this report card…?"

"Better than last time," I snapped.

"Oh?" Her voice sounded higher than usual. "Do people pass with those kinds of grades? I mean, will you be able to go to sixth grade with us? I thought you and Eddie were already partners for the science fair next year. And what about nature camp?"

I felt like slugging her, but I kept it under control, especially with dad nearby—no longer banging on his bolt. "What do you usually get?" I asked her.

"Mostly As," she mumbled. "Last year I got a B in history because I turned my folder in a day late. It was in Mom's car at work."

All As. As easy as that. And that one awful B. "I'd give anything to get a B in something that wasn't P.E. or Conduct." I sighed as my heart kept tumbling down.

"Okay." Her fists were clenched, not a good sign.

"Okay, what?"

"Let's choose a subject, and we'll fight like cats to get you a B."

"How will we do that?"

"You pick the subject, one you think you've got a chance of improving to a B, and I'll think of a plan when I go home tonight."

I opened the report card. I'd gotten the Ds in history and spelling. Maybe I should work on one of them, spelling. Miss Finch had just reduced my list to fifteen words so I could concentrate on studying a few of them extra hard instead of being overwhelmed by the whole list. "Spelling."

"Spelling it is," she said.

Two more things I knew about Elizabeth. One, she drove me crazy, and two, she didn't give up. She would probably half-kill me in the process of getting a B in spelling.

Miss Finch took me aside one day during recess. "Luke, I'd like to try something. It has to do with the today's history test."

I was all ears.

"You'll take the test like everyone else. Then, later, I'll let you go out in the hall with Mrs. Harris. She'll read the test to you, and you can tell her the answers and she'll write them down."

This seemed strange, but I wasn't going to argue. "Okay."

"Then I'll record both grades and average them for your final score."

"Okay." It couldn't hurt.

So, on that day I struggled through the multiple-choice test with everyone else. Then later, during art, which I hated to miss, I went out in the hall with Mrs. Harris, Jack's mom, who helped in the classroom sometimes. She read me the same questions and I answered them easily.

Before I went back into the room, I noticed Eddie's jacket was on the floor of the cloak room—and several others. One by one, I loaded them onto their hooks. I probably shouldn't have done that because while I was there, I heard Mrs. Harris beside the door, whispering to Miss Finch.

"You'll never believe this," Mrs. Harris said.

"What?" I heard Miss Finch answer.

"Your...uh, dumb kid—he just aced the test."

Dumb kid? I stopped breathing, my hands clutched against my chest. Turning, I shoved my way out of the cloakroom, knocking jackets to the floor and stumbling over boots. I ran out into the hall, then down to the boys' restroom, stopping with my hands against a sink, gasping for air.

The words "aced the test" held no joy for me because of the other words, "dumb kid." I kicked the sink a few times, then the back of a metal door, making a dent. The kicking felt good, but the big dent stopped me. I had damaged school property. My dad would be disappointed. I hung my head. I was such a loser.

Pretty soon Eddie came into the restroom, looking for me. "Miss Finch wants to know what happened to you."

"Nothing," I growled.

"Are you okay?"

"Yeah." I went to the sink and washed my hands.

He didn't seem to notice the dent. At least he didn't say anything.

"We better get back to class," he said.

We returned together, and I slumped into my seat. I had missed the entire art project. The other kids were finishing animal paintings and starting their math homework.

Thankfully, Mrs. Harris was gone. As I pulled my math book out of my desk, Miss Finch motioned for me to come see her.

"Where were you?" she asked.

"Restroom."

"You know you're supposed to check with me first. We can't have kids just wandering all over the school."

"I'm sorry. I'll ask next time." I couldn't get the picture of the door dent out of my head. Guilt was seeping in, making my stomach hurt. I would have to go apologize to…who? The principal? I would have to offer to pay for the door.

"You got a high D on your written test, and an A+ on your oral test. That averages to 84, a B."

"Okay." A B. I should've been rejoicing. Instead, I felt like someone was smashing my insides with a hammer.

"You don't seem very happy about this."

I wanted to clam up and go hide. But I needed to do something about the guilt battling in my gut. I took a deep breath like I'd seen Maggie do when she was about to say something bold, just like she'd done last night in the kitchen: "William, I backed into your truck when I was turning around in the driveway today. You have a new scratch near the left front tire."

Dad and I were in the barn at the time of the incident, and we heard the big scraping sound when it happened. Dad had peeked out the window and groaned.

"I'm so sorry," Maggie had continued last night. "I'll pay to get it fixed."

I thought Dad had a pretty good answer ready. "There's already about sixty other scratches on my truck. Why don't you just tape a big white hanky bandage on it like you do me?"

I could still hear her burst of laughter.

"Luke?"

Miss Finch brought me back to reality. I was in front of her desk, ready to make a confession.

"Luke?"

I drew in another deep breath. "Miss Finch, I wrecked the door in the bathroom."

"You what?"

"I kicked it."

"You did that? You? Luke Bradley?"

Obviously, people weren't used to me being destructive. I wasn't used to it myself. "I need to go to the principal's office. I need to pay Mr. Potter for the door. Maybe I can work it off." This day was getting worse by the minute. "Maybe I can carry books or wash chalkboards or something." What if Mr. Potter suspended me from school? Dad would be devastated, and Maggie too.

Did kids go to jail for kicking school restroom doors?

"Luke, what's going on with you?"

I sucked in a big breath. "I don't want to do tests with Mrs. Harris anymore."

Her eyebrows lifted. "Why not?"

I'd already told her about the door—I might as well keep talking. "She called me the dumb kid."

Miss Finch gasped. I could see the silent words, *Oh, no,* flash across her face. She remembered.

"Maybe Eddie or Elizabeth can give me the test. They're honest. You can trust them."

"I'll think about it," Miss Finch said.

I turned to go.

"Luke?" she said gently.

I faced her.

"Mrs. Harris was wrong to say that. You are far from dumb."

"Okay." I shrugged. She probably told that to all the kids whether they were dumb or not.

As I walked past Kathleen and Michael doing their math on graph paper, I felt a little better, but not much. I trudged down the hall to the principal's office to make my confession.

Later, when I got on the bus, Mr. Potter handed me a sealed white envelope, addressed to "William Bradley." I sat down on the bus, feeling like a soldier returning from the war, beaten.

Back home, I didn't have the gumption to see Dad right away. Instead, I walked into the kitchen, threw my books on the table, and flopped down on a chair. No matter what position I was in, I could feel the sharp corners of the folded white envelope in my pants pocket.

Maggie got the big manila envelope Mr. Coleman had given her on our trip to Richmond. "We always seem too busy to look at this stuff from Mr. Coleman," she said. "Maybe now would be a good time."

Maybe not.

She sat down across from me. "Remember at your school conference when we talked about the flickery fluorescent lights?"

I nodded, but I really, really didn't want to think about school right now.

"There are colored overlays in here." She undid the envelope clasp.

I had no idea what colored overlays meant.

"Some people use them to help settle the wiggly movement on a page. You know, when the letters look like ants marching in the margins."

Yes, I knew.

"So, we'll have you read until your eyes get tired, and the wiggling gets bad. Then we'll set each colored overlay on the page, one at a time, and see if one of them makes things settle down."

Tears welled in my eyes. I'd had the most horrible, terrible, miserable day. I didn't want to think about ants marching across the page, or bathroom doors, or tests in the hall, or the sealed envelope poking pocket. I gulped down the sob that was rising in my throat.

"If you find a color that helps you, then you can use it when you read." She stopped. "What's wrong?"

"Nothing."

"Do you want to talk about it?"

I shook my head.

She raised the manila envelope. "Do you want to do this some other time?" Her voice had become soft, gentle.

"Yes."

"I'll stick these overlays on the shelf over the washer." She gathered them up. "Are you sure you're okay?"

"I need to go see Dad." Sliding off my chair, I stood to my feet and trudged out the door to the barn.

The next morning, Dad put his toolbox in the truck and drove me to school. While I went to class, he met with Mr. Potter.

After history, I got permission to use the restroom, and Dad was in there putting his tools away.

"Dad," I whispered. "Did Mr. Potter kick me out of school?" I almost wished he had. Then I could go home and shoot baskets.

"No." Dad examined the door.

Even though it looked better, there was still a scratch around the part I'd kicked. I knew that whenever I came here, the scarred door would blare out at me like a big fat reminder of that terrible day. "Do I need to pay Mr. Potter for this?" I asked.

"No, I'm fixing it for free. You'll have to pay me." Dad rubbed his forehead and sighed.

I wanted him to be proud of me instead of sad like this. "How can I pay you, Dad?" My voice quivered. "You can make it a really big punishment—anything."

"Let me think on it, son."

"All right."

"Shouldn't you be in class?"

"Yes." I'd be so glad when I grew up and didn't have to go to school anymore. "Dad, I'll never do that again, just so you know."

"I know, son."

"How do you know?"

"Because I know you, son, very well. You are a man after my own heart."

Starting the next day, I helped Dad milk cows every morning for two weeks.

We never spoke of it again, even while we were milking the cows. He just woke me up every day at 5:00 and ushered me out to the barn, silently in the crisp morning air. I knew it cut his usual milking time short because there were two of us. He must've liked that because he always thanked me before sending me back to the house. When the two weeks ended, he stopped waking me up.

I would much rather have been milking cows as a favor, not as payment.

A few nights later Maggie went somewhere with Keith Sanders. Before she left, she fed us round steak and mashed potatoes and gravy but didn't eat any herself.

When Dad sat down to the table, he was grouchy. "Why'd you fix all this food?" he growled. "Doesn't it cancel out the fun of you going somewhere else for dinner if you have to cook a meal for us?" He poked at a slab of meat and tossed it on his plate. "I told you I'd make sandwiches tonight."

Maggie untied her apron. "I wanted to make you guys a nice meal. The sarge has spoken." Her voice didn't have its usual spunk.

She set her apron on the table. "I put Alice's pajamas on the dresser by her crib. I hope she's not fussy for you. I think she's starting to teethe already."

"Yeah," I said. "This morning she about chewed my hand off."

Dad held Alice on his lap, wiping baby food cereal off her chubby little cheek. Then he turned to Maggie. "Do you want me to save today's *The Secret Garden* chapter until tomorrow?"

"If you don't mind."

"Hey!" I complained. "I've been waiting all day to find out about that scream down the hall."

Maggie looked at Dad. "Go ahead and read it to him, William. Don't make him wait on account of me."

Now I was angry. Why was she messing up our reading time by being gone? Why was she going to get into Keith's car and leave?

"Where are you going, anyway?" I snapped.

"Luke…" Dad began.

We heard a knock on the front door.

"Me—me!" Stevie jumped out of his chair and ran to the living room.

Maggie glanced at me. "We're going to Keith's sister's house for dinner. Then Bonnie and I are going to work on her quilt while Keith and George putt."

"Huh? Putt? What's putt?" I asked.

"Golf—putting. George made three golf holes in his back yard."

"Why does Mr. Sanders have to drive you there? Can't you just go by yourself?"

169

"Well, I live halfway between his house and Bonnie's. It's convenient." She grabbed her purse, picked up her sewing bag, and walked out of the room.

I stood to follow her. "Dad, we need more details about this."

He grabbed my arm. "Son, it's none of our business."

"Yes, it is."

He held me fast. "Stay here, Luke."

Hearing the front door shut, I jerked my arm away. "Maybe you should explain to Maggie that she shouldn't be going places with Mr. Sanders. Elizabeth says you two need to discuss your personal lives."

He sighed. "Sit down."

We ate in silence. There was nothing to talk about, nothing good to say. Nobody smiled except Alice who always liked to be in Dad's strong arms. Stevie wasn't in the mood to do the cool dish dance tonight, so I did the dishes alone.

Dad offered to read *The Secret Garden*, but I said no. I went outside and shot baskets for a while, working on an amazing spin move Maggie had taught me yesterday when Dad was working on a tractor out in somebody's field.

Finally, I turned off the yard lights and came inside. Stevie must've already been put to bed because the living room was silent except for the squeak of the rocker and Dad humming to the baby.

As I set my basketball on the washer I noticed the envelope on the shelf—poking out from underneath a pile of folded clean rags. Yuck. Color overlays. I pulled them out, grabbed Eddie's Hardy Boys book that was sitting there like a fossil, and went outside.

I walked through the dark barn to my dad's desk, and I switched on the old fluorescent light that was tacked against the wall. It flickered on, then off, then on again, then off. Sometimes it stayed on, sometimes not. I tried it again. More flickering and finally, it stayed on, steady, with the familiar buzzing hum that drove Dad crazy.

I opened the envelope and pulled out the six colored sheets. They were like cellophane, only stiff, and separated by clean white pieces of regular paper. Each overlay had the words *This side up* on it, and the name of its color. I set them to the side of the desk.

I read the title of Eddie's book, *The Tower Treasure,* and cracked it open. Carefully, I began to read, not allowing myself to shade the book with my head.

As I knew they would, the letters began to dance, mixing among themselves. Along the edges of the page, letters marched like ants. I kept forcing my eyes to focus on the page, trying to identify certain words and putting them into their phrases. I read aloud. "Watch your step, Frank."

I blinked. Don't rest your eyes. Keep trying, keep your eyes on the page.

Without looking away from the book, I took an overlay and set it on top of the page. Blue. Nice color. Nothing happened. I pushed the blue sheet to the other side of the desk and tried to keep reading.

"'Why not?' Joe reg…replied with a slow prin."

No. It was "replied with a slow grin."

Yellow next. No difference. This was hogwash.

Goldenrod. Hogwash.

"'Isn't he one of the fam…'"

Green…Wait.

Wait!

The letters were still, settled on the page like the rows in a marching band…and in groups. They were in groups—words. Individual words! "Wow!"

Some letters continued to wobble, and some of the words still ran together, their shapes unfamiliar. The overlay didn't cure everything. But much of the page was still, with letters settled, meshed into tight little clusters with spaces between. Words.

I stood. "Holy cow!"

I stared at the page again. Is this what Eddie saw when he read? And my Dad? And Elizabeth? Something like this?

I leaned over the book and tried to read more. Still, I struggled, but this was better—much better!

I picked up the overlay—*This side up. Green.* I clutched it to my chest and danced around the tractors, slapping at the tires and shouting, "Cool green! Cool green!"

Then I settled down long enough to slide the plastic sheet between the pages of my closed book. I needed to tell Maggie.

I raced to the house, then stopped halfway.

Wait—she wasn't home. She was with Keith Sanders. After all the months of her effort to fix me, she wasn't here now.

I forged ahead, up the porch steps and into the semi-dark kitchen, lit only by the nightlight by the sink.

Dad stood at the window, looking out over the moon-washed driveway. Holding Alice against his chest, he swayed back and forth. I heard slurping sounds as the baby sucked on her fingers. Dad turned to me and gave me the shush signal. He mouthed the words, "Almost asleep."

I was bursting to tell him about the overlay, but I didn't want to disturb Alice, so I took a deep breath and held it inside.

As Dad turned back to the window, Alice's eyes peeked over his shoulder, and her little round cheek rested against his ear. She smiled at me.

I didn't have the heart to tell him she was wide awake. They both seemed pretty comfortable standing there. I realized then that Dad's problems with females didn't apply to babies—at least not this one.

While I waited for Dad to finish taking care of Alice, I walked down the hall and climbed the stairs to my room. Flopping down on my bed, I stared up at the slanted ceiling. I needed to stay awake until Maggie came home. I needed to tell her about the green overlay.

The overlays! I'd left them scattered all over Dad's desk. I would straighten them up in the morning, and I'd try the last two, just in case they were better than the green.

Flipping on my light, I picked up the book, placed the green shield over the first page, and started again. Even though the letters held still, no magic happened when I tried to read the unfamiliar words. I tried breaking them down into little pieces like Elizabeth made me do when we practiced spelling, her voice echoing in my head.

Syllables, Luke. Think syllables.

Slowly, I stumbled through the first few lines, trying to understand the meaning.

Then I read aloud.

"Frank and Joe Hardy clutched the grips of their motor...cycles and stared in horror at the onco...oncoming car. It was car...careening from side to side on the narrow road."

It was not going to be easy, reading a whole book. But I would try. By the time I finished this one, Eddie would be on number 627. But I didn't care. A bubble of excitement was rising in me. I could read this book. I really could. And to prove it to myself, I battled my way through the entire first page, word by word until I had them all figured out, and then I read it aloud from top to bottom.

I put the overlay between the pages and dropped the book to the floor. I was worn out in the best possible way.

Stretching my hands behind my head, I listened to our house. In the bed across the room, Stevie, asleep, made his snarly rhythmic noise, the one that sounded like a low-pitched bumblebee. He turned to the side, and the sound stopped.

His birthday quilt lay crumpled on the floor. At first Maggie had tried to keep the quilt on his bed, but he always yanked it off and carried it around the house. Now there were other blankets tucked around him, and his quilt was "free to roam," as Maggie said.

Once, he'd left it at church. He'd cried all afternoon until Dad found someone to unlock the building so he could get it—just a quilt. How long would Stevie cry when Maggie left us for good? My heart started aching.

Bosco slipped off Stevie's bed and landed with a soft thunk. Panting, he padded across the room and jumped onto my bed. I scratched his ears while he snuggled against me.

I supposed if Maggie married that woman-stealer, Keith, she would take her dog with her, and the basketball hoop. Oh, and of course, Alice, who was getting cuter every day. What would our house be like without her? I didn't want to think about it.

Sighing, I pulled my dog quilt up to my chin. I guess our household was like a quilt, the patchwork kind where the pieces come together from all different places. Tonight, Dad stood at the kitchen window, holding Alice. Bosco and Stevie were upstairs with me—all of us in this house, stitched together with edges touching in a mismatched pattern that somehow worked.

Except tonight one piece was ripped out of the middle—Maggie.

Sometimes life stunk.

Tomorrow when Elizabeth came, I would call an emergency meeting to alert her to the urgency of our situation. My dishwashing tactic, alone, was not enough. We needed to set a new really effective plan in motion immediately. This time I had no idea what kind of a plan. But I was sure my creative friend would think of something.

TWELVE

*This was probably the most cheating ever
done in one basketball game.*

I was sleeping in the living room the night Dad and Maggie talked about the fire-flood. Well, actually, I wasn't sleeping. I was feeling sick to my stomach after eating two giant helpings of cherry cobbler, and Maggie wanted me close to the bathroom. I settled on the couch with my pillow and blankets, shut my eyes, and tried to work on memorizing my Paul Revere poem for school.

"William, why is this part of the wall behind the stove patched up— and a different color?" Maggie's voice trailed in from the kitchen.

The fire-flood.

I heard something clunk softly on the table, maybe a cup. Dad often ended his day with coffee and a book at the kitchen table. He hadn't answered Maggie's question. Her footsteps pattered, and a pan clanked against the sink. The water ran for a moment.

I started the poem in my head. *Listen my children and you will hear of the midnight ride of Paul Revere. On the eighteenth of April, in Seventy-Five: Hardly a man is now alive...*

"The fire-flood." Dad's voice stopped my silent words.

"The what?" Maggie asked.

"Fire-flood."

She turned off the water. "What fire-flood?"

No sound from Dad. I held my breath.

Her footsteps padded to the table and I heard her pull out a chair. It creaked as she settled on it. I could see her in my mind, wiggling into a comfortable position like she usually did.

The fire-flood happened two years ago, and Dad never, ever, mentioned it. Neither did I. It was a dark, scary, sad day that nobody wanted to remember.

Back to Paul Revere. *On the eighteenth of April, in Seventy-Five: Hardly a man is now alive who remembers...*

"William, tell me."

Dad sighed. "Stevie tried to cook oatmeal on the stove."

Hardly a man is now alive who remembers that famous day and year.

Dad cleared his throat. "Two years ago, Stevie pushed a chair up to the stove so he could reach it. He poured oatmeal into a pan and turned on the burner. Blasted the flame on high—caught a dishtowel on fire, and books on the counter. Stevie jumped back in time to avoid it and screamed. By the time Luke got in here, flames were licking up the wall."

Maggie gasped.

Dad continued. "There were always dirty dishes soaking in the sink back then, so Luke ran back and forth, sloshing pans and bowls full of water on the fire until it stopped burning, then added some more to be sure."

Things were totally silent in the kitchen.

"Then what?" Maggie asked.

"The boys got dressed and went to school. No teacher ever called, no nothing. Luke must've held it inside all day. I can only imagine what he was feeling."

Worst day ever. The teacher asked me why I smelled like smoke. I told her a lie about burning the trash. I sat at my desk and tried not to think about Stevie jumping in front of the fire, crying and flapping his hands. I tried not to dwell on what could have happened, and I worried about my dad—who hadn't jumped up from the couch to help me. This couch, the one I was on right now, with cherry cobbler grumbling angrily in my stomach.

Her voice was soft. "William, where were you when this happened?"

I sat up. No, don't tell her!

Silence.

He was asleep on the couch, and I couldn't wake him. Well, I tried. I told him what happened, and he'd mumbled, "Hmm," but he hadn't opened his eyes.

Now I heard something rustle in the kitchen, and a sniff.

"William?" Maggie whispered.

"Sorry." His voice was garbled.

Was he crying? What? I sat up.

"Maggie, give me a minute."

"Here's a napkin," she said.

He blew his nose.

I did not want to hear my dad cry, and in front of her of all people.

He cleared his throat. "I was on the couch—dead drunk."

What?

"Oh, William." A chair scooted. I wondered who moved. Was it her? Did she move toward him or away from him? I wished I could see in the room, and then again—not.

"I'd been drowning my sorrows at that time, more and more. I was a worthless drunk." Dad's heavy footsteps plodded toward the counter. He stopped there for a moment, blew his nose again, splashed coffee into his cup, then went back to his seat. It squeaked under his weight. "The next thing I remember was Uncle Ned literally dragging me through the kitchen, which smelled of gas and smoke, sliding across the floor puddles and out to the porch. While I lay there, he ran back inside and opened windows and doors. When he came out, I was sitting on the steps, my head splitting. He shoved me out of the way and stood before me, my liquor bottle in his hand, and emptied what was left on the dirt. I've never seen him so angry."

Silence, again.

I stood now. I'd never heard this part of the story, the part about the liquor bottle. I knew there was something bad going on back then, times when Dad didn't pick me up from school so I walked home, or he slept at the wrong time or in the barn all night. And our house was a worse mess than ever. I ended up taking care of Stevie, feeding him, and dressing him for school in dirty clothes.

Dad's voice broke into my thoughts. "Ned told me that somebody left the burner on with no flame, and the house was filling with gas. He broke down in front of me and sobbed, and then he went out to the barn to milk my neglected cows."

Silence, again.

I wondered what Ned meant about the burner with no flame. Oh, wait. He probably meant that when there's no flame the gas goes into the air, and if people breathe it, they will fall asleep and…die.

My stomach lurched.

My dad could've died. I clutched my stomach. "Oohhh."

Bending over, I walked away from the couch.

I'd put out the fire. I'd dumped panfuls of water on the fire, on the counter, on the wall, on the stove. I'd stopped it, every flame. But I didn't turn off the gas burner.

I gasped, my breath frozen in my throat. I didn't turn off the gas burner.

I had almost killed my dad. "Noooooo. Oh, nooooo." I couldn't stop the words from oozing out of my mouth in a slow low moan. "Ooooo-hhh."

I stumbled to the kitchen doorway, my stomach reeling on the inside, upward, rolling forward as I stared at my dad sitting at the table with his head bowed over the coffee cup, Maggie's hand on his shoulder, tears rolling down her cheek.

They both turned to see me, and that's when the cherry cobbler left my body.

What happened next was a blur of activity, mostly coming from Maggie. In a matter of minutes she had me washed down and in clean pajamas, with Dad sitting at the table with a look of petrified horror on his face. At first I thought it was because I threw up all over the floor.

But soon I realized he was feeling like that because I'd heard the rest of the story for the first time, the terrible part where I almost killed him.

So I threw up again.

I ended up on the couch, only this time Dad was sitting beside me, his arm tight around my shoulder. He'd helped get me into an old shirt and shorts because I didn't have any more pajamas.

Maggie did some cleaning in the kitchen, started the washer, and disappeared while I sat with Dad. "I'm so sorry," I said to him. "I didn't know."

"It wasn't your fault, son. It was mine. I was the responsible adult—and you were only nine. You saved all of us and the house, then Ned saved me."

I leaned against him for a while. The only movement he made was breathing in and out. The rest of him was stiff and silent like a robot with no batteries.

Dad spoke quietly. "And later—don't forget this—you saved me in the blizzard."

He was trying to make me feel better, but for some reason it wasn't working.

Finally, I asked him the question that was on my mind. "Dad, why were you drunk?"

"People have different ways of handling their grief...and guilt. You're hoping that the drink makes you forget the sadness in your heart, to make you numb." He sighed. "When you wake up the next day, it's still there—the pain. Meanwhile, you neglect the ones you love the most." He sighed again. "After that fire-flood day I stopped drinking. It's also when I knew we needed help around here and that's when I hired Mrs. Beecher."

"I almost forgot about her."

"Didn't stay long."

"Why not?"

"Stevie—his messes, sneezing, daycare issues. And I couldn't pay her enough."

"Oh." I brought my knees up and tried to pull my long shirt down over my cold legs.

"Then Nelda's Aunt Rose, followed by Mrs. Lendon, Clara Johnson, Hilda Mickelsen, Nellie Randall…" I felt him take a deep breath. "And now Maggie."

"Maggie's different from all those other people."

"You're right." He reached across the back of the couch and pulled my quilt down, wrapping it around my legs. "Here."

I tucked it around me. "Dad, who all knows the whole fire-flood story?"

"Only Ned—until tonight. Now Maggie and you. I wish you hadn't heard it."

"Me, too. Dad, do you think Maggie will leave us now that she's learned our worst secret?"

"She knows all our worst secrets. Sometimes she'll sit down next to me, and before you know it, my worst secrets come flowing out of my mouth."

"You gotta stop doing that."

He rubbed my arm. "It just happens."

"What does she say afterwards?"

"She says that you can't just bottle it up inside of you forever. You gotta let that awful stuff come out."

"Sorta like what happened to me tonight."

I felt him relax. "Nice analogy."

"Huh?"

"And she made me memorize a verse where Jesus says, 'Come unto me all ye who are weary and heavy laden, and I will give you rest.' She told me that when I start to feel bad, think about the verse."

"Does it help?"

"Haven't tried it yet." He rubbed his forehead. "Sometimes I get such an awful feeling when I think about the bad things I've done. It just eats away at my insides—like a big ugly blob inside of me. I suppose the words, 'Come unto me all who are weary and heavy laden' isn't just referring to physical burdens. He's talking about my heavy heart."

I knew what he meant. My own insides were grinding. "Maybe that's what the pastor said when he took those ugly paper blobs and set them at the foot of the cross."

He rubbed my shoulder. "When did you get to be so smart?"

Maggie came walking through the room and stopped in front of us. "How're you two doing?" she asked.

"Been better," Dad answered.

"I'm glad God was watching over you that day with the fire. He's in control, you know. I suppose he has a plan for you both." She dabbed at her eye with a hanky. "I've thought about how I came to this house after I lost my Ted, how much I needed you guys to take care of me and make me feel safe."

Her words comforted me. A purpose for my dad. A purpose for me. A purpose to keep us alive so we would be here for Maggie.

My stomach continued to ache that night, but not because of the cherry cobbler. I knew that in the days ahead, I would have trouble every time I looked at the stove. I would think about how I almost killed my dad. I would need to work on giving Jesus my heavy heart, to ask for His forgiveness, to help me feel better.

Finally, I leaned against my dad's chest, both of us breathing softly against each other, both feeling responsible for what could have happened the night of the fire-flood.

A numbness crawled into my heart, and I gave in to thankful tiredness as I lay against the rhythm of my dad's breathing.

"What's this?" Maggie pulled the shiny green overlay out from between the pages of my history book.

"I did the color test thing like you asked me to."

"When?"

"When you were gone that night." I was part excited to tell her, and part mad that she wasn't there when I made the discovery. I pushed it aside and started to label my math graph paper.

She sat down. "You tried the sheets?"

"Yeah. I took them out to the barn and used the stupid flickery light on Dad's desk. I did what you said, let my eyes get tired, then tried the different colors. Green stopped the letters from wiggling."

Her eyebrows went up. "Really?"

"It helps me read."

"Good." She reached her hand across the table and covered mine. "Hank Coleman will want to know about this for his research. He says it helps some people, and not others."

I nodded.

"He'd like to call you and discuss it with you. Is that alright?"

"Okay." Since our trip to Mr. Coleman, she always asked my permission about him and his research.

She withdrew her hand.

I bent down and finished labeling my graph paper. I wrote number one and started to copy my first long division problem.

"How did you do on last night's homework?" she asked me.

"Missed five problems. It was because I copied them wrong."

Maggie pulled the graph paper toward her and turned the book around so she could see it. "Let me copy the problems for you. And I'll write a note and ask Miss Finch if that's okay."

I looked up and watched her as she carefully wrote the numbers, one per square, leaving space under each problem for me to do the figuring. Her short brown hair fluffed around her head. There was a dab of flour on her cheek. I could smell the biscuits in the oven.

She smiled at me and winked, then got back to work.

"Stop doing that." Elizabeth groaned.

"What?"

"Stop fixing my bike for a minute."

"Your chain guard is still bent." I leaned her blue bike against the barn.

"How do I look?" she asked.

Her yellow hair was stringing around her glasses like it always did. She hadn't grown since yesterday, and she didn't have dirt on her face.

"You look the same as always."

"I'm not the same as always," she said.

"What's different?"

"I'm a basketball player—an official basketball player."

"What?"

She stood straight and lifted her chin. "I made the spring league team." Then, she squealed.

I put my hands over my ears.

She jumped up and down. "Thank you, thank you, thank you!" she screeched.

Oh, great.

"Guess what else."

"What?"

"You're coming to my first game."

"Huh?"

"I already invited your dad, and he said he would bring you."

A girls' basketball game?

"It's not really a game," she said. "The coach called it a skimmage."

"A what?"

"Skimmage." She made a motion with her hand like it was skimming across the ice. "Skim-mage."

"Skimmage? How about—scrimmage?"

"Scrimmage?"

"A scrimmage is a game that doesn't count. It's a practice game," I said.

"Oh, well, that makes sense. I was trying to figure out what skimmage had to do with basketball."

"I don't think there even is such a word as skimmage."

Elizabeth was looking proud of herself, and with good reason, I suppose. Maybe I was a decent basketball teacher. She'd made it on the team, hadn't she?

And maybe she was a decent spelling teacher, forcing me to try her experiments all week. We would find out on Friday's test.

Dad and Maggie both walked out of the house and down the porch steps. Dad was bouncing the basketball, and Maggie was holding a clothes basket against her side.

"It seems to me like your dad and Maggie are getting along just fine right now," Elizabeth said. "Maybe they'll fall in love today."

"You're crazy."

"They may act like they're just friends, but who knows?"

"They are just friends." At least, if you compared them to the TV show we watched last night where the man in the suit was dancing with a lady, staring right at her face. When the song ended, he leaned her back so far she almost bonked her head on the floor, and he kissed her. I'm sure that if anything like that was going on around here, I would've noticed.

Elizabeth broke into my train of thought. "I wonder what they're talking about."

I looked at Dad and Maggie. "Maybe she's challenging him to the big one-on-one game. She practices when he's not home." Against me, in fact. And she'd taught me some impressive moves.

"Hi, you two." Maggie stopped by the barn, Dad close behind her. "Did you get the bike fixed?"

"Not yet," I said. "But I'm still working on it. The chain guard is bent."

She smiled at me. "You'll get it done." Then she turned back to Dad. "So, after I talked to Bo-Wad's mother, we decided to get the boys matching shoes, and just let them wear whoever's. Their feet are the same size. That would end all this confusion we're having with the trades they do all day long. The bad part is when they come home with one kid wearing right-right and the other wearing left-left."

Shoes? They were talking about shoes?

Elizabeth rolled her eyes and sighed. She probably didn't think shoe talk was all that romantic.

Dad tossed the ball to me, but he was looking at Maggie. "Too bad nobody makes shoes that fit on either foot, like socks."

"Where's Alice?" Elizabeth asked Maggie.

"She's in the playpen. Would you like to bring her outside? It's such a beautiful day. Put the pink sweater on her."

"Sure." Elizabeth ran into the house.

I shot the ball and it landed in the hoop. My hours of practice were paying off. After chasing the ball down, I passed it to Dad.

He shot it through the hoop, and I snagged it on the first bounce.

Maggie set down her clothes basket and held out her hands.

I tossed her the ball.

She shot and missed. "Wait, let me try that again," she said.

I threw it to her.

This time it hit the rim, bobbled around, and rolled off.

Dad grabbed the rebound and banked it in.

"Okay," he said. "Who's ready for a little one-on-one?" He was looking straight at me.

I turned to Maggie and cleared my throat.

"Me," she said, catching my signal. "I'll play a little one-on-one."

"Huh?" Dad looked at me.

I shrugged.

"Okay, one-on-one." As Dad bounced the ball, I saw the twinkle in Maggie's eye.

She looked so little, and quiet, and innocent.

"I'll be the ref," I said, trying not to smile. "First to ten. One point baskets."

"Okay," Maggie agreed. "What's the bet?"

Dad raised his eyebrows. "What kind of talk is that? A bet? I'm a foot taller than you."

Maggie bristled. "So, you're chicken?"

"No, I just can't think of anything to bet, or a reason to bet."

I decided to take things into my own hands and make an announcement. "The loser does tonight's dishes."

"Okay," Maggie said.

Dad looked down at her and scratched his chin. "Um, sure."

I walked to the edge of the imaginary court and drew a line in the dirt with my foot. "Here's where you go when you change possessions. Behind this line."

Elizabeth walked out the back door, lugging the baby.

"We'll start with a jump ball," I said.

"Wait. Where's Stevie?" Maggie looked around.

Dad answered. "He's in the barn making an airport out of silverware."

"What?"

"He's using spoons and forks to mark his runways."

"What? Spoons and forks from the kitchen? How did that happen?"

Suddenly Dad looked nervous. "He's been carrying them out in bits and pieces. I wondered why you were allowing it."

"I've been giving the baby her bath."

"Okay, then. My mistake."

"Uh..."

"It's okay, Maggie," Dad said. "We'll get it all back in the house in time for supper."

"So," I added, "the loser, *she* will clean up the cool silverware airport and do the dishes." You'll notice I emphasized the word *she*. That was for Dad's benefit.

He was grinning and Maggie was trying not to.

I wouldn't have missed this game for a million bucks.

Elizabeth came and stood beside me, Alice squirming in her arms.

I tossed the ball high. Dad pulled it out of the air without jumping, dribbled to the basket and made a bucket.

"One to nothing," I stated. I figured I'd be both referee and score-keeper.

Dad and Maggie jogged around the court with him being real easy on her, practically handing the ball over, and guarding her from eight feet away.

Then Maggie made a lob from the line that sailed through the hoop without touching the rim.

Dad rubbed his chin and gave me a puzzled look. As he started toward the basket, Maggie stripped the ball from him, dribbled a crooked pattern around him and flipped an off-the-backboard lay-up on the other side.

That's when I think Dad started catching on to Maggie. And that's when the game changed. The two of them battled on the dirt court— two people with completely opposite styles, one a lanky jump shooter and the other a short, quick trickster. By the time the score was eight to nine, with Dad ahead, he and Maggie were both out of breath—and

I don't mind telling you, neither of them was goofing off. The stakes were high. Not the dishwashing stakes, but pride.

Elizabeth and I stood breathlessly on the side, watching the battle unfold.

As Dad drove to the basket, Maggie came out of nowhere and punched the ball upward out of his hands. It whacked into his jaw and ricocheted off.

"Owww!" he yelled. "Foul!"

Ball in hand, Maggie zipped around him and dribbled toward the basket. I swear, she was faster than a garter snake. One second she was right in front of you, and the next—gone!

"Foul!" Dad repeated.

"I did not…touch…you!" Maggie said between breaths. "I touched the ball."

Dad tried to fake-steal the ball, but Maggie spun the other way, sped past him, and put up the tying point. Panting, she handed the ball to Dad, whose one cheek was bright red.

"Win by two, or…sudden death?" she asked.

"Sudden…death," he gasped.

Speaking of death, they were going to die. Both were out of breath— ready to just keel over, leaving us orphans to fend for ourselves.

"Time out!" I yelled.

They ignored me.

Dad crouched as he dribbled toward Maggie. "You can't do that punching thing again."

Eye-to-eye, they moved with the rhythm of the ball.

He stepped to the basket the exact same way he'd done on the last play, the play where Maggie thumped the ball out of his hands. He started to rise up—and stopped.

As her hand came under his, he grabbed her, and after a tussle, wrapped his arm around her, pressing her against his side and lifting her off the ground like he always did to Stevie and me. "I've had enough of you, varmint, buzzing around me like a bee!" he shouted.

"Oh, no, Dad! Not that!"

"What are you doing?" she yelled, trying to peel herself off him.

With his other hand, he dribbled toward the basket.

All the while, Maggie was whacking at him and kicking her feet above ground. "Talk about fouls!" she yelled.

"Foul!" Elizabeth shouted in my ear. "Foul!"

I jumped to the side. "Get away from me! You're hurting my ear!"

"Ouch! No pinching!" Dad yelled at Maggie. "Foul on you!"

"Foul!" I shouted. "Foul! Hey! I'm the referee here!"

Alice squealed. Her eyes were huge.

With Maggie clamped against his side, Dad tossed the ball up to the basket. It hit the underside of the rim and banked straight down on his head like a bullet.

"Wrong hand," he muttered. "Can't shoot lefty worth beans." Grabbing Maggie in both arms, he shifted her to the other side, and went for the ball again.

"You are such a cheater!" Maggie yelled as she tangled her foot between his knees, tripping him and sending them both down to the ground like wrestling tigers.

The ball rolled away.

Dad dove forward and tucked it under his chest like a football player. He sat up.

With lightning speed, Maggie stripped it from him and dribbled back to the line.

They were both gasping for breath.

"Time out!" I shouted.

Dad jumped to his feet and crouched in front of her, his arms out.

Oh boy, I thought. She's going to make a move on him. He'll swing one way, she'll zip past him on the other side.

As I was thinking it, she did it.

In a flash the ball went up, rolled around the rim and fell off to the side.

Dad yanked the rebound out of the air. He held it above his head so he could catch his breath. "Oh, man," he said, dribbling to the line, then back toward the basket.

He stopped midcourt when Maggie came toward him. I could see the fear in his eyes. He stood tall, held the ball over his head, bent his knees, and sprung up with a desperate shot.

The ball fell in.

He dropped to the ground and lay on his back, arms outstretched. "Oh…man," he gasped. "This game…about killed me."

"That's the most cheating I ever saw," Elizabeth announced.

Maggie retrieved the ball and walked toward Dad. "Two out of three?"

"Heavens to Murgatroyd." Dad closed his eyes.

She set the ball in my hands, picked up the laundry basket and carried it to the clothesline—with Elizabeth close behind, still holding the baby. I could tell by the movement of Maggie's cheek that she was smiling.

"That was amazing," I heard Elizabeth say.

"She almost beat you, Dad," I said, plopping down beside him. "You won, but you cheated, so it doesn't count."

"Maybe I'll help her do the dishes and the cool silverware airport cleanup."

"Good idea."

"But first I need to find the energy to stand up."

Across the yard, Maggie finished hanging a sheet on the line, then put her hands on her hips and took a deep breath. She reached into the laundry basket, picked out a small towel and wiped the back of her neck.

"So, son," Dad said. "How long have you known that she's this year's number one draft pick for the American Basketball Association?"

I grinned. "A while."

He groaned. "Sometimes that woman just drives me crazy."

The way he said it I couldn't tell if he meant her driving him crazy was a good thing or a bad thing.

Later that night while we worked on our homework, Elizabeth informed me that if there was a thermometer that measured romantic progress, my dad's temperature would be twenty below zero. Her exact words were, "He cheated at basketball."

THIRTEEN

Maggie's birthdays should come with a survival guide.

N o cooking on your birthday," Dad announced to Maggie when she walked into the kitchen on the morning of March 29. We'd already eaten our cereal while Maggie had tended the baby.

"What did you just say?" she asked.

Dad pulled out her chair. "Have a seat."

Her eyebrows went up. "But…"

"No cooking on your birthday," I chimed in as I walked to the refrigerator. "I'll get you some juice."

She started to stand. "Oh, but William…"

"Nope, nope." Setting his hand on her shoulder, he pushed her back down. "No cooking on your birthday. We're taking care of you. It's all planned."

Showing her my best smile, I held up the orange juice in one hand, and a glass in the other.

A slow grin spread across her face. "Okay, then."

The cereal and bowl were already on the table, so Dad brought the milk while Stevie handed her a spoon. Two pieces of wheat toast, Maggie's favorite, popped out of the toaster, and the coffee pot percolated on the counter. We were in business.

Maggie looked around the room. "You guys are something else." Her eyes sparkled.

We were off to a good start. I even hoped that a day like this would help Maggie know how wonderful it would be to stay permanently in our family.

I hummed Amazing Grapes while I walked down the lane with Stevie to wait for our buses. Dad had packed us peanut butter and jelly sandwiches and Ritz crackers, and he'd made extras at home so Maggie wouldn't need to make lunch. While he was fixing the sandwiches, he explained to me that he would cook chili for supper. He'd pulled the recipe card out of Maggie's little blue file box. He'd decided it didn't look too difficult, and all the ingredients were in the house.

I could tell he was excited to make the day special for her, and I was anxious to get home after school to help him cook. He said this would be a team effort.

When Elizabeth and I walked into the house after school, she explained to me, for the umpteenth time, that tonight was the perfect opportunity for Dad to finally win Maggie's heart. After all, he was cooking for her. Our job was to encourage him as much as possible, and to help in any way we could.

The problem was, I wasn't sure that Dad's cooking could win anyone's heart. Besides hotdogs, all I'd ever seen him do was open cans and pour stuff into pans.

When we arrived in the kitchen, Dad stood at the stove wearing Maggie's yellow daisy apron, the ties hanging down his back from a lopsided knot. There were green and red juicy splotches all over the bib part of the apron, as well as on his shirtsleeves, stove, and countertop—which was littered with cans, pots, spoons, and Maggie's recipe card. It looked like someone had flung tomatoes and green slime into the air and let it all rain down.

He turned to me with a satisfied look, sort of a victory smile—with red splotches on one eyebrow. He was really cooking, and proud of it.

Elizabeth's mouth dropped open as she viewed the kitchen scene.

I nudged her arm and whispered. "Close your mouth."

Dad stirred a pot that was filling the air with its beefy-tomato aroma, just like when Maggie made chili. I thought we were off to a great start.

Elizabeth took a deep breath. "Smells good, Mr. Bradley."

He nodded. "Thank you,"

"Where's Maggie?" Elizabeth asked.

"Taking a nap—she and the baby."

"Good, because I have an idea."

Oh, no. Now what?

She set her thick, always-organized school binder on the table and unzipped it. "Miss Finch let me bring home some leftover construction paper so we can make birthday cards for Maggie." She pulled out several sheets of white paper, already folded in half so they looked like blank cards. She dumped crayons, rulers, and pencils out onto the table.

With an inward sigh of relief, I sat down. This idea wasn't so bad. Within a few minutes we were joined by Stevie, who was thrilled to make a cool card for Maggie.

"You, too, Mr. Bradley," Elizabeth said.

"Oh, I'm not good at that sort of thing. Just let me cook."

Elizabeth held up a blank card. "I think Maggie would like one from you."

He stood helplessly for a moment, his hands twisting a dishtowel. "I wouldn't know what to write on it."

I decided to help. "I know, Dad. Draw stuff on it that she likes. You know how she made Stevie and me those quilts for our birthdays, and they had dogs and airplanes on them? You can make her a card with things on it she likes."

"That's good, Luke," Elizabeth said. She pushed Dad's folded paper down to the end of the table nearest him. Her card already had a straight row of purple flowers across the top and the words *Happy Birthday* in pink letters.

I looked down at my own card, hoping I'd spelled *Happy Birthday* right, but not sure. At least Elizabeth hadn't tried to fix it yet. Anyway, I drew a dog and baby under the words because I knew that's what Maggie liked. I opened the card and puzzled about what to say.

Beside me, Stevie's card was turning into a mass of black, blobby swirls. It looked like an ink tornado had landed on it.

I stared at my blank page. I wanted to write something really nice and fancy for Maggie, but nothing came into my mind. So I wrote, *I hope you have a nice birthday, beceus you are realy nice.*

When I looked up, Dad was sitting at the table, writing on the inside of the card Elizabeth had given him. He focused hard, his eyebrows scrunched together. Finally, he set down his pen and shut the card. He'd drawn a basketball and hoop on the cover.

Elizabeth cleared her throat. "Mr. Bradley, most ladies don't expect to have basketballs on their cards."

I looked at Elizabeth's card where a row of pink hearts now ran along the bottom. It looked good enough to be sold at Woolworth's.

Dad stood up, card in hand. "Maggie likes basketball." He took it to the little shelf by the window and set it there. "Let's keep the cards here for now."

I placed mine on top of his and got to work getting out bowls that someone had washed since breakfast. Elizabeth set her card and Stevie's along with the others and began to clear the table.

I wondered what Dad had written in his card. I wanted to take a peek, but not with him right there beside me, staring into a bowl of shiny green soup. "What's that, Dad?"

"Lime Jell-O."

"It looks more like lime Kool-Aid."

"You're right."

"It smells like it too. Maybe we should just pour it in our glasses and add ice."

Dad jiggled the bowl and watched the green liquid splash against the sides. "Probably needs to set a bit longer." He returned it to the refrigerator.

"I feel well rested for once," Maggie announced as she slid into her seat at the table. "Hmm. Smells good in here." She took a long look at Dad in the food-splattered flowery apron. The corners of her mouth twitched.

Stevie pounced on her with a flurry of napkins. He carefully arranged one on her lap, patting down the edges and corners so it lay exactly flat. One by one, we each settled in our seats so Stevie could take care of everyone's napkin. Elizabeth was last because she'd been busy finding an envelope in her binder. She gave it to Maggie. "Here's the payment from my mom."

"Thank you." Maggie took it. "I almost feel guilty accepting money from your mom these days. You are such a blessing."

Elizabeth beamed.

You are such a blessing. What good words to tell somebody. I wished I would've written on my card, You are such a blessing.

After Dad thanked God for the food and the occasion, he stood and ladled chili into our bowls. Along with that, we had crackers, bread and jelly, and the green Jell-O soup, which sat uselessly by Dad's elbow.

"What's this?" Maggie asked as she reached for it.

I answered. "Jell-O soup."

"It didn't set?"

"Nope." Dad gave it a stir. "I did everything like I've seen you do— two cups of hot water, stir, then two cups of cold."

"When did you make it?"

He checked his watch. "Two hours ago."

Maggie picked it up, covered it with a clean plate for a lid, and set it back in the refrigerator. "It'll be good with lunch tomorrow."

Dad was silent for a moment. "How long does Jell-O usually take?"

"Six hours to overnight."

"I missed that part."

Elizabeth was staring down at her chili, and not eating it.

I glanced at mine and gave it a stir. It looked shiny. I lifted the spoon to my face, sniffing to enjoy the rich tomato smell, and took a sip. Tasty, yet slimy. It slid down my throat like it was on roller skates.

As we ate, I glanced around the table at the others, noticing how their lips seemed glossy. Each person ate quietly, slowly, politely. Elizabeth, her eyes wide, licked her lips. Something was wrong.

I tried another spoonful. Sort of yummy, and sort of greasy.

Stevie was dragging his spoon around his mouth, trying to scrape off the slime.

"Okay." Dad set down his spoon. "Everybody with slippery lips, raise your hand."

I lifted my hand along with Maggie and Elizabeth. Stevie took a big slurp off his spoon.

Dad eyed my brother for a second, then turned to Maggie. "What's wrong with this chili? I followed all the directions on the little card. Why is it like an oil slick?"

Maggie let her spoon rest in the bowl. "What card?"

"The one I used from your recipe file box." He went to the counter and picked it up. "I did everything it said." He brought it to her.

She took it. "Did you drain the hamburger?"

"Huh?" He scratched his head.

"Oh, boy."

He looked over her shoulder at the card. "It just says to brown the hamburger."

She pointed at something on the card. "Is this blob here tomato sauce?"

"Yeah, it splashed a little."

"More like a tomato bomb," I said.

Maggie licked her finger and rubbed a spot on the card. "Look here."

Dad leaned down closer and examined it and read. "And drain." He stood up straight. "I was supposed to drain the meat. We are digesting hamburger grease that should've been skimmed off."

Maggie nodded.

He turned to the table. "Everybody stop eating."

As I set down my spoon, I hoped Dad didn't hear the little "whew" that escaped out of Elizabeth. Then she looked at me with sad eyes. I knew Dad's birthday supper was not being the victorious matchmaking success she had hoped for.

Maggie smiled up at Dad. "It's okay, William. I did the same thing once." I knew by now she hated to see anyone be embarrassed, especially when they were trying so hard to do something nice.

Dad took a deep breath and let it out. "Okay, I have an idea. There's a new place in town called Beulah's Cheeseburger Barn. Let's go try it."

"Yeah!" I shouted.

"Yeah!" Stevie sputtered an avalanche of grease down his chin.

"I'll get the baby," Maggie said, and left the room.

Dad started ordering us around. "Luke, go get my wallet off the dresser. Elizabeth, see if Maggie needs help with Alice. I'll degrease Stevie's face."

Lickety-split, we all gathered by the car—Elizabeth with the baby, and me with Stevie, who was jumping up and down and clapping because we were going somewhere. His face was shiny clean.

"Okay, everybody, get in the car," Maggie ordered. She turned to Dad. "Not you."

"What's wrong?" he asked.

I climbed in first and sat by the back window while Elizabeth loaded in Stevie and Alice. Looking out, I watched the sarge put her hands on Dad's shoulders and turn him around. She carefully undid the knot in his apron. Then she wheeled him around again and finished peeling it off his front, neither of them talking, yet their eyes were sending messages loud and clear.

His eyes, if they could speak out of his bright red face, were saying something like, *I'm a lousy birthday giver—one who ruined supper and almost wore a frilly, tomato-splattered apron out in public.*

And her eyes responded with kindness.

She smiled up at him, and he smiled back.

They stood there for just a moment like that, face to face, as if they were alone together in a really good place—far from a car full of wiggly kids, lubed liked the tractors in the barn.

"Eww!" Elizabeth shrieked. "Alice just hiccuped and now there's spit-up all over my arm!"

That pretty much broke the spell. After mopping up the baby and Elizabeth, Dad and Maggie got into the car and we took off.

While we waited for our cheeseburgers, Dad, who seemed to have recovered from his cooking disaster, pulled a paper out of his pocket and unfolded it. "In honor of Maggie's birthday, I did a little research. Now we can know how Maggie came to us."

"What do you mean, Dad?" I asked.

"Remember when she first arrived, and we didn't know who knew the person who knew the person who knew Maggie?"

"Oh, yeah. With the kangaroo."

Dad grinned. "Right."

"What kangaroo?" Elizabeth adjusted the squirming baby on her lap. "What are you guys talking about?"

Maggie smiled. "The kangaroo part is a joke, honey. We just always wondered what chain of people connected me to this family." She turned to Dad. "Where did you do your research?"

"Well," Dad confessed. "I got Aunt Nelda working on my end of the chain, and I called your Aunt Joyce about the other end."

"Oh, really? Is Aunt Joyce the one who told you today was my birthday?"

Dad grinned. "As a matter of fact, yes."

"Okay. That explains—"

Dad interrupted her. "After you gave the boys such great birthdays with special dinners and those nice quilts, we thought we'd like to make your birthday special too."

The corner of her mouth quivered upward.

He sighed. "Yes, special, like slimy chili and dead Jell-O."

"I didn't say anything." Maggie's smile was growing.

"You didn't have to." He looked around the table, held out his paper, and cleared his throat. "Are you ready? Here goes."

And he began to read. "My Aunt Nelda's sister, Louisa, has a cousin named Carolyn Penner. Carolyn's sister, Nichole Scanlon, is a friend of Clarissa Adams who lives in Richmond. Esther's niece, Adriane Frye, lives next door to Martha Taylor who went to school with Caryl Curless."

Maggie sat up. "Oh, and Caryl is my second cousin. She must've said something to Aunt Joyce."

"Right."

"Guess what," I said. "No kangaroos."

We all laughed—well, except for Elizabeth who didn't know what was going on, but she was busy arranging Alice on her lap anyway.

Then, since our cheeseburgers still weren't ready, Dad handed Maggie her cards.

Good job, Dad. Even in the middle of the confusion with the stupid Jell-O and greasy chili he remembered to bring the cards.

First, she opened Elizabeth's and took a minute to admire the fine artwork on the front before reading what was inside. "Oh, Elizabeth, I love this. And you wrote the poem?"

Elizabeth nodded.

"I'll read it to everyone.

"'The Beautiful Sarge' by Elizabeth Mitchell

"You're the best cook in the state

"That we could ever find.

"You whip everyone into shape

"In a way that's very kind."

Elizabeth sort of glowed while Maggie read the poem.

Of course, Stevie's card had no words, just big black tornado tracks. Maggie pretended to read it, then grabbed my brother and hugged him, making him burst into giggles.

I was glad she opened my card after Stevie's instead of after Elizabeth's. This way the comparison wouldn't be so bad. Maggie looked up from it, her sparkling brown eyes smiling into mine, pushing a rush of warmth through me. That's what Maggie does to people. It's almost like she can touch your heart from across the room.

After reading Dad's card, she pressed it to her chest for a moment. "Thank you, William."

I could tell he was feeling the heart touch, too, his eyes lingering on her while she carefully tucked the cards into her purse.

Again, I wondered what Dad's card said.

Elizabeth gave me a quiet smile to let me know she thought that now the evening might possibly be moving along okay.

Things ran smooth through the cheeseburgers and ice cream parts of our supper, probably because Dad didn't cook them. Then the bill came. Dad pulled out his wallet and opened it.

His mouth dropped open. "Where's my money?" His eyes were open like saucers. "I had fifty dollars in here yesterday."

Elizabeth groaned.

Dad slapped his forehead. "Oh, wait. I told Uncle Ned to take some cash out of my wallet when he went to town for parts this morning. I thought he would just take a twenty, not everything." Anguish crossed his face.

I looked around the room at the other diners, their silverware clanking against their dishes. "Will we need to wash dishes to pay for our meal?" I asked softly. "There are a lot of dishes in here."

That's when Maggie started to laugh, muffled behind her hand at first, peeking over her fingers with watering eyes. Then she just let loose, and Stevie joined in because, well, if somebody laughs, Stevie laughs with them.

I got tickled, myself, and soon we were all a bunch of laughing hyenas, sitting around a table in a restaurant where we couldn't pay for our supper.

When things died down a bit, Maggie dug around in her purse, pulled out the envelope from Elizabeth's mother, and handed it to Dad. "You can pay me back later."

Dad sighed. "Okay."

I was relieved that we didn't have to wash dishes.

After the bill was paid and the dishes cleared, the sarge made us stay in place. Since Alice was squirming all over Elizabeth, Dad took the baby and settled her in the crook of his arm.

That done, Maggie folded her hands on the table. "Okay. Now I need to tell you something that I wish I didn't have to say. Honesty is the best policy."

What? On her birthday? Something bad?

She looked around at each one of us, then took a deep breath. "This isn't really my birthday."

"What?" Dad bellowed, causing the baby to jerk. "Oooh, sorry, Alice."

Maggie cleared her throat. "Aunt Joyce confuses all of the family birthdays in March and May. My cousin Irma's birthday is today, March 29. My birthday is May 29."

"Oh, no," I said. "Do you mean we have to do this all over again?"

Maggie tightened her lips and glanced at Dad, who was smiling at me. Taking a deep breath, Maggie lifted the baby into her arms before she spoke again. "I just want all of you to know that this, even though it really isn't my birthday, has been wonderful. I loved having someone else cook." She glanced at Dad. "The cards, the special treatment—all of it." Her eyes got kind of misty. "I feel so honored. I'll never forget this day."

"Me either," Dad stated.

Elizabeth leaned forward. "In my family, we always say our birthday wish. What's yours?"

Maggie took a thoughtful pause, then looked around the table. "My wish is that on my real birthday, I can celebrate it with all of you again."

That means she's a keeper for two more months. My heart lifted.

Dad seemed to relax. Maybe he was thinking the same thing as me.

Maggie turned to him. "So, William. Did you bake me a cake?"

"No." His eyes crinkled. "A man can only do so much."

Maggie displayed her birthday cards on the top of our bookcase by the television. The next morning when no one was around, I took a peek inside the one from Dad.

Sarge,
I'm thankful that God brought you to us.
You are a blessing.

Well, at least one of us knew how to say it right.

FOURTEEN

Dad hits himself in the face with a wrench.

The fourth graders were outside the window, using magnifiers to examine buds and leaves. Last year, Mrs. Randall had made us do the same thing. Science was fun in her class. I wished I could be outside right now instead of sitting at my desk—not studying the spelling list that rested on top of my reading book with a green clear overlay page sticking out.

Then I realized I was wishing I could be with the fourth graders. A sharp pang stabbed me in the gut. No, I did not want to be with fourth graders.

Elizabeth nudged me and whispered, "What's that green thing you use when you read?"

"Nothing. An experiment."

"You should be studying your words instead of daydreaming."

Thanks, Elizabeth.

Last night she'd made me paint the spelling words with water on the side of the barn four times each—with big swooping letters. Then I'd gone into the house and typed each word twice. Because of that, it was 9:00 before I even started my other homework. I yawned.

Elizabeth started to pull the colored overlay out of my reading book.

I smacked her hand. "Stop that."

She looked around. Miss Finch was bent over Kathleen's desk. "What is it?"

"It kinda helps me read, settles the movement caused by lights." At least, that's the way Maggie had explained it, and Miss Finch said she would allow it.

"I want to try."

Groaning, I handed it to her. "Be careful with it."

She set it over her open reading book and looked down. "It's pretty. Does it come in pink?"

"Yes." Sighing, I returned it to my book. "I'll bring you a pink one tomorrow." Girls—weird.

"We want you to go on a blind date," Elizabeth announced to Dad after school.

He slid out from under the tractor and sat up on the barn floor. "What?"

"We want you to go on a blind date," she repeated. She didn't even blink. I decided she could be one of those British palace soldiers who stay focused no matter what.

"Are you talking to me?" Dad chuckled and looked at me. "You agree with this?"

I nodded.

"For what reason?" he asked.

Elizabeth took a deep breath. "It's time for you to fall in love."

He raised his eyebrows. "Oh, really? Why?" He rubbed his chin. "And who exactly am I going to fall in love with?"

"Dad, blind date. It's a surprise."

He narrowed his eyes at me.

"Don't be suspicious, Dad. You'll like her a lot."

"Let me guess. Miss Finch?" He shook his head. "I already have one woman trying to whip me into shape. Don't think I can handle two." He glanced at Elizabeth. "Three."

Elizabeth giggled. "No, not Miss Finch. She's not your type."

"Good." Dad leaned down and slid back under the tractor. "I don't have any blind date clothes."

"I'll get you fixed up," Elizabeth offered. "I can borrow the clip-on tie I gave my dad for Christmas. He won't mind."

I think I heard Dad chuckle again.

"Just this once, Dad. Go on the blind date."

"There's nobody I want to go on a blind date with." His voice sounded a bit weary. "Hand me the big red-handled wrench, son. It's by your foot."

I gave it to him.

"You'll like her," Elizabeth said. "She's lovely."

"My, but you're persistent."

"It's for your own good," she said.

"I appreciate the thought, Elizabeth, but..." he sighed, "...the thought of going on a blind date just scares the heebie-jeebies right out of me. I don't do dates. I don't have date clothes. She might not like me—all valid reasons."

"She will like you."

"You have a specific person all lined up? She will like me? Who is this she?"

Elizabeth put her hands on her cheeks. "You're driving me crazy. I can't say who it is. It's a blind date." She rolled her eyes.

"Then sorry, but—no." He moved around underneath the space between the back wheels of the tractor.

"She's very nice," Elizabeth said to his feet.

"No."

"She's pretty."

"No."

"I know you would have a good time. You could go to a fancy restaurant and have a romantic dinner."

"I won't know what to talk about." He seemed determined to not go on a blind date.

Elizabeth frowned at me.

I needed to help. "You can talk about tractors and stuff," I volunteered.

"Aaauuuggghhh!" Elizabeth smacked her forehead. "You guys are impossible!"

"Huh?"

"No, Luke." Elizabeth took a deep breath. "That's not what he should talk about."

"Well, what then?"

"He should say something like, 'You look beautiful in the candlelight.'"

I tried to imagine my dad saying, "You look beautiful in the candlelight." A giggle was rising in me like a big strange bubble.

Elizabeth took a deep breath. "What if it was Maggie?"

Something thudded under the tractor in the area of Dad's head, followed by the clang of heavy metal on the concrete floor. "Ouch!" He shoved the wrench out from under the tractor. "Ooouuuuchhh."

"What happened?" Elizabeth asked, leaning down.

"Dropped the wrench on my head. Give me a minute."

I leaned down too. "Are you okay, Dad?"

"Fine and dandy."

"How about the blind date thing?" Elizabeth pressed.

"Okay, let me get this straight." Dad's empty hand rested on the floor. "Maggie, the nosiest, bossiest person in America, would agree to go on a date with someone without knowing who it is? You could talk her into that?"

"Yes," Elizabeth said.

Elizabeth, the pushy, strong-willed miracle worker. I didn't doubt her for a second.

Dad continued to talk from underneath the tractor. "We are talking about Sarge—the woman with eyes in the back of her head, who can throw rocks over barns and whip all of us into shape in five seconds without blinking an eye. You could talk that woman into going on a blind date—with no questions asked?"

"Yes. I can do it." Her voice was confident.

Maybe Elizabeth was crazy enough to make this work.

Dad laughed again. "And she would show up, and she would look at me and say, 'Oh, brother! It's you?'"

"Dad, it's time for you to face your Goliath."

Maggie appeared in the doorway. "Oh," she said. "I wondered where you kids were. Elizabeth, your dad called. He'll be an hour late tonight, honey. Said you should get all your homework done here." She walked into the barn and stopped by Dad's feet. "William, you had a phone call, too, someone named Eugene Anderson."

"What'd he say?"

"His tractor broke down in his field. He wonders if you can come there tomorrow. I wrote down his number. He'd like you to call before nine tonight." She placed her hand on her hip. "Your skills are in such demand."

"What time is it now?"

"Seven-thirty."

Dad scooted out from under the tractor and sat up. His left eye was all red and there was fresh blood above his eyebrow.

"What did you do now?" Maggie asked, kneeling beside him. "Here, let me see." She turned his face toward her. "You're bleeding. What happened?" She pointed at me. "Luke, get the first-aid kit from the kitchen and a clean washcloth."

Dad protested. "No, no. Not here, not now. I'm coming into the house in a few minutes to make the phone call. Then you can fix me."

She grabbed a clean rag off the workbench and pressed it against his eye. He held it in place.

"Okay." She stood. "What did you do?"

"I dropped a wrench on my face."

"You did what?"

"I was thinking about you, and I dropped a wrench on my face. There, now you have the whole truth." He scooted back under the tractor. "I'll finish this, and I'll come make the phone call, and you can put a splint on my head or whatever."

Maggie didn't move. "You were thinking of me, so you hit yourself in the face with a wrench?"

"Yes, exactly like that."

Maggie turned to me.

I shrugged.

"Really?" she asked.

Nobody answered.

"Okay, then." She scratched her head and left.

Elizabeth stared at my dad's long legs sticking out from under the tractor. "Mr. Bradley," she said. "When should we schedule the blind date?"

Dad started to chuckle. He laughed for several minutes, alone under the tractor, and finally settled down. Then he sighed. "Oh…Saturday."

I was feeling pretty good on Friday afternoon. Miss Finch graded my spelling test during lunch, and before school was out, she showed me the big red A- on top. A miraculous A-. I carried it in my pocket now while I waited for Dad to pull up in the school parking lot. We were on our way to Elizabeth's scrimmage.

"You look pleased about something," he said as I climbed into the truck. "I didn't know girls' basketball meant so much to you."

"It doesn't." I pulled out the test, unfolded it, and handed it to Dad, wondering if he would believe it. I could hardly believe it myself.

His eyebrows rose. "Wow, maybe we should frame this." He grinned. "It looks like your hard work is paying off. I'm proud of you, son." He gave it back and drove down the street.

After carefully folding it, I returned it to my pocket so I could show Maggie later.

"Let's celebrate with ice cream after the game," Dad said.

"That sounds like a good plan." Something inside of me was swelling. "Oh, and guess what."

"What?"

"Elizabeth talked Maggie into doing the blind date."

The color left his face.

"She said Maggie argued at first by saying she didn't want to go on any dates at all. But Elizabeth kept pressing on, and told Maggie that this blind date was really, really important."

For some reason, Dad's upper lip was sweating, and I think he was holding his breath.

"Elizabeth said that all of a sudden Maggie stopped arguing. She just clammed up, then said, 'Well, okay.'"

Dad wiped his lip on his sleeve. "Oh, boy." He shifted gears, then accidentally bounced over the curb on his way into the youth center parking lot.

When we walked into the gym, the teams had already warmed up and were ready to play.

We climbed the bleachers and sat down beside Elizabeth's dad and a few other parents.

Elizabeth smiled and waved to us.

We waved back.

Her basketball game was not what I expected. For one thing, it was noisy—not because of crowd shouts and referee whistles, but because the players on the bench were doing cheers, really loud ones.

Another thing I noticed was that the basketball game, itself, was not the only thing that was important. What was also important was that the girls all had pink ribbons to match their uniforms, and pink finger-nail polish, and pink socks and shoelaces. When most boys would be stretching and jogging in place to stay loose, Elizabeth and her team-mates were fixing each other's ponytails and comparing fingernails.

Once the game began though, things changed. A couple of the players, like Elizabeth, were sort of awkward. Others, including a short black-haired girl from my class named Marie Palos, were terrors. I fig-ure Marie was something like Maggie must've been at that age. She tore up and down the court and scored a lot of points. I hated to admit it, but I might be afraid to take on Marie one-on-one for fear she would do to me what Maggie did to my dad.

I glanced at Dad. He was absorbed in a conversation with Eliza-beth's father about truck tires, so I turned back to the game.

At one point, Marie threw a pass to Elizabeth who shot it into the basket just as the buzzer sounded. Then she screamed and jumped up and down. Her teammates gathered around and did this with her, all of their pink bows bouncing like butterflies on milkweed during an earthquake. That part was different from boys' basketball too.

Here's the bottom line. The end score was twenty-one to twenty-four, with Elizabeth's team winning. Elizabeth actually shot a few times, made a couple of buckets, dribbled down the court a lot, and threw several passes, one of which hit a parent who was carrying an armload of full soda cups. This resulted in a time-out that required mops.

Elizabeth also squealed every time one of her teammates hit a basket, and once she accidentally squealed when the other team made a basket.

My observation about Elizabeth and basketball was this: she had fun. I guess that's what counts.

Afterwards I told her I was proud of her, and I showed her my test, which resulted in more squeals just like when somebody made a basket.

Later, as I sat beside Dad in the ice cream shop, I realized that with a lot of hard work and creativity, Elizabeth had become an almost half-way decent basketball player. Maybe, with a lot of hard work and creativity I could pass fifth grade. And possibly, with some coaching from Elizabeth, Dad could win Maggie's heart.

On Saturday mornings Dad went to town to replenish his regular tractor parts inventory, and Stevie and I often went with him. So, on the Saturday of Dad's blind date, he loaded Stevie and me into the truck. For some reason, Dad stopped and picked up Elizabeth along the way. We ended up at Mrs. Johannson's flower shop next to Apple Valley Hardware and Tractor Supply.

"Dad, what are we doing?" I asked.

Shoving his hands into his pockets, he scanned a row of flowers. "What are those, I wonder."

"What are we doing?" I asked again.

"My consultant, Elizabeth, has advised me to purchase flowers for the blind date. She said to come here, pick out flowers, and let Mrs. Johannson arrange them all pretty."

Mrs. Johannson was busy helping another customer.

I looked along the rows of multi-colored flowers. I picked a small, perfect daisy and showed it to Dad. "This one has yellow like the kitchen curtains."

He took it. "I guess it's okay to match curtains. Isn't it?" He looked at Elizabeth for help.

She was poking at a cluster of roses down the aisle.

"Can the daisy be from me, Dad?" I asked.

"Sure. Let's let Stevie pick a flower, too. It'll be a combination bouquet—from all of us." He reached for a pink rosebud. "This can be from Alice." He put it with the daisy.

Elizabeth came over and noticed the flowers in Dad's hand. "That's not very color coordinated, Mr. Bradley. You're supposed to pick a theme color, and work around it."

Dad examined the flowers in his hand. "I like these." He added a red rose. "This'll be from me. Maggie likes red, I think." He looked at me. "Doesn't she?"

"Well," Elizabeth said. "There are different meanings to each color of rose, and normally, people don't do a lot of pink and red together…"

That's when I noticed Stevie was coming our way, holding a thick purple floppy flower with black lines on it.

"Oh, no," I said. I'm not even sure it was a flower. It looked like a giant's hand with no bones in the fingers. They just waggled around.

"Maggie cool flower." He handed it to Dad.

Elizabeth's eyes were huge. "Stevie, let me help you find a smaller one."

"No!" he snapped. "Maggie cool flower!"

Dad stared at his bouquet, several small multi-colored flowers and a big, floppy purple one—which if it could talk would be saying, "Cowabunga!"

Dad grinned. "Thanks, Stevie."

Stevie beamed.

Elizabeth's mouth was open, a look of panic on her face.

"It's okay," I whispered to her.

Dad took the flowers to Mrs. Johannson, whose eyebrows lifted high as she viewed them.

"Can you fix them up all pretty?" Dad said.

"I'll try." She added some little fluffy plant things.

"Maybe they should be in a vase with water," Dad suggested.

She set them in a simple glass vase and tied a white bow around it. "Like this?"

"Perfect." Dad got out his wallet.

Then we went to the hardware store.

As Elizabeth and I wandered around the shelves of nuts and bolts she let out a huge sigh. "Those flowers are not what most ladies would expect on a date."

For once, I wasn't worried. "I like 'em. I think they look like us."

FIFTEEN

The tie didn't help that much.

So, does my blind date plan to be here soon?" Maggie sat on the bench by the front door. She looked at her watch and grinned at me.

I wondered if she knew what was going on and was just playing along. I couldn't tell, and I really didn't want to know.

Even though she wasn't dressed up all fancy-dancy, she looked good in her new yellow blouse. Elizabeth had donated some of her mom's perfume, and Maggie smelled like the lilac bush behind our house. I decided Dad would like her this way.

She peeked at her watch again. "Make sure you feed Stevie and your dad after I leave. They didn't come to the table at all. I left macaroni and cheese in the pan."

"Okay." I winked at Elizabeth.

After we'd bought the flowers this morning, Stevie had walked around giggling into his hands. Dad grabbed him and took him out to the barn for the day so he wouldn't give away the surprise.

Maggie sighed. "Where is William? You know, I need to talk to him before I leave. Alice seems a bit fussy. Is he still out there with that old wagon full of field corn that Uncle Ned parked in the barn? Why did he do that, anyway?" She stood. "I should go out there and talk to William."

"Sit down. Relax," Elizabeth said. "We'll take care of Alice. Everything's fine."

Maggie sighed again as she settled on the seat.

I nudged Elizabeth and pointed to the kitchen.

We went together and looked out the back window. The barn was silent, the door still open.

"I thought you said he was ready," I whispered.

"I had him all fixed up, tie and everything. I told him he was handsome—you know, to give him confidence." She smiled at her own wisdom, then shook her head. "He refused to wear the cologne I brought. He said he didn't like how it smelled."

"Me either." It reminded me of dish soap mixed with vinegar.

Elizabeth sighed. "I told him it didn't matter if he liked the smell, because ladies like it, and he should wear it for Maggie. Do you know what he said?"

"What?"

"He said that Maggie likes the smell of the bubblegum that comes with baseball cards."

"Maybe you should rub baseball cards on his head," I offered.

Elizabeth rolled her eyes. "Anyway," she continued. "I told him to sneak around the side of the house and knock on the front door. He was all set to go."

"Did he follow you out of the barn?"

"He started to. Then he said he needed to do one more thing."

Oh, no. "What thing?"

"He said he needed to make sure the paint can lids were on tight, and something about a wagon latch peg, whatever that is."

"That should've only taken a minute."

We stared out at the barn while I heard the sound of a car come down the lane and stop in front of the house where we couldn't see.

"I wonder who that is," Elizabeth said.

Footsteps pounded on the front porch and someone knocked on the door.

What was going on?

Elizabeth frowned. "Did your dad take the truck somewhere earlier?" Her eyes widened. "Wait! Maybe he hid the truck down the road, and just now—he got in it and drove it here so he could pick Maggie up for the date at the front door like a real date-person would do. Impressive!"

"Why would he do a dumb thing like that?"

"To be romantic, silly."

"Not my dad. Trust me."

From the sounds in the front hall, Maggie had opened the door and greeted someone, and the voice that answered wasn't Dad's.

Elizabeth and I wasted no time in rushing into the hall, only to find Keith Sanders standing there, his eyes on Maggie in a very approving way. "You look nice," he said as he handed her a pile of fabric squares. "These are from my sister."

What was he doing here—at this exact minute?

"Thanks." She seemed surprised to see him.

We needed to get him out of here now!

"Are you…uh, going somewhere?" he asked.

"I think so." Maggie shot a quizzical look at Elizabeth.

"Are you going to the art fair downtown? That's where I'm headed. Do you…uh…"

Oh, no. Keith Sanders was going to kidnap Dad's blind date! I poked Elizabeth, who seemed to be in her own state of open-mouthed shock.

Maggie, who usually ramrodded her way through everything, had a look on her face that said she had no clue what she was supposed to do. She took a deep breath and faced Keith. "Would you excuse us for a second?"

"Sure."

She grabbed Elizabeth and me by our shirts and marched us into the kitchen. "What is going on?" she whispered.

I shrugged, relieved to have Maggie away from Mr. Sanders.

"Is Keith my blind date?" she asked.

"No," I answered.

"Well, who is?"

"You'll find out," I said weakly.

"I'm through playing games. Tell me now, or you'll wash dishes for the rest of your life."

Sadly enough, I'd be happy to wash her dishes for the rest of my life—if that would keep her here.

Elizabeth's tiny voice came from behind me. "Mr. Bradley's your blind date."

Maggie took a deep breath. "If I'm supposed to go somewhere with William, then who will take care of the baby and Stevie?"

"Aunt Nelda is coming over to help us right after you leave," I said. "She's part of the surprise."

After a thoughtful pause, Maggie wheeled around. "I need to speak to William."

"I'll go get him." I headed out the kitchen door. Someone probably needed to warn him that his blind date had already hit a snag. "You wait here."

The big light inside the barn wasn't on, but bits of late afternoon sunshine lit my way through the shadows as I wove between the farm equipment. I could hear Stevie making his little play car sounds outside the open side door.

Dad, clenching four-inch nails in his teeth, stood with his arms extended, chest high, facing Uncle Ned's big ancient wagon, holding a loose board against its side so all the field corn wouldn't escape.

"Dad?"

"I knew this thing was falling apart," he said out of the side of his mouth.

"Dad, Keith Sanders is at the house trying to kidnap Maggie."

"Who?" One of the nails fell out of Dad's mouth and landed in the shadows by his feet. "What are you talking about?"

"Mr. Sanders is in our hall and he's trying to kidnap Maggie right now."

He tucked the hammer under his armpit and let the mouthful of nails drop into his free hand. "Luke, relax a minute and help me. Would you stick a new bulb in the big light? There's a pack of bulbs on the shelf by the extension cords. Turn it off first."

"But, Dad…"

"Hop to it, son."

Why was he worrying about a stupid barn light? He needed to get over to the house!

"Dad…"

"Just do it. Fix the light. Then we'll talk about Keith Sanders."

I flipped off the switch. Then I climbed up on the tractor directly beneath the light fixture, bulb in hand. When I got down and turned it on, a yellow glow washed the interior of the barn. "Is that better?" I turned to Dad.

He was standing in a sea of corn kernels. No, it wasn't a sea, it was a snowdrift as deep as his ankles, billowing out around his feet. He focused on the side of the wagon, patched together with pieces of old wood, and hammered another nail into place. Bits of corn flowed through the cracks.

"Dad?"

As he turned toward me, a loose board gave way and hit him in the chest, releasing a flow of dry corn. Whipping around, he smacked it back into place. "Whoa."

"I'll help." I reached up and held it while he quickly nailed it, bracing it with his body. Together, we slowly backed away.

It bent a little but held.

"Temporary, for sure," he mumbled. "I need to reinforce it on the inside. Have to shovel some corn around in there first."

"Hello?" Maggie stood beside the tractor under the light.

Elizabeth was right behind her, Alice balanced on her hip.

"What happened here?" Maggie asked.

As Dad turned toward her, I noticed many things about him. I noticed that his entire right side—including his face, hair, and new shirt—was dotted with corn, sort of like they were stuck there with glue. No, not glue—white paint. For some reason, there was paint all over his side, like it had spilled from above. Glancing at the high shelf behind him, I saw a paint can overturned, still dripping. He must've bumped the shelves during the corn avalanche. His clip-on tie dangled from his neck like a flag at half-mast, declaring whatever half-mast declares.

He didn't seem to notice me anymore. His eyes were burning straight ahead at Maggie. "What're you doing out here?" His voice sounded strained.

"I'm supposed to be on a blind date," she said. "Apparently with you—I just found out. At first when Elizabeth talked about it, I assumed you were the one, and I played along to see what would happen. But then nothing seemed to indicate:" She scratched her temple. "You hadn't asked for a clean shirt, or…"

"I took care of his clothes," Elizabeth interrupted.

Maggie gave Elizabeth a tender look, but it lasted just a few seconds because Alice was squirming in Elizabeth's arms and whining.

"What is Keith doing at the house?" Dad asked Maggie.

"Dropping off quilt squares from Bonnie."

"Is that all?"

Maggie gave Dad a weird look, one I didn't understand.

"He wants to take her to an art thing," I broke in. We needed to get this settled right now.

Dad drew his hand across the unpainted side of his face as he looked down at his clothes. He seemed to realize, for the first time, that he was a mess.

We heard a car roll across the gravel in front of the barn and come to a stop. I guess Keith had decided it was lonely in the front hall all by himself so he'd come to join the party.

Maggie turned and looked outside, then back at Dad.

Dad stood tall. "I've just made a decision." He yanked the tie off his neck, tossed it away, and pressed his hand against the side of the creaking grain wagon. A trickle of corn slipped off the bed, rolling down his arms and dropping off. Another creak, a snap of wood, and a rush of grain flooded around him as he released the boards, stepped back, and let it all flow to the ground.

Everyone was pretty much petrified as Dad stood like a frozen soldier in the middle of his growing grain pile. It was knee deep when it finally slowed down and stopped. There was nothing any of us could do.

"Hello?" Keith's cheerful voice floated into the barn. "Where is everybody?"

The overhead light flickered and died, plunging us into half-lit shadows.

Keith stopped. "Whoops. Lost the lights. Maggie, what did you decide about the art fair?"

Oh, please, no.

A long sigh passed through my dad. He looked at Maggie, eye-to-eye in the soft glimmer of sunlight reaching from the open barn doors. "Go."

"No." She shook her head.

"Right now. Just go." His voice was firm. "I have a mess to clean up. There'll be no blind date for me tonight."

"No."

"Yes."

"No, William." Maggie's eyes dug into Dad's, who looked like he was in some sort of pain.

"I'm not going to argue with you, Maggie. Just go."

After a pause, she turned and wove through the tractor maze and out of the barn. I heard a car door open.

Dad glanced to Elizabeth and me. "Nice try," he said. "I couldn't ask for better kids."

Elizabeth looked down at the tie. "Maybe if we put your tie back on and straightened your shirt…"

Alice cried in her arms.

"No, Elizabeth. I'm covered in paint. Thank you." His voice sounded like he had something stuck in his throat. He reached out and took the baby, who was fussing, and put her up to his least messy shoulder. He patted her back while she squirmed in his arms.

I was getting angry. "You should go chase Maggie, Dad. Go stand up for what's yours."

"She's not mine. She's not a possession." He turned back to the wagon, and with his free hand, pulled off the rest of the broken, dangling slats. As more corn rained down on him, he spread his fingers and mumbled, "Splinters everywhere."

Alice spit up on his ear. White slime rolled down his neck and into his collar.

I felt our future just falling down, sinking like the grain that continued to slide off the wagon. Maggie was slipping away in a red convertible.

219

"You didn't even try," I complained. I knew I was speaking out of turn, but I couldn't stop myself. "If you really cared about her, you'd be chasing her down the road like a knight in shining armor."

He wheeled around. "Do I look like a knight in shining armor to you?" His eyes flashed with frustration. "Look at me." He held his free hand out to his side. "What do I have to offer a fine woman like her? She's beautiful, and smart, and full of kindness. She could have any man in America. Don't you think she deserves..." he thrust his hand out farther, "something better than this?"

I was speechless.

He shifted the baby up on his shoulder. "I have nothing to offer her but peeling wallpaper and cows and tractors—and Stevie, a son who will never be able to take care of himself. That's a lot to ask of any woman, Luke. Just think about it."

I struggled to accept what he was saying to me. "You're just going to let her go, then?"

His eyes blazed into mine. "Son, when you really love someone, you want her to have what is the best, the very, very best—even if it isn't you."

I felt a hand bump my shoulder from behind.

Maggie's eyes met mine as she grabbed her sweater off the tractor seat.

Dad's face, the part that wasn't covered in paint and spit-up, turned a deeper red. He swung away.

Something inside of me died. I wished I could go back in time and undo this whole blind date thing.

Maggie stared at his back, then left the barn. I heard Keith's car door slam shut, the motor rev, and gravel crunch in the driveway.

Dad didn't move.

"Do you want me to help you with the corn?" My voice quivered. "I'll get a shovel."

"No."

Elizabeth tugged at my sleeve. "We'll take care of Stevie and Alice for you." She picked up the tie.

I reached for the baby, and Dad handed her over. "If you need me, call on the intercom. Take the flowers into the house. I don't want to look at 'em right now. And grab Stevie, too. He's outside."

We got the flowers off the ledge, slid the barn door shut, collected Stevie from where he was lining rocks and toy cars along the side of the barn, and trudged to the house.

SIXTEEN

Go, Sarge.

Elizabeth was crying by the time we reached the porch steps. She ran into the kitchen and stood by the window, gasping, looking out at the barn. "I ruined your dad's life." She sobbed.

"No, you didn't." I adjusted my grip on squirmy Alice. "He'll be fine. He was okay before Maggie came, and he'll be okay after this. You'll see." I said it, but I didn't believe it.

Elizabeth continued to bawl her eyes out while she fixed a bottle for the baby. I didn't know what to do. Actually, I knew what I wanted to do. I wanted to cry right along with her or dig a hole and fall in it. But I couldn't because I had too much responsibility right now. I needed to help watch Stevie and Alice so Dad could be alone in the barn. Part of me wanted to go out and tell him what a great guy he was, and how Maggie deserved him. But right now he just needed some alone time—and that, I could give.

The phone interrupted my miserable thoughts—Aunt Nelda. I explained to her that things hadn't worked out, and she should stay home. I could tell she wanted to know more, but I didn't have the heart in me to talk about it just then.

After hanging up the phone, I gave the baby to Elizabeth and took Stevie to the living room. Holding back my tears, I helped him take down his lopsided Lincoln Log truck garage so he could start something new, pulling the wooden pieces apart so he could stack them by size. That would keep him busy for a while.

Returning to the kitchen, I walked past Elizabeth and Alice on my way to the dirty dishes beside the macaroni and cheese pan.

Dishes. My gift to Maggie. She wanted a dishwasher, and I was it. Anger bubbled in me. I thought of Dad out in the barn, miserable, standing in a pile of grain. Actually, if I knew my dad, he had already found some good pieces of wood from the pile in the shed out behind the barn, probably slats from the barn stalls he'd taken down to make room for more tractors. I supposed he was whacking away at nails, thinking about the only date he'd tried to go on in umpteen years, and how terrible it had turned out.

I flipped the intercom switch once to listen to him work, but all I heard was silence. I flipped the switch off. Private silence.

Dishes. Maybe I needed to whack at some dishes. I walked to the sink.

After Dad got the slats repaired, I figured he would get the shovel and start tossing the corn back onto the wagon bed. He'd feel better while he was doing that, fixing something—even though it wasn't his life.

Dishes. There was still macaroni in the pan. I left it on the cold stove and began to run water in the sink. I'll do dishes for my dad. He deserved clean dishes. I squirted the detergent into the sink, and I set the glasses in first, like I always do, because of what Maggie had taught me.

Out where I couldn't see, the gravel crunched, and a car pulled up near the house. I heard footsteps on the front porch while a car drove back down the lane.

I recognized Maggie's church shoes, clicking, as she walked into her room and shut the door. Taking a deep breath, I turned to Elizabeth. "What's she doing now?"

She shrugged, her moist blue eyes full of worry. Elizabeth, for once, was being silent.

I set a glass in the drainer.

"I never knew a boy who did dishes all the time like you do." Elizabeth's voice quivered.

"I don't want to talk about it."

She held the baby close while I plunged my hands into the warm water.

Almost immediately Maggie's door opened, and she strode into the kitchen wearing overalls and her pink tennis shoes.

I turned completely around.

Elizabeth's eyes widened even more.

Maggie reached out and rubbed Alice's back. "Thanks for helping with the baby, Elizabeth. She seems happy now."

"I fed her," Elizabeth said.

As Maggie straightened up, she eyed the flowers on the table. "Where'd those come from?"

"From Dad," I said. "We each picked a flower to go in it."

She touched the ugly purple one. "Cool flower."

My insides were in knots. What was going on? "That sure was a short date."

"You're right." Maggie smiled sadly. "We just drove to the end of the property so we could talk. Then I came back." She put her hands on the sides of her overalls. "I'm still going on my blind date that you planned—with that man out in the barn. How do I look?"

I thought she looked great. "Perfect."

Turning to the stove, she picked up the macaroni pan. "Still some of this left?" She reached into the silverware drawer, picked out two forks, and stuck them in her front overall pockets. "A dinner date then."

I was starting to feel sort of nervously giggly.

She put her hand on my shoulder. "Keith is a very nice man."

"I know. Dad told me."

"And I like the dishwasher in his house."

"I know."

"But I love the dishwasher in this house." She smacked a big wet kiss right on my cheek. Her eyes watered for a minute, then she faced the door. "Now I'm going to go talk to that impossible man out there who says he loves me so much he thinks he should give me away."

I was afraid to try my voice—it might just croak.

"He has corn glued to the paint on his head and spit-up running down his neck." She smiled and spoke softly. "How romantic is that?"

Man, I tried not to show it, but there was a glow surging inside me.

"If the baby needs attention, just flip on the intercom and call for help." As she walked out the door, her voice floated through the screen. "Oh, boy. Here I go."

With a goofy grin, Elizabeth shifted Alice in her arms and followed me to the door, both of us looking out the screen.

Maggie, macaroni pan in hand, walked to her garden patch. Reaching over the fence, she grabbed her shovel and marched to the barn. She set the shovel beside the door, stood tall for a moment under the basketball hoop, took a deep breath, and shut her eyes.

Praying, I supposed.

Then, sliding the door to the side, she picked up her shovel and stepped inside.

"Go, Sarge," Elizabeth whispered.

About half an hour after Maggie marched through the barn door with her macaroni pan and shovel, two things happened. First, Elizabeth's mom called and said her car was flat-tired in their driveway. Then Alice filled her pants. Neither Elizabeth nor I was willing to tackle that project. In fact, we argued about it.

Finally, when neither one of us could stand the smell any longer, Elizabeth found the guts to flip the switch on the intercom and interrupt the date by saying, "I need a ride home, and Alice stinks."

Soon Dad and Maggie walked into the kitchen, both smelling like turpentine. The side of Dad's head was scrubbed clean of paint, and his ear and cheek had a raw red tinge like someone had used an ice scraper to pry off a glacier.

As Maggie carried the stinky baby to her room, Dad told Elizabeth to go get in the truck, and that he'd be out there in a minute to drive her home.

After she went outside, he turned to me. "Son, are you okay?"

"I don't know, Dad. Mostly, I'm confused."

He set his hand on my shoulder. "While Maggie was out there

scrubbing the skin off my face, she became the sarge and took charge of the situation. She sort of announced stuff at me."

"Like what?"

"First off she told me she isn't ready to be going on dates right now. She's still in mourning."

"Oh." My heart sank.

"She still needs closure."

"Dad, what's closure?"

"Well, son, closure is like saying good-bye…here." He tapped his chest.

"Oh." I guess Maggie was still trying to say good-bye to her good husband.

"She went on to say that when someday she is ready to go on a date—I'd be the first to know." A slow grin crept across his face.

I couldn't help but smile back.

He continued. "Maggie agreed to Elizabeth's blind date plan simply because she wanted to see what you two had cooked up. Thought it might be interesting."

I sighed. Yes, definitely interesting.

"That's not all she said." He took a deep breath. "She told me she's happy here in our house with us. She says she came to take care of us, but we're taking care of her too."

"Really?"

"She has a purpose here—to take care of two boys she loves."

"Wow."

"And she says that with me she feels safe."

I looked into his true-blue eyes. Yes, safe.

"Not just physically safe, but safe here." He tappped his heart again. "And she said that the next time I try to give her away to somebody else, she's going to wallop me across the head with Stevie's whiffleball bat."

"Good."

His eyebrows lifted.

"Good, sir."

"That's better. She also told me to get some ice cream after I drop off Elizabeth. We're going to finish out our blind un-date with ice cream here."

227

"She likes butter pecan with fudge sauce on it."

"Thanks for the tip." And with that, Dad walked out the door, his stride like that of someone who'd just won an election.

As I stood by the window and looked out over the moonlit yard, a warm feeling washed over me. Dad's truck bounced down the lane, taking Elizabeth, my basketball success story and friend, home to her family. An A- spelling test was taped to the front of the refrigerator right beside the progress report that showed an upswing in all my grades because of things like Maggie's pushiness, the colored overlays that helped my ants stop marching across the page, Elizabeth's ideas, and mostly, my own hard work. Last week Miss Finch referred to me as "Mr. Determination" and offered to tutor me during the summer to get me ready for sixth grade. That was right before she said, "Luke, because of you, I'm learning to be a better teacher."

These thoughts had me glowing from the inside out just as Stevie snuck up beside me at the kitchen window and snuggled against my side. I stretched my arm around him and listened to Maggie's voice down the hall, talking to Alice. "You are so cute, and so stinky."

"Cool moon," Stevie said.

I agreed. "Cool moon." Something warm flowed through me. Serendipity.

EPILOGUE

At the end of April, Miss Finch went to Richmond and met with Hank Coleman. She came back loaded up with ideas and plans to help prepare me for sixth grade. Then she started keeping me after school twice a week, and together we tried different creative experiments to help me learn reading and math. We used little tiles with letters and numbers on them, colored cards with syllables, and chalkboard writing so I would use different muscles while I learned. She took notes on everything we did so she could report back to Mr. Coleman. And while we worked, we ate pretzels. I started to like Miss Finch a lot, and I think, maybe, she was starting to like me.

In May, for the first time, I made a Mother's Day card in school like the other kids. Mine said, "To Maggie." We celebrated her birthday again, only this time we skipped the Jell-O and chili altogether, and went straight to Beulah's Cheeseburger Barn. Dad brought money.

In June, Maggie and Alice went to Aunt Joyce's house in Richmond for a week to do some special things to remember her fireman husband. June was the anniversary of his death. Every day that week at supper Dad and I prayed for Maggie because we knew she would be sad while she was doing her remembering. And secretly, I prayed that Maggie and Alice would, for sure, come back to us. It was too lonely at our house.

They did come back, bringing a memory book Maggie had made with her husband's mother. It had pictures of Ted from babyhood all the way to his firemen days. They made it for Alice so she could learn about her dad when she was old enough.

In September, Dad and Maggie went on their first real date. Aunt Nelda and Uncle Ned came to stay with us. I got out the chess board, and we played until it was pretty late, but I fell asleep before Maggie and Dad got home.

The next morning, I woke up to Maggie humming in the kitchen. I asked her how the date went, and she tousled my hair. "Great."

That lifted my heart.

After a quick bowl of cereal, I walked out to the barn to help Dad. This summer, I usually was his assistant, managing his tools and holding things. He said the extra pair of hands made his work easier.

Today he sat on a stool, working on a rusty old tractor, his long legs stretched out.

"So, Dad," I said. "How was the date?"

"Good."

"Where'd you go?" I asked.

"First, Ben's Steak House, then Lucky Charm Putt Putt Golf."

"Lucky's golf? Man, I want to go."

He laughed. "No kids on Friday nights. Just me and the sarge."

Too bad. "Hey, who won?"

He cleared his throat. "She did."

"Did she cheat?"

"Well, sort of." He handed me a wrench. "Can you trade this for the next size up? I grabbed the wrong one."

I took it to the workbench area and stared at the tools hanging up against the wall—largest to smallest. While I compared wrenches, Dad kept on talking.

"She bet me she could beat me at golf with one hand tied behind her back, so I took her up on it."

Trading for the right tool, I turned to see Elizabeth standing quietly in the doorway.

Dad's voice continued from where he was beside the tractor, his eyes focused on his work. I knew he couldn't see Elizabeth from where he sat. "So, I pulled out one of my shoelaces and tied Maggie's hand to the back of her belt."

Elizabeth rolled her eyes and shook her head.

Dad shifted his feet. "What is wrong with me? Why do I make bets with a woman who seems to have spent her entire youth in some kind of sports training?"

I came and stood near him, wanting to hear more. "So, how bad did she beat you?"

"Twenty points."

"Twenty points? Dad, there are eighteen holes at Lucky's golf! She beat you by more than one point per hole."

"Where's that stupid wrench?"

"And with one arm tied behind her back?" My voice screeched.

He jerked out his hand, palm-side up. "Wrench."

I placed the tool in his hand. "Dad, did you do your usual cheating?"

"I tried nudging the ball with my foot once, but she caught me and docked my score. It's hard to be sneaky with a floppy shoe."

Elizabeth clapped her hands on top of her head, and mouthed, "Hopeless, hopeless, hopeless."

I ignored her. "Dad, next time you should probably use the shoe that was laced tight when you cheat—not the loose one."

"Oh, now that's a nice thing to say to your honest father."

"You just told me that you tried to cheat. Don't blame me."

Elizabeth leaned her forehead against the doorjamb and shut her eyes.

He continued. "After we finished the golf slaughter, we went to Frosty's for ice cream." He turned toward the tractor, but he didn't seem to be using the wrench yet. "Guess what I learned while we were there?"

"What?"

"When Maggie was thirteen, her parents worked at a camp for an entire summer. They were the missionary speakers. While she was there, she broke her arm. She couldn't do any of the camp activities, so she spent her long summer days on the homemade miniature golf course, hitting the balls with one arm." He sighed. "I asked her, why didn't you tell me that before I made the bet?"

I laughed. "So, Dad, what was the bet?"

"The usual. Dishes. I seem to be doing dishes quite a lot around here these days." His voice didn't seem very upset about it. "Looks like you're getting a break from that chore."

"At least you won't have to wash them with one arm tied behind your back."

Dad chuckled. "Hey, don't ever let Maggie hear you say that. She doesn't need any more creative ideas about her sneaky bets."

I could just see Dad trying to wash dishes with one hand tied behind his back, and it made me smile.

Elizabeth walked away, shaking her head.

"So, Dad. Are you going to take Sarge on another date?"

"Next Friday. It's already planned."

"Golf again?"

"No, I think this time we'll go to the band concert at River Point Park."

"I want to go."

"No kids on Friday nights."

"Oh, yeah." I guess that was okay. "A band concert is probably a safe date. You know, non-competitive."

He chuckled. "That's what Maggie said."

Even so, I figured that a non-competitive, safe date with Dad and Maggie would probably still turn out to be some kind of adventure.

But that was okay. If Maggie didn't like adventures, she wouldn't still be here with us. We were just an adventure package.

Dad continued to chuckle beside the tractor, and when I'd left the kitchen, Maggie had been humming. And me? I was just plain thankful that last September, Dad decided to buy us a woman.

NOTE TO READERS

Our schools are full of students who have a wide variety of problems that block their success. They don't understand why they can't function like their peers, and silently self-label themselves as stupid when, in truth, they aren't. Many are gifted in areas that enrich our society. This book was written to show the effects learning difficulties have on school life, social interactions, family, and most of all—the students' perception of themselves. The path to success starts with identification of the specific problem, acceptance, help from outside resources, consistent creative methods, and a loving touch by those who are close to them.

ABOUT THE AUTHOR

Connie A. Williams is a retired teacher in California. She is blessed with three kids and their spouses, ten grandkids, a husband who loves his flip phone, and a Labrador Retriever who refuses to retrieve anything. Connie enjoys reading, writing, playing the piano, and making creative messes with her grandchildren.

Surviving Carmelita

When Josie's world implodes
there is only one place to go.

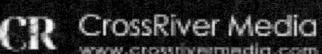

More great books from…
CrossRiverMedia.com

Love Final Sunrise

New Yorker Ruth Jessup and Amish-bred Joshua Stutzman live in different worlds, but their lives collide as they battle wits against a psychopath and the New World Order. Suffering from amnesia, Ruth finds herself in a world without TVs, cell phones, or computers, only buggies and lanterns, planting and canning. If not for Joshua, Ruth would be lost and homeless. An attraction blossoms, but the chaos of the biblical seven-year tribulation blankets the world. Can Joshua's Amish ways help them survive the next three-and-a half years without the mark of the beast?

Claiming Her Inheritance

A shooting, a stampede, a snakebite… Sally Clark has received an inheritance of a lifetime, but first she has to survive living on the ranch in Montana. Chase Reynolds is astounded that his father has willed one-third of their ranch to a total stranger. Who is this woman and what hold did she have over his dad? What Sally and Chase discover is beyond their imagination and wields far greater consequences than the inheritance.

Lottie's Gift

She's a little girl with a big gift. Lottie Braun has enjoyed a happy childhood in rural Iowa with her father and older sister. But the quiet, nearly idyllic life she enjoyed as a child ended with tragedy and a secret that tore the two sisters apart. Forty years later, Lottie is a world-class pianist with a celebrated career and an empty personal life. One sleepless night, she allows herself to remember and she discovers that memories, once allowed, are difficult to suppress. Will she ever find her way home?

Books that build battle-ready faith.

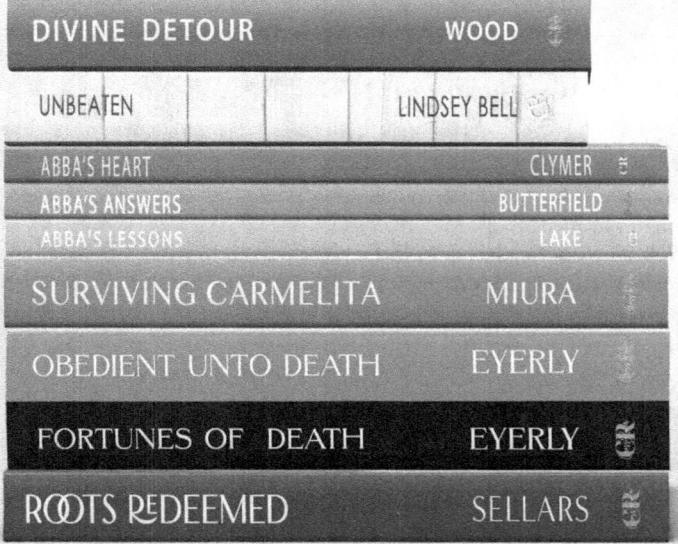

If you enjoyed this book, will you consider sharing it with others?

- Please mention the book on Facebook, Instagram, Pinterest, or another social media site.

- Recommend this book to your small group, book club, and workplace.

- Head over to Facebook.com/CrossRiverMedia, 'Like' the page and post a comment as to what you enjoyed the most.

- Pick up a copy for someone you know who would be challenged or encouraged by this message.

- Write a review on your favorite ebook platform.

- To learn about our latest releases subscribe to our newsletter at CrossRiverMedia.com.

www.ingramcontent.com/pod-product-compliance
Lightning Source LLC
Chambersburg PA
CBHW060633260626
47161CB00008B/2881